THE
PENDERWICKS
AT
POINT
MOUETTE

Awards for
THE PENDERWICKS

Winner of the National Book Award for Young People's Literature

A Junior Library Guild Selection

A *Child* Magazine Best Book of the Year

A *Kirkus Reviews* Best Book

A *Publishers Weekly* Best Children's Book

A *Booklist* Editors' Choice

A *School Library Journal* Best Book of the Year

Awards for
THE PENDERWICKS
ON GARDAM STREET

A New York Public Library 100 Titles for
Reading and Sharing Selection

A *Publishers Weekly* Best Book of the Year

A Book Sense Children's Summer Pick

A Texas Bluebonnet Award Master List Title

THE PENDERWICKS AT POINT MOUETTE

JEANNE BIRDSALL

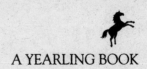

A YEARLING BOOK

Text copyright © 2011 by Jeanne Birdsall
Cover art and interior illustrations copyright © 2011 by David Frankland

All rights reserved. Published in the United States by Yearling, an imprint of Random House Children's Books, a division of Random House, Inc., New York. Originally published in hardcover in the United States by Alfred A. Knopf, an imprint of Random House Children's Books, New York, in 2011.

Yearling and the jumping horse design are registered trademarks of Random House, Inc.

Visit us on the Web! randomhouse.com/kids

Educators and librarians, for a variety of teaching tools, visit us at randomhouse.com/teachers

The Library of Congress has cataloged the hardcover edition of this work as follows:
Birdsall, Jeanne.
The Penderwicks at Point Mouette / Jeanne Birdsall.
p. cm.
Summary: When the three younger Penderwick sisters go to Maine with Aunt Claire and are separated from oldest sister Rosalind for the first time in their lives, an uncertain Skye is left in charge as the OAP—oldest available Penderwick.
ISBN 978-0-375-85851-2 (trade) — ISBN 978-0-375-95851-9 (lib. bdg.) —
ISBN 978-0-375-89898-3 (ebook)
[1. Sisters—Fiction. 2. Vacations—Fiction. 3. Family Life—Maine—Fiction.
4. Maine—Fiction.]
I. Title.
PZ7.B51197 Pef 2011
[Fic]—dc22
2011005806

ISBN 978-0-375-85135-3 (pbk.)

Printed in the United States of America

10 9 8 7 6 5 4 3 2 1

First Yearling Edition 2012

For Quinn

CONTENTS

CHAPTER ONE
Going, Going . . .

THE PENDERWICK FAMILY was being torn apart. The tearing wouldn't last long—only two weeks—but still it was uncomfortable. Mr. Penderwick was the first to go, flying off to England with his new wife, Iantha, for scientific conferences and a bit of a honeymoon. With them went Ben, Iantha's son, who was too small to be without his mother, honeymoon or not.

That had been two days earlier, and now the remaining Penderwicks—four sisters named Rosalind, Skye, Jane, and Batty—were about to tear apart even more. Early the next morning, three of them would leave for Maine with the sisters' favorite relative, Aunt Claire, while the fourth headed to New Jersey with her best friend. The girls had never been apart for an entire two weeks, and though all of them were nervous about it, the one going off on her own was the most nervous. This was the oldest, thirteen-year-old Rosalind, and she was having a terrible time accepting that her sisters could survive without her.

Right now she was waiting in her bedroom for them to arrive. She didn't want to be in her bedroom—she wanted to be with five-year-old Batty, getting her ready for bed just like she always did. But tonight Skye and Jane, the two middle sisters, were helping Batty with her bath and pajamas. Practice, Aunt Claire called it, or a dry run. She'd thought it would calm Rosalind to see that indeed she wasn't absolutely needed when it came to Batty. And Rosalind would have been calm, except that the others were supposed to come to her room as soon as they were finished, and that should have been at least ten minutes ago. How could a simple bath take so long? They knew she wanted to have one last MOPS—that is, Meeting of Penderwick Sisters—before Batty had to go to sleep. One last MOPS before they were all separated for two weeks.

"Two whole weeks," groaned Rosalind, then looked up hopefully, because she heard footsteps in the hall. They were here.

But it was only one of them—twelve-year-old Skye, the second sister—and she didn't have the look of someone who'd just conducted a successful bath. Her blond hair was hanging in damp clumps, and there were wet spots on her T-shirt.

"It's not as bad as it looks," she said. "Batty's fine. She didn't drown or anything."

"Then what happened?"

"Hound got into the tub with her."

That explained why Skye was so wet. The Penderwicks' large black dog was clumsy and enthusiastic—getting him out of a bathtub would make anyone wet. But it didn't explain why he'd been in the bathroom in the first place.

"Hound always tries to get into the tub," said Rosalind. "That's why he's not allowed near Batty at bath time. Didn't you know that?"

"Nope, and neither did Jane. But we know it now, and we'll clean up the bathroom later. I promise."

A dry run! The irony wasn't lost on Rosalind. She was determined not to scold, though, not this very last night. "Where are the others?"

"Jane is helping Batty with her pajamas. They'll be here soon." Skye shook her head violently, tossing droplets of water across the room. "Where's your Latin dictionary? I need to look up *revenge*."

"On my bookshelf, though I wish you wouldn't." Rosalind knew why Skye was thinking about revenge, and that she'd been thinking of little else for the last twenty-four hours. Which was absolutely not the best way to prepare for the next two weeks. With Rosalind off in New Jersey, Skye would be the OAP—Oldest Available Penderwick—and she needed to concentrate

3

on taking care of her two younger sisters, not on carrying out revenge. "Daddy says the best revenge is to be better than your enemy."

"I'm doing that, too. Almost anyone could," said Skye, leafing through the dictionary. "Here it is. Revenge: *ultio* or *vindicta*. Then it says: to take revenge on is *se vindicare in*. *Se vindicare in* Jeffrey's loathsome mother. How do I say 'Jeffrey's loathsome mother' in Latin?"

Skye's desire for revenge was justified—Rosalind knew that. Jeffrey was Jeffrey Tifton, a boy the Penderwicks had met the previous summer while renting a cottage at his mother's estate, called Arundel. By the time that vacation was over, Jeffrey was their excellent friend and honorary brother, and since then the sisters had seen him as often as they could, which was nowhere near often enough. He was always too far away—either at Arundel, a couple of hours west of the Penderwicks' home in Cameron, Massachusetts, or at his Boston boarding school, a couple of hours east of Cameron. It had been natural, then, for the younger three sisters to want Jeffrey in Maine with them, and with great hope they'd invited him.

After much dillydallying and back-and-forthing by his mother, permission had finally been granted, spirits raised, ecstatic phone calls exchanged—until suddenly, just that morning, a mere twenty-four hours before departure for Maine, the permission had been withdrawn.

Jeffrey's mother had decided that he wasn't going with the Penderwicks. No reason had been given. He simply wasn't going anywhere. He was stuck at Arundel for the whole summer.

Even through their agonized disappointment, the sisters weren't all that surprised. Jeffrey's mother was capable of endless awfulness—the real surprise was that she had a son as wonderful as Jeffrey. The Penderwicks' only explanation was that Jeffrey had inherited his good qualities from his father, but this was guesswork, since Jeffrey had never met him, nor did he know his name, or even if he was alive or dead. Which was all sad and terrible enough, but in the last year he'd also been saddled with a stepfather, the selfish and stupid Dexter Dupree.

"Loathsome. Here it is: *foedus*," said Skye. "Jeffrey's *foedus* mother, Mrs. Tifton-Dupree, known to us as *foedus* Mrs. T-D. I like it."

"You need to use the feminine accusative form of the adjective," said Rosalind, momentarily in the spirit of things.

"An unimportant detail." Skye wouldn't study Latin until she started seventh grade in the fall. "Maybe I should include Dexter. Help me translate this: *To take revenge on Dexter and foedus Mrs. T-D, I consign them to a life of guilt-racked agony, like a serpent in their entrails.*"

"Guilt-racked agony! Did you write that?"

"No, Jane did, after you shot down her idea about voodoo dolls."

"As well I should have. And I think we can skip the serpent in their entrails, too." Rosalind shut the Latin dictionary and slid it back onto the bookshelf.

"But we have to do *something*, Rosy—it's Jeffrey!"

"I know. I'm sorry."

Skye stomped around the room. "I suppose I have to be a good example and all that while you're gone."

"Yes. And please stop stomping. Thank you," said Rosalind. "Now let's think. Have I told you everything you need to know about Batty? Like brushing her hair?"

"You've told me about Batty's hair a hundred times," said Skye with great dignity. "And I do know how to brush hair."

Of course she did, thought Rosalind. It was just that Skye's own blond, straight hair was so easy to take care of, and Batty's dark hair—just like Rosalind's and Jane's—was thick and curly, and needed serious attention. Especially now that it was getting long, which was Rosalind's own fault, because she was growing her own hair long, and Jane, then Batty, had decided to follow suit. And Batty seemed to get knots in hers even when standing still, and then she hated having the knots brushed out, so much that sometimes she even cried.

"Oh, Skye, you will be careful with her in Maine,

won't you? You won't ignore her while you think about math or stars or whatever it is you think about? And you won't get frustrated or lose your temper when she cries?"

"I've been working on my temper, and I promise to be careful with Batty." Skye's dignity was even greater now. "If you'd like, I'll get my Swiss army knife and take a blood oath."

"No blood, but thanks." Rosalind did trust Skye to do the best she could. And of course Aunt Claire, that most wonderful of aunts, would be there, too. Though since Aunt Claire had never had children of her own, her practical experience was limited. While no one had actually expired under her care, when the girls were small, Aunt Claire had once brushed Rosalind's teeth with shampoo and dabbed Skye's scraped knee with toothpaste. And she had never quite gotten the hang of putting on other people's shoes—the right and left were often mixed. Oh! Rosalind had a terrifying image of Batty limping around Maine, shampoo foaming from her mouth.

The bedroom door opened again, and again it was only one sister—this time, Jane. She was even wetter than Skye, her dark curls wild, and she was carrying a pile of books.

"Where's Batty?" asked Rosalind sharply.

"Right here." Jane looked behind her, but the hall was empty of five-year-olds. "Oh, now I remember.

She said she needed to go to her room first. Rosalind, do you think Iantha would mind if I borrowed some of her books to take to Point Mouette?"

Rosalind looked through the books. They were barely suitable for her, let alone for Jane, who was only eleven.

"You're not old enough for any of these. Besides, why would you even want to read"—Rosalind picked a particularly odd title—"*Bilgewater?*"

"It's about love. They all are," answered Jane, as though that explained it perfectly.

"She's doing research for a new Sabrina Starr book," said Skye, her hand over her heart like a fainting heroine in an old-time movie. "She thinks it's time for Sabrina to fall in love."

Sabrina Starr was the heroine of many books Jane had written. Rosalind had never thought of her as the falling-in-love type. She'd always been too busy rescuing anyone who needed it, from a groundhog to an archaeologist. And Rosalind thought that Sabrina should continue the rescuing for a while longer. She didn't want Jane doing research on love while in Maine. She wanted her being a good backup OAP.

"Yes, I think Iantha would mind you borrowing these books. Wouldn't Sabrina be better off rescuing a moose or something?" She took the books from Jane and put them on her desk. It was time—past time—for the MOPS, and the littlest sister was still missing.

"I'll get Batty," Rosalind said. "Nobody wander off."

She went down the hall to Batty's room, hoping to see Batty there, neatly pajamaed and ready for a MOPS. Here is what she saw instead: an open suitcase on the floor, empty except for Asimov—the Penderwicks' orange cat—who had curled up inside and fallen asleep. The clothes that just hours ago had been folded into the suitcase were now in untidy heaps on the bed. Also on the bed was a still-wet Hound, happily chewing on the new hairbrush that Iantha had bought specially for Batty to take to Maine.

And Rosalind saw one more thing—the door to the closet seemed to be trying to shut itself.

"I know you're in there, Batty," she said.

There was a long silence, then: "*How* do you know?"

"I just do. Batty, it's time for the MOPS. Skye and Jane are waiting for us."

"I don't need to go to the MOPS, because I'm not going to Maine."

Rosalind picked up a red-striped bathing suit from the floor, refolded it, and put it back into the suitcase next to Asimov. "Is it because of the bath Skye and Jane just gave you?"

"No, that was fun. Hound jumped into the tub."

"I heard." Next into the suitcase went a half dozen

shirts. "And you're not upset about Asimov again, are you? Because we've gone over that. He has to stay home, and Tommy's going to take very good care of him. You trust Tommy, right?"

Tommy Geiger was Rosalind's boyfriend, who lived across the street, and though sometimes he could drive her crazy, he was quite good with Asimov.

"Yes."

"And I know you're disappointed about Jeffrey not going to Maine." That blow had fallen hard on Batty, already devastated at being separated from Ben. She'd been the youngest in the family for so long—even Hound was a year older than she was—that the addition of a little brother had come as a delightful relief. "And I could understand you wanting to stay home if Ben were here—"

"And Daddy and Iantha."

"—but they're in England and won't be back until you're home again from Maine."

Rosalind took hold of the hairbrush Hound was chewing and tugged until he let go. The damage was minimal, so she wiped it down and put it into the suitcase, too. This woke up Asimov, who leaped gracefully out and onto the bed—steering clear of the wet dog—where he immediately fell asleep again. The space he'd left behind was just the right size for a pile of shorts, two sweatshirts, and another bathing suit.

"Rosalind, are you still there?"

"I'm still here." Socks, underwear, an extra pair of pajamas, more T-shirts, and the suitcase was once again full. "Why don't you come see me?"

The closet door opened itself back up, and out crept Batty, well scrubbed and pajamaed, yes, though Rosalind noticed with a pang that the shirt was inside out.

"You're packing my stuff again," said Batty, her forehead scrunched with concern.

"Listen to me." Rosalind knelt beside her on the floor. "I'm so sorry that I'm not going to Maine with you. I promised Anna to go to New Jersey with her, and then it was too late to change the plans. You know all that, right? I know this is the longest you and I will have ever been apart, and I've told you over and over how much I'll miss you, so you must know that. Tell me you know how much I'll miss you."

"I do know."

"Here, let me fix your pajamas." With a minimum of wriggling, the shirt was turned right side out so that the dolphin showed. "Now you look better. Do you think you're ready for the MOPS now? Good girl. Go tell Skye and Jane I'll be there in a minute."

Batty left, with Hound trailing along after her. Asimov stayed behind, waking up in time to see Rosalind tuck a yellow sunhat in with the rest of Batty's clothes, then pull down the lid of the suitcase and shut it tight.

"Meow," he said.

"I am not crying," she answered. "Come on, let's go to the MOPS."

Back in her room, Rosalind found the others seated in a circle on the floor. She sat down with them, pulled Batty onto her lap, and waited politely while Asimov gave Hound a friendly swat on the nose, then stretched out beside him.

"MOPS come to order," she said.

Skye seconded the motion, Jane and Batty thirded and fourthed it, and Rosalind went on. "All swear to keep secret what is said here. . . . Actually, we can skip the bit about secrets. This isn't that kind of a MOPS."

"So we don't need to swear?" asked Batty, who liked that part.

"No swearing." Rosalind now took a moment to gather herself. She'd been thinking about this MOPS for days and wanted it to go just right. She had a list of rules to go through, and some cheering thoughts, and she'd end with a brief statement about how much she trusted Skye. "As you all know, early tomorrow morning I'll be handing over my OAP responsibilities to Skye. Before that happens, I want to give you some rules to follow in Maine. Rule One is . . ."

She stopped, and it seemed to the others as though she'd gone a little green.

"What is it?" asked Skye.

"I've warned you about the rocks, right? How

Maine has huge rocks along the coast, and in some places people have built seawalls to keep the ocean away from the land, and if anyone falls off a seawall, they would smash onto the rocks."

"You have indeed warned us about the rocks," said Skye.

"And the seawalls," added Jane. "By the way, you're squashing Batty."

"Sorry." Rosalind relaxed her grip on Batty, who started breathing again. "I've mentioned drowning, of course. Maybe I should start with the next-to-last rule."

"How many rules are there?" asked Skye.

"Six." Rosalind reached under her bed and pulled out a bright orange life preserver. "Rule Five: Batty wears this whenever she's near the ocean."

"We're staying on the coast. Batty is always going to be near the ocean."

"Then she will always wear it."

"Even when I sleep?" asked Batty.

"Of course not, honey." Rosalind buckled the pre-server onto Batty and felt safer just seeing it there. Many dangers might lurk for Batty in Maine, but drowning wouldn't be one of them. "All right, I'll start over. Rule One: Help Aunt Claire with meals and cleaning up. Rule Two: No squabbling with each other. Three— What, Skye?"

"We've already worked this stuff out."

"We made pacts about no fighting," added Jane.

"And we've divided up the meal chores. I'll help with cooking. I know I'm not much good at it, but Skye is worse. Sorry, Skye."

"It's true, though, so I'll do the cleaning up."

"And I'm going to set the table," said Batty. "Skye said I could."

"Oh, well, good." Rosalind took another moment to gather herself all over again. "Rule Three: Don't let Hound eat things he shouldn't, but of course you already know that. What about Rule Four? Be polite to strangers, because you're representing the Penderwicks in Maine, which is an entirely new state for us."

"We hadn't thought about meeting strangers," said Jane. "That's a nice idea, Rosy."

"We've done Rule Five. Rule Six—"

She was interrupted by a clunking sound, which turned out to be Asimov diving into Rosalind's wastebasket in search of who knew what. Feeling left out, Hound tried to go in after him, but only his nose fit, which was quite enough to annoy Asimov, and soon the floor was littered with old tissues and such, and Asimov had been banished to the hallway and Hound told to stay still or else.

"It's because they'll miss each other," said Batty.

Rosalind tossed the last tissue back into the wastebasket. "Now, where was I?"

Her answer was the sound of the doorbell, announcing a visitor at the front door. Rosalind knew exactly who'd arrived, because she'd asked him to come to say good-bye. She had a list of rules for him, too, though she knew better than to give them to him.

"Tommy?" asked Jane.

"He's a little early." Rosalind started talking more quickly. "Rule Six: No revenge on Mrs. T-D or Dexter, either the magical or actual kind."

The doorbell chimed again.

"Go see Tommy," said Skye.

"For your romantic farewells," added Jane.

Rosalind was determined to keep control over her own MOPS, but even Batty seemed to be against her, yawning suddenly.

"I'll put her to bed," said Skye. "You can say good night to her after Tommy goes."

"You'll tell her a story?" asked Rosalind piteously.

"Jane will, won't you, Jane?"

Jane nodded, and Skye declared the MOPS officially closed. Defeated, but happy to be on her way to Tommy, Rosalind left the room. Listening to her clatter down the steps, the others sat quietly, missing her already. Only Hound went on as if nothing important had happened, sneakily shoving his nose back into the wastebasket.

"No revenge," said Jane after a while. "Didn't she like the curse I wrote for Dexter and Mrs. T-D?"

"The part about entrails upset her." Skye stood up. "Let's get Batty to bed."

"Nrgwug," said Batty in a strangled sort of voice.

She'd tried to get out of the life preserver without unbuckling it and was now hopelessly entangled, her face hidden and her arms sticking out of all the wrong places. Freeing her took a while, what with her hair catching on one buckle and Hound tugging unhelpfully on another, and by the end all three sisters were grumpy. Skye was the worst.

"This is going to be a very long two weeks," she said, and no one contradicted her.

CHAPTER TWO
Gone

IN THE MORNING Rosalind departed for New Jersey, leaving her younger sisters waving their good-byes from the front yard. Hound was also there, trotting anxiously from one sister to another, determined to prevent any more Penderwicks from straying.

"Now I really am the OAP," said Skye faintly.

She hadn't wanted to be. Taking care of anyone, especially Batty, had never been a skill of hers—why would that change now? She'd told her father and Iantha so when the plan for separate vacations had first come up, and when they'd insisted that she had their absolute trust, Skye called Aunt Claire and explained it all over again. Surely, she'd thought, Aunt Claire would take measures to stop this calamity.

After all, if Skye made a mess of everything in Maine, Aunt Claire would be the one cleaning up.

Aunt Claire, too, had let Skye down. "You'll do fine as the OAP," she said. "You'll find it in you," she added, and Skye went off to research multiple personalities, hoping she could find a new person inside who would be good at caring for Batty. When she discovered that extra personalities couldn't be ordered up on demand, she considered locking herself in the basement—or maybe faking a coma—until everyone had gone away to New Jersey, England, and Maine without her.

It was while she was working on slowing her heart rate for the pretend coma that her father came to her and asked her to please buck up and gracefully accept OAP-dom. He explained that the separation would be good for Rosalind, that she'd been in charge of her sisters for too long and badly needed a vacation. He also hinted that if Skye—and Jane and Batty, too—could convince Rosalind they'd be fine on their own, it would be easier for her to have a good time in New Jersey. How could Skye say no to that? Rosalind had indeed been in charge for a long time—more than five years, ever since the girls' mother had died of cancer—and she'd done it well and without complaints. So Skye canceled her coma, presented a carefree exterior to Rosalind, and told Jane to do the same.

However, agreeing to be the OAP wasn't the same

as having the knowledge to do so. If she'd been paying attention over the years, there would have been nothing to learn. But Skye hadn't paid attention, and though she was trying hard to do so now, none of it seemed to stick. Geometry theorems, or the names and positions of constellations—these she could memorize effortlessly. But how to care for Batty? Impossible. So secretly she began to make a list. Everything her father did or mentioned, or Rosalind, or Iantha, went onto it. By the end, the list was six closely written pages, and Skye kept it with her at all times.

It was in her back pocket now, which Skye patted, trying to reassure herself that she really had gathered all the information she needed to keep Batty alive and undamaged for two weeks. The reassurance didn't come.

"We're doomed," she said.

"No, we're not," said Jane. "Batty and I have complete faith in you, don't we, Batty?"

"I guess so." Batty snuffled and wiped her nose.

To Skye, the sound of that snuffle heralded disaster. It meant that Batty was crying about something, probably Rosalind. And since neither Skye nor Jane was good at stopping Batty's crying once it started, they were in for a painfully tearful drive to Maine. But then—oh, miracle—Batty sneezed! She wasn't crying but only truly snuffling. Maybe it was a sign, thought

Skye, that they weren't doomed after all. Onward, then. She told the others that it was time for the final countdown to departure, and that they should go to their rooms and make sure they hadn't forgotten anything. Skye herself went through the packed car, stuffed to its limit with suitcases, boxes of books, Batty's life jacket, Hound's food and water bowls, several soccer balls, and Skye's own personal necessities—a pair of binoculars and *Death by Black Hole*, a book that explained certain fascinating aspects of the universe. Then she went inside to the kitchen, where Aunt Claire was making lunch for the trip. Asimov was there, too, glaring balefully into his full-to-the-brim food bowl. He did this often, in the hope that someone would take pity and give him a piece of cheese.

"I've been the OAP for ten minutes now, and Batty is still fine," said Skye.

"Congratulations." Aunt Claire was wrapping up peanut-butter-and-jelly sandwiches. "Don't give that cat any more cheese. I've given him two pieces already."

Insulted, Asimov began to knock the food out of his bowl, one piece at a time.

"You still think I'll be able to handle this responsibility?"

"Yes, Skye, I do. Besides, you keep forgetting that you won't be doing it all alone. Jane and I will be there, too."

"I know." Skye got a piece of cheese out of the refrigerator for Asimov. She couldn't help it. She was going to miss him. "I checked the car. I think everything's packed."

"Everything but this food and us. Are you ready to go?"

Skye gave Asimov one last rub on the head. "As ready as I'll ever be. I'll get the others."

Their destination in Maine was Point Mouette, a tiny slip of a peninsula jutting into the Atlantic Ocean. To get there, they had to drive across Massachusetts, cut through a corner of New Hampshire, and wander more than a hundred miles up the coast of Maine. It was too long a drive for people not to get weary and cranky. Added to that were a few incidents that tried everyone's patience, like when Hound fell in love with a poodle named Penelope at a rest stop and refused to leave until he was given half a peanut-butter-and-jelly sandwich, and when Batty suddenly decided she'd left Funty, the blue elephant, at home and was so upset that Aunt Claire pulled over to the side of the highway to allow a full-out search for Funty, who was found hiding in a box with a soccer ball and a large inflatable duck. But before anyone actually murdered anyone else, Skye spotted the sign that said TO POINT MOUETTE, and they were turning off the state highway and onto the peninsula. Now they had only a few miles left to go, and all of it downhill.

Weariness and crankiness flew away as they gazed

avidly around, trying to drink in everything at once. Tall trees crowded the sides of the road, except where brightly painted houses sat in clearings of well-tended grass, and where—even better—the trees parted briefly for quick glimpses of the glistening ocean below them. Although everyone wanted to stop and explore each new sight, especially the rambling wooden Moose Market with a colossal stone bull moose out front, his dignity not at all impaired by the FRESH PIES sign hanging off his antlers, they wanted even more to rush on, eager to see where they'd be living for the next two weeks.

So on they went, until they came to the road that skirted the end of the peninsula. This was called Ocean Boulevard, a fancy name for a narrow road only a few miles long. Most of it was off to the left, but Aunt Claire turned right and a minute later pulled into the last driveway, just before Ocean Boulevard dead-ended at a pinewood. The driveway was short and narrow, with barely enough room for the car, and in front of it was their house.

"It's called Birches," said Aunt Claire. "I hope you like it."

Birches was tiny—not much bigger than a garage—and looked even smaller, nestled as it was next to a half dozen of the tall white-barked trees for which it was named. The girls had been prepared for its lack of size, but not for how charming it was, like a dollhouse, with gray clapboards, red shutters, and window boxes full of bright pansies. And it had a screened porch that the girls had already heard all about, where Skye and Jane would sleep.

"It's great, Aunt Claire," said Skye. "Thank you."

"I've always wanted to sleep on a porch," added Jane. "I will be one with nature."

"How about you, Batty?" asked Aunt Claire. "Do you like our little house?"

But Batty was busy rolling down the window to give Hound a breath of fresh air, and all at once the car was filled with the wild scent of salt, seaweed, marsh grass, and a breeze that had been around the world a thousand times, and the sisters were gripped by ocean fever. So when Aunt Claire said that she was going to explore Birches, and did they want to come with her, they all said no, thank you, because they had to get to the water as quickly as possible.

There was a delay as Skye and Jane maneuvered a protesting Batty into the orange life jacket, buckled it the wrong way, then had to do it over again, but before too long the sisters and Hound were following a flagstone path to the tiny green lawn behind Birches. And there was the ocean, sparkling blue and spread out before them in its vast glory, and above the ocean and vying with it for splendor was the summer sky, just as blue and filled with great heaps of white clouds. When the sisters had looked at all that, which took a long time, they could pay attention to what was on the water—small boats, some moored and some in full sail, and farther out a cluster of islands, most of them just big enough for a clump of trees and a house or two.

Skye hadn't forgotten Rosalind's warnings about seawalls. Indeed, at the edge of the lawn was a low wall, built from rock and wide enough to sit on. Nothing frightening there, except when Skye peered over it, she saw a six-foot drop to a jumble of ominous gray boulders, certain to smash any Penderwick who fell. She mentioned this several times to Batty, until Batty broke away to race Hound around the lawn and up to the deck—Birches had a wooden deck, perfect for picnic dinners—and back down to the lawn, but neither of them jumped onto the wall, for which Skye was grateful. Meanwhile, Jane had discovered steps at one edge of the yard, and she called the others over. Aunt Claire had told them there was a beach, and here it was.

Down the steps they ran. At first look, it wasn't much of a beach, just a narrow strip of sand that ran along the seawall for about forty feet. Skye knew about tides, though, and could tell that the tide was high. When it went out again, the beach would be a decent size, with plenty of room for soccer and anything else three girls and a dog could come up with. And no matter how small the beach was at high tide, they could still take off their shoes and wade into the shallow wavelets. The water was so cold that Batty screeched and Hound barked, but that made it all the more exhilarating, and just what everyone wanted after those long hours in the car.

Skye not only wet her feet, she splashed the cold water onto her face, reveling in the salty smell. She liked this place—and they had it almost all to themselves. Off to the right, the pinewood marched down to the rocks—they would have no company from that side. In the other direction, Skye could see a red house, half hidden by the birches, with its own set of steps leading down to the beach. Maybe the people who lived there would be quiet beach haters. That would be nice.

When the cold drove them out of the water, Jane made an announcement. "Batty and I have a speech for you, Skye. I tried to write it as a poem, but the only thing I could rhyme with OAP was *therapy*, and I didn't think that was the right way to go."

"Thank you." Jane's speeches could be overwrought enough without the added burden of poetry.

"You're welcome. Batty, begin the Skye speech."

Batty folded her hands over her orange life jacket. "Skye, we know you don't want to be the OAP, and we know you won't be good at—"

"No, no," interrupted Jane. "We know you don't *think* you'll be good at it."

"Oh, sorry. But we know . . . but we know . . . I forget, Jane."

"But we know in our hearts, Skye, that you'll be great, and we pledge to act with honor and restraint while in Maine, so that you'll have nothing to concern you."

Skye applauded, hoping that was the end, but Jane went on.

"Sundered from many of our loved ones—including Jeffrey, who would have been here if not for Mrs. T-D and her despicable Dexter—we're desolate in our hearts and souls. But Rosalind is connected to us by this ocean, which also brushes the fair shores of New Jersey." Jane picked up a tiny shell and tossed it into the ocean. "Maybe this shell will get washed to Ocean City and Rosalind will pick it up and know it came from us."

Batty enthusiastically threw in several more shells for Rosalind, and then a clump of seaweed that Hound retrieved, a new kind of treasure for him. But Jane still wasn't done.

"And we have not forgotten our father or Iantha or our little brother, Ben. Now everyone face this way." Jane and Batty turned to the ocean and pointed to the horizon. "Doubt not, there is England in the utter east—Skye, you're supposed to point, too."

"Except that you're pointing to the utter southeast. Maybe to Africa, but definitely not England."

"Now?"

"Better."

"Doubt not, there is England in the utter east, across the vast and lonely sea—oh, look at the seagulls!" Jane pointed in a new direction, more toward Iceland this time.

Her sisters pointed with her at the three seagulls bobbing on the water just yards away. The seagulls looked back at the sisters—and at Hound—and for one pleasant moment all was serene communion among species. But then the serenity was wrecked by a yelping streak of black and white that came out of nowhere to fly past the girls and into the ocean and after the birds.

Chaos erupted. Hound launched into a barking frenzy, Jane lunged at him to grab his collar, Batty wailed about the birds, and Skye, who had identified the streak of black and white as a small dog who didn't seem to be much of a swimmer, plunged into the ocean on a rescue mission.

Now it was a girl chasing a dog who was chasing seagulls. The seagulls soon wearied of that game, however, and took to the air. Skye called to the dog, hoping he'd have the sense to turn back, but no, his frantic doggy paddle was still taking him away from the shore. Her only chance was to cut him off, so onward she raced until, just as she caught up, the sand dropped out beneath her and suddenly Skye was up to her waist in very cold water.

This wasn't pleasant, and some people might have

let the dog work out his own fate at that point. Skye wasn't given the chance to decide whether she was one of those people, because the dog now changed direction and plowed right into her, trusting her to catch him. Which she did, though it's not easy to catch a thrashing dog when you're waist-deep in icy water, even if he's barely past puppyhood and weighs only fifteen pounds. And it's even harder to keep hold of him when he thinks it's all a terrific game and keeps twisting and squirming and the whole time licking your face with a pink tongue that seems much too large for such a small dog. And especially when your younger sisters, for whom you're supposed to be presenting a figure of calm authority, are screaming at you about birds and dogs and drowning and heaven knows what else, and your own dog hasn't stopped barking for even a second.

When Skye managed to get her face away from the bug-eyed, squishy-nosed, madly licking dog, she could see that a bearded man had joined her sisters on the beach. Where had he come from, and was he shouting "Hoover"? They're all nuts, thought Skye, and wished like anything that Rosalind were in Maine instead of New Jersey. She took a few wobbly steps and tossed the wretched dog as far as she could toward the shallower water.

And in doing so lost her balance and collapsed, freezing and furious, into the sea.

When she managed to get her face out of the water and the water out of her mouth, she shouted, "Did I kill him?"

The answer came back from several people. "No, he's okay!"

"Too bad," muttered Skye, then started the long slosh back to the beach.

CHAPTER THREE
The End of the List

JANE WAS DELIGHTED with the sleeping porch. It wrapped around one corner of the house, L-shaped, with bamboo shades you could roll down to cover the screens for privacy and one more extra-large shade to separate the two legs of the L. Skye had claimed the longer leg with two cots in it, as was her right as the OAP. Jane didn't mind. Her shorter leg, with enough space only for a cot and a squat green cupboard, was the perfect place to be a writer—spartan, yet when the shades were up also romantic and inspiring, like sleeping outside without mosquitoes. She tested the cot—it was sturdy and made up with white cotton blankets, quite different from her bed at home. A different bed can bring you different dreams, she thought.

"I'll do great work here," she called out to Skye on the other side of the separating shade.

"Humph" was all that came back.

Jane wasn't surprised at Skye's lack of enthusiasm. Getting dunked in the ocean by a small dog could be annoying, even if, as Jane thought, it was a cute small dog with a funny name. Hoover. She'd complimented his owner—the man with the beard—on the name and had also found out the man's name. He was Alec McGrath, and he lived in the red house next door to Birches. Jane had also found out that Alec had no children, which was unfortunate, since he seemed about old enough to have some the same age as the Penderwicks.

"I wish Alec had children, don't you, Skye?"

"Not if they were as obnoxious as his dog."

Jane hoped that Skye would cheer up soon. If only Jeffrey had been able to come to Maine. He was always a good influence on people, unless those people happened to be his mother or stepfather. It was hard to imagine anyone being a good influence on them. They were incorrigible.

Incorrigible was an excellent word. Jane decided to make a note of it. And maybe that thing about different beds and different dreams. She dug through her suitcase to find a pen and notebook. All this could come in handy for her new Sabrina Starr book, which would be about love no matter what Rosalind said.

Jane had touched on love in a play she'd written the previous autumn, and it was time for her to go further. It would stretch her as a writer. The problem, unfortunately, was that she knew so little about love. Not by choice but because of her age—she'd just turned eleven in June, which made her too young to have a history of serious romance. There had been a few promising episodes in the last year, like when Mateo Phelan gave her a card on Valentine's Day and when Marcus Jefferson asked her to go bowling, but these ardors petered out before they began, and Marcus had been a terrible bowler on top of it.

Until now Jane's biggest crushes had been on boys in books, especially Peter Pevensie, who became High King of Narnia. There'd been others—Tom Hammond from *Leepike Ridge*, Finn Taverner from *Journey to the River Sea*, and, though he was so small, Spiller from the Borrowers books, but none of these had inspired the same adoration as Peter. Many nights Jane had put herself to sleep with lovely imaginings of adventures with him. Sometimes she was a maiden of Narnia, a dryad perhaps, who fought shoulder to shoulder with Peter in his battles, and sometimes an English girl who found her way through the wardrobe with him. Once she'd been a Calormene maiden who left her people to swear true love and devotion to the High King, but Jane hadn't liked that as much, never having understood the Calormenes.

She worried about coming up with a boy as thrilling as Peter Pevensie for Sabrina. And without someone for Sabrina to fall in love with, there could be no book to write. It was frustrating, and being frustrated with her writing was a new experience for Jane. Usually the books had just poured out of her. Sighing, she closed her notebook and tossed it onto the green cupboard.

Above the cot was a window that looked back into the house. Jane knelt and peered through to the main room, which had lots of wicker and brightly colored cushions, and big sliding glass doors that opened onto the rear deck. Off to one side was a round wooden table for meals. Batty was sitting there now, drawing with a set of new markers that Iantha had given her for the vacation. The minuscule kitchen was around the corner and out of sight, and Aunt Claire could be heard banging around in there, putting away the supplies they'd brought from Massachusetts. Soon Jane would go in and explore the kitchen, since she'd promised to help with meals.

But first to finish unpacking. Jane stuffed a pile of T-shirts into the cupboard, then paused, distracted by noises coming from the other part of the sleeping porch. Skye was muttering to herself over there, not happily, and there were thumps, too, as though she were tossing things. Jane peeked around the bamboo shade. Skye had dumped the contents of her suitcase onto the floor and was frenziedly pawing through her clothes and, yes, tossing them from one side of the porch to the other.

"What's wrong?" asked Jane.

"I can't find my secret list." Skye was now flipping through the pages of *Death by Black Hole*, forward and backward, once, twice, three times.

"What secret list?"

"Everything Rosalind, Daddy, and Iantha told me about Batty, all written down so that I could remember. I thought it was in my pocket, but I can't find it." Skye jammed her hand into one of the pockets of her jeans, then another, and then another. "See, nothing."

"Those jeans are dry. What about the ones you wore into the ocean?"

"I hung them outside on the— Oh, no." Skye whirled around and crashed out through the screen door. A moment later, she was back with a pair of sopping jeans in one hand and a sodden wad of paper in the other.

"Now we really are doomed," she said, looking sick.

Jane wasn't in the mood for doom. She took the wad from Skye and tried to gently separate the pages, but where the paper didn't rip, the ink had run so badly that nothing was legible. But wait, here were a few blurry words.

"*Blow up,*" she read. "I wonder what that means. Maybe that Batty could blow up, with hives or something?"

"We're sure to find out, since we can't read what we're supposed to do or not do about it! This is a nightmare. What was everyone thinking, Jane? I make a terrible OAP."

"Daddy thinks you'll grow into it. I heard him tell Iantha so."

Skye looked like she'd been thrown a lifeline. "He really said that?"

"Yes, he really did." Jane was telling the truth—she had heard him say that. She'd also heard him say he wasn't sure exactly when Skye would grow into it. But Skye didn't need to hear that part. "Maybe you can remember what the list said."

"Stuff about brushing her hair and which vitamins to give her."

"Which vitamins?"

"I don't remember details! I thought I'd have the list!"

"Maybe I can hypnotize you into remembering." Jane waved her hand like a pendulum in front of Skye's face. "You are getting sleepy. You are getting very—"

Skye swatted her away. "Jane, this is serious."

"Taking care of Batty can't be all that hard. We've watched Daddy and Rosalind do it for five years now."

"I haven't been paying attention," said Skye. "Have you?"

"No, not really." Jane refused to give in to hopelessness. "So whenever we have a question, we'll just call Rosalind and ask."

35

"We can't do that. If Rosalind figures out I don't know what I'm doing, she'll be on the next bus to Maine." Skye sank onto one of the cots. "I'll have failed in everyone's eyes."

Jane wanted to help. But short of staging a near tragedy so that Skye could dramatically rescue Batty, thereby boosting her self-confidence, there was nothing she could do. Unless they went back to the hypnosis idea. Jane thought that Skye had dismissed this too readily and was about to tell her so when they heard a phone ringing inside the house.

Skye grabbed Jane's arm. "That's Rosalind, I know it is. Please don't say anything about this."

"I won't. But, Skye, you should try to sound happier if you don't want her suspecting trouble."

Now Aunt Claire was calling for them to come inside.

Skye pitched her voice higher. "Do I sound happier?"

"No, just weird."

"That's the best I can do. Let's go talk to her."

But when they went into the living room, Aunt Claire had already hung up the phone and Batty was dancing around Hound.

"There's a very good surprise," she said, hopping over Hound's tail. "Guess!"

"Ice cream for dinner," said Skye, wondering if there was a flavor of ice cream that blew up children. "Wasn't that Rosalind on the phone?"

"Not ice cream and not Rosalind." Batty danced in the other direction. "Guess again. Starts with a G."

"Giraffe, gnu, goldfish," tried Jane. "Green beans, grass skirt, George Washington."

"Not even close."

"Batty, the surprise doesn't start with a G," said Aunt Claire. "Now everyone sit down so that you don't fall over when I tell you what it is."

Neither Skye nor Jane could imagine a surprise good enough to fall over for. But they sat down at the table, because it seemed the quickest way to stop Batty from dancing. She was a loud dancer.

"Good," said Aunt Claire, sitting, too. "First I have to apologize for not telling you last night when I found out, but I was afraid she would change all over again. Heaven knows it's happened enough times already."

The girls were used to Aunt Claire not making sense when she was excited or nervous, but usually their father was available to straighten her out. Skye took a deep breath—it was up to her now.

"You were afraid who would change all over again?" she asked.

"Starts with an M," said Batty, jiggling in her chair.

"Oh, my!" Jane jiggled a little, too. "I'm having an idea."

"I'm not," said Skye crossly.

Jane turned to Aunt Claire. "Did Batty mean *J* instead of *G*?"

"She did indeed."

"Oh, Skye, don't you see? J is for Jeffrey and M must be for Mrs. T-D. Did she change her mind again, Aunt Claire?"

Skye was back on her feet, so full of hope she couldn't stand it. "Is Jeffrey coming here after all? Don't tease. Please just tell us."

She didn't need an answer—Aunt Claire's big smile was enough. And then there was lots of shrieking, and when Aunt Claire said that not only was Jeffrey coming but he would arrive any minute, Skye dashed outside into the late-afternoon sunshine, then stopped so abruptly that her sisters and Hound, who were also dashing, slammed into her.

"Go ask Aunt Claire how he's getting here," Skye told Jane. "If his mother is driving—"

Jane didn't need to hear the rest of the sentence. She knew as well as Skye that the sight of actual Penderwicks could be enough to make Mrs. T-D turn around and drive all the way back to Arundel. But Aunt Claire had the right answer—Jeffrey was being delivered to them by a hired driver—and now there was nothing to keep the girls from running down Ocean Boulevard to meet him headlong.

So they ran, Skye and Jane carrying Batty between them, with Hound following, barking at all the excitement. They ran and ran, and would have kept on running forever to be with Jeffrey, but way before that, a long black car appeared. Hound barked even more,

Skye and Jane waved frantically, the car came to a stop, and out of its window popped Jeffrey, looking exactly as he should, with his freckles and his hair that had trouble staying down, and just as happy to see them as they were to see him.

"Get in!" he cried.

They all crammed into the car, gleefully scrambling over each other and Jeffrey, though they did manage to say hello to the driver, a cheerful-looking man named Mr. Remillard. Then, with everyone talking and laughing at once, they rode back to Birches. Hound helped by barking the entire time, because he worshipped Jeffrey and was amazed to have him turn up so suddenly in Maine.

"The house is awfully small, Jeffrey," said Skye when they'd arrived and tumbled out of the car. "Do you mind?"

"Are you kidding?" Jeffrey picked up Batty and spun her around until she squealed with laughter. "I'll sleep on the floor if I have to."

"No, no," said Jane and Skye together, then went on interrupting each other to explain the sleeping porch and how they would share one leg of it, and Jeffrey could have the other leg all to himself, and how they didn't mind sharing at all, since it meant they'd have him there. In the meantime, Mr. Remillard had opened the trunk of his car and was unloading it. First came a suitcase and then a cardboard box tied with a ribbon.

"Food from Churchie," said Jeffrey when the box appeared. "As soon as Mother decided to let me come, Churchie started baking."

The sisters had gotten to know and love Churchie, who was Mrs. T-D's housekeeper, the summer before at Arundel. She had many excellent qualities—her fierce devotion to Jeffrey among them—but in the realm of the kitchen she was beyond excellent and all the way to phenomenal. Skye peeked into the box and almost swooned. Three loaves of Churchie's famous gingerbread! Jeffrey and gingerbread, all at the same time. Perfection.

Now Jeffrey reached into the trunk and brought out a small black clarinet case. This wasn't unexpected, since Jeffrey was a musician and would be miserable without some instrument or another. His first love was the piano, which he'd been playing for years; he'd been studying clarinet for only six months. But pianos don't fit into trunks of cars, so the clarinet was an excellent choice for Maine.

Skye started to close the trunk but saw one last thing, crammed way into the back and half covered with an old towel, as though Jeffrey had tried to hide it. And when she looked closer, she understood why. Back there was a fancy leather bag full of golf clubs. The sisters knew this bag well—they'd been with Jeffrey the previous summer when his mother and Dexter gave it to him for his eleventh birthday. Jeffrey had loathed golf then, and Skye was quite sure he loathed it still.

"Why did you bring this?" she asked him, saying "this" as she would say "putrid garbage."

Jeffrey grimaced. "Dexter says there's a golf course around here. There could be a hundred golf courses for all I care. Stupid sport."

"Never mind," said Jane. "We'll stick the bag under one of the cots and you can ignore it for the whole two weeks."

"You can stay for the whole two weeks, can't you?" asked Skye anxiously. Now that he was here, it would be horrible to have him swept away again.

"Every minute," said Jeffrey. "Mr. Remillard will come back for me on the morning you're all leaving."

"Even if your mother calls and says she's changed her mind again?" This was Jane.

"Even if she and Dexter drive here themselves and try to tear me away."

Batty took hold of his arm. "Promise?"

"I promise," said Jeffrey. "Do or die."

Skye dragged the golf bag out of the trunk and slung it over her shoulder. It was just as heavy as it was unwanted, but Skye stood up straight and strong, determined not to let Dexter, Mrs. T-D, or golf bags—or even the loss of her precious list—wreck their vacation. Jeffrey was here now, and they were going to have the time of their lives.

CHAPTER FOUR
A New Song

BATTY'S BEDROOM WAS SO TINY that the narrow bed and small bureau filled it up. There wasn't even space for a closet—just a row of hooks on the wall, too high for Batty to reach. She didn't mind that the room was small, and she especially didn't mind about no closet. You never know what scary monsters might be hiding in the closets of strange houses.

Earlier, Aunt Claire had helped her unpack and put her clothes into the bureau. Now—almost bedtime—Batty had to do the next, most important part of moving in, which was to figure out what to do if a monster managed to appear, even without a closet to come from. Rosalind always helped her with this part. Rosalind knew all about monsters, and how to keep away from them. But Rosalind was far away in New Jersey, and Batty was on her own. Just thinking about being on her own made her want to hide under the covers, but she couldn't, not without first working out about the monsters.

So how *would* she get away from one? She looked out the window. There were the birch trees and, past them, a patch of red that was the house where Hoover the dog lived. Batty was impressed with Hoover. It wasn't everyone who could knock Skye into the ocean. But back to monsters. Batty supposed that if she had to, she could jump out the window. It wasn't far to the ground. She'd have to figure out how to take out the screen, though, and she'd never done anything like that in her whole life. Maybe she could convince Hound to tear a hole in the screen big enough for her to crawl through.

"If a monster comes, will you wreck the screen for me?" she asked Hound.

Hound didn't answer. He was too busy chewing a hunk of seaweed he'd sneaked into the house. Batty sighed. If he wouldn't help her with the screen, there was only one place in the room to hide: under the bed. Of course there could always be a monster down there. Seaweed or no seaweed, Hound had to help after all. So Batty pulled him at one end and pushed him at the other until about half of him was beneath the bed.

"Any monsters?" she asked him. "No?"

Now it was safe for her to wriggle in after him and squash herself against the wall. It was clean under there except for something large and plastic, which turned out to be the big duck that Iantha had given her for Maine. The duck, flat now because it had no air in it, must have been put there by Hound. He loved hiding things under beds.

Batty heard the door open, and Skye came into the room—Batty recognized her black sneakers—and started questioning the part of Hound that was sticking out.

"Are you eating seaweed, you silly dog? And where is Batty? Good grief, I've lost her already."

Usually, Batty would have stayed hidden, but there was an unfamiliar note in Skye's voice, as though she *minded* that Batty was lost.

"I'm down here."

Skye's face swam into view, looking relieved, and disappeared again. "It's time to get into your pajamas."

"I've already put them on." Batty was proud of this. She was even prouder for having already washed her face and brushed her teeth.

Skye's face came back. "So you did. Well, you still need to brush your teeth."

"I did that, too."

"Oh." Skye stood up again. After a moment, the

bed sagged over Batty, which meant that Skye had sat on it. "Batty, do you happen to know which vitamins you take?"

"The ones in the yellow bottle."

"Right. And do you know what would make you blow up?"

This felt like a trick question to Batty. She'd never been blown up and didn't like thinking about it. She hoped it wasn't something that happened a lot in Maine.

"Why?" she asked.

"No reason," said Skye. "Oh, hi, Jeffrey. She's under the bed."

Now Jeffrey's face appeared, but Batty was already squirming out into the open. She'd hoped that Jeffrey would be part of her good-night routine, and now here he was.

"Hey, goofball," he said. "Hiding from monsters?"

She beamed up at him, her favorite boy in the world. "Are you going to tell me a bedtime story?"

"Jane has one all ready for you. Maybe tomorrow night, okay?"

"Okay." Batty hopped onto the bed and slid under the covers.

"I hope you sleep well," said Skye, self-consciously patting the part of the pillow that Batty didn't have her head on. "Jane will be here in a minute."

Jeffrey said good night; then Skye pulled him out

the door and the room was quiet again. Through the open window, Batty could hear the gentle murmur of waves breaking on the rocks. She could also hear a squishy chewing noise. That was Hound and his seaweed. Squish. Squish. Batty found it soothing. She snuggled in among her stuffed animals—Funty and several others, including Ellie, the small green elephant, Funty's special friend. Ellie had been a goodbye present from Ben, but Batty was certain her father had really bought her. Her father always knew just what stuffed animals Batty liked the best. He'd promised to bring another new one home from England, and Batty was pretty sure it would be a tiger.

While she was experimenting with good tiger names—Gibson, or maybe Chip—Jane arrived. Batty hoped that she had a cozy story ready. Sometimes Jane's stories could be too exciting for bedtime.

Jane perched on a corner of the bed and began: "Once there was a beautiful maiden named Sabrina Starr."

"This is about love, isn't it?" Batty had learned to spot Jane's romantic stories coming on—"beautiful" was one hint and "maiden" was another.

"Yes. I'm working on ideas for my next book. You're my trial audience."

Batty gave up on getting a cozy story, or even an exciting one. However, she'd been Jane's trial audience before, and was always proud to do it. She waited for Jane to go on, but Jane just sat there, twiddling with her hair. After too much of this, Batty tapped Jane on the arm.

"I'd better begin again," said Jane. "Once there was a beautiful maiden named Sabrina Starr who had never been in love."

The hair twiddling started up again, but Batty wasn't going to wait so long this time. "Then what?" she asked.

"That's all I have so far. What do you think?"

"It's okay," answered Batty carefully. This seemed as much a trick question as the one about blowing up. "But not very long."

"I know. I just can't figure out how to start this book."

Batty was trying to be patient, but this was disappointing. Rosalind would never have told her a story with only a beginning and no middle or end. But no, she wasn't going to think about Rosalind, because if she did, she would cry. And she wasn't going to cry in front of Jane, or in front of Skye, especially not Skye. Not once, not for the whole time she was in Maine. So she yawned instead, then remembered the present that Iantha had given her for Maine. It was a real book with chapters, and Batty had already learned to read the two names in the title—one was Ivy and the other was Bean. She had high hopes of learning to read even more of the words one of these days.

"Since your book is still so short," she said to Jane,

"maybe you could read *Ivy + Bean* to me. It doesn't have love in it, though."

"I don't need love in everything," said Jane.

Batty didn't believe her, but Jane read her the first chapter of the book anyway, and it was an excellent chapter, and she also taught Batty to read one new word: *girl*. Then Jane drifted away, once again pondering Sabrina Starr, and there was only Aunt Claire left to say good night.

"I brought you a night-light," she said when she came in a few minutes later.

"It's a pig!" Batty was fond of pigs, and this one was wearing sunglasses, which was even better.

When Aunt Claire plugged it into a socket on the wall, the pig gave out a pink glow that was sure to discourage even the boldest monster.

"How's that? Good?" Aunt Claire sat on the bed and surveyed the stuffed animals. "You have a new friend."

"Ellie," said Batty, gently pulling the green elephant's trunk. "Ben gave her to me."

"Ben has excellent taste for a toddler."

"Yes."

"You miss him, don't you?"

"*Yes!*"

"I do, too."

Batty stowed Ellie carefully beside the pillow. "Do you think Ben misses me?"

"Are you kidding? I *know* Ben misses you. And so do your dad, Iantha, and Rosalind. Everyone misses you—Asimov, Tommy, the whole neighborhood. I'll bet even the president of the United States misses you."

"I never met the president."

"Which just shows how special you are, that someone you've never met would miss you anyway."

Batty tried to puzzle this out, but it made her sleepy. "I guess so," she answered, her eyelids drooping.

"Trust your aunt," said Aunt Claire, kissing Batty first on one cheek, then on the other. "Good night, honey bug. Sleep well, and call me if you need anything."

Then she was gone, and Batty and Hound were alone again. Batty waved good night to the new pig and told Hound to come be with her. Being a true and loyal friend, he abandoned his seaweed and jumped onto the bed, and before Batty could remember how far she was from home and from Rosalind, she was fast asleep and dreaming about tigers.

Being woken up in the middle of the night can be scary, especially when you're in a strange place and when what wakes you sounds like a train going through your room. It took Batty only seconds to realize that of course the thunderous rumbling was Hound's snoring, but it took her longer to remember that she was in Maine, and that the odd, looming shadows cast by the pig night-light didn't come from monsters but from her own animals sitting atop the bureau. It wasn't their fault, Batty knew. It was probably her own for bringing so many of them with her to Maine. Skye had wanted her to leave everyone but Funty and Ellie behind, but Daddy had said she'd need as much comfort as she could get. Daddy hadn't known Batty was listening when he told Skye this, and she hadn't meant to, but she'd just happened to be under the kitchen table playing cavemen with Ben when he'd said it.

Oh, Ben! Who would play cavemen with him when he wasn't with Batty? Did people even play cavemen in England? England was a great mystery to her, almost as much as New Jersey. Aunt Claire had tried to explain it all, and had even taped postcards onto the refrigerator here at Birches—down low so that Batty would be able to see them without standing on a chair. It would be nice to look at those postcards right now, thought Batty, but it was a long way to the refrigerator in the dark, and she didn't know if she had the courage to go. So she closed her eyes and tried to picture them. The New Jersey one showed a wide beach full of umbrellas, and the England one—she couldn't remember what the England postcard looked like. Now she just had to go look at it. But not without Hound. She poked at him until he got the idea and jumped off the bed to await further instructions. Batty slid down after him and saw that underneath her door was a strip of light, which meant that Aunt Claire had left a lamp on out there, just in case someone desperately needed to go look at postcards. Batty squared her shoulders. Aunt Claire had expected this to happen, so there was nothing to be frightened of.

With Hound beside her, she tiptoed out into the living room and was startled to see a little girl and a big dog just outside the sliding glass doors, staring back at her. Ghosts? No, silly, Batty told herself. Maybe Ben would think they were ghosts, but Batty was much too big for that. It was just her and Hound reflected in the sliding glass doors.

Hound was already on his way to the small kitchen. Now that he'd been dragged out of bed, he'd check for spilled food, since the seaweed hadn't been very filling. Batty followed him, ignoring the dark corners of the living room. She cared about only one thing now—seeing the all-important postcards. She made it to the refrigerator, and there they were. First she looked at the England postcard. It showed a tall red bus going over a stone bridge, and across the top was a word that Batty spelled out for Hound.

"O-X-F-O-R-D," she said. "That's where Daddy is with Iantha and Ben. Iantha told me about the red buses."

There was no answer from Hound, because his nose was jammed under the stove, continuing his search for food. Batty turned to the shiny New Jersey postcard, with its wide white beach and blue ocean. It was looking at the New Jersey ocean that gave Batty her idea. If a shell could float all the way from the Maine ocean to the New Jersey ocean—and Jane had said so—a letter could, too. Batty would float Rosalind a letter, and she would do it right now to give the letter time to reach New Jersey by tomorrow. She needed only her drawing pad and markers, and they were over there on that bookshelf. In a moment, Batty had the pad open on the floor, and all the markers spread out, ready for letter writing. She had so many things to tell Rosalind—about how much she missed her, and about Jeffrey and Hoover and the shadows on her bedroom wall—that she hardly knew how to begin. And, too, there was that problem with spelling. She did know how to spell her sister's name, though, so she started there. In big blue letters, she wrote ROSALIND, and although she'd gotten too close to the edge and had to make the N and D small, she was very proud of what she'd done so far.

She thought for a while, trying to figure out how to spell *miss*, as in *I miss you*, but when she couldn't work out whether it was *mis* or *miss* or something else altogether, she used a gold marker to write LOVE instead. Then, since somehow she'd managed to fill up most of the paper, she finished off with BATTY in red letters. Rosalind would know what she meant. She always did.

And now came the hard part—throwing the letter into the ocean. Batty pushed open the heavy sliding door, shoving with all her strength, then stepped out into the night. How dark it was outside, and how much louder the ocean sounded all of a sudden! Clutching her letter, Batty crept to the edge of the deck but could go no further. Not without Hound, who had stayed inside, and not, she realized now, without the orange life jacket. Rosalind had made it clear that Batty would drown without that life jacket, but now she was too tired to go back for it. She wasn't going to be able to send her letter and Rosalind would never know how much Batty missed her.

Out there on the cold deck, Batty started to cry, and once she started she couldn't seem to stop, even when Hound gave up on the stove and came outside to find her. He licked her face, but she sobbed on and on and thought she might sob forever, or at least until breakfast. But she didn't have to wait that long, because Hound, finding that he couldn't soothe her, wisely went looking for the one person who could, and soon he came back with Jeffrey, who sat down beside Batty and put his arm around her, and that was wonderful. She told him everything, about the shadows and the postcards and how she needed to throw the letter into the ocean, and he didn't laugh at her or even smile, and then he offered to throw her letter into the ocean for her, which he did, just like the hero she'd known him to be since the very first day she met him.

"There," he said, coming back to her on the deck. "Letter launched."

"And you won't tell Skye and Jane, right?"

"Penderwick family honor." He inspected her for traces of further crying. "Do you feel better now? A little bit? Wait—I know what else we can do. Stay here."

Jeffrey disappeared back into the house, but before Batty had time to get scared all over again, he was back with his clarinet case and a small silvery something that he handed to Batty.

"It's a harmonica. If you like, you can keep it, and I'll teach you how to play. Think how surprised Rosalind will be when you play a song for her."

Batty turned the harmonica over and over and let Hound sniff it. She'd seen one before, and had even blown on it, but no one had ever offered to teach her a real song. Penderwicks didn't play songs on instruments. Rosalind and Skye had both tried music lessons when they were younger, and they'd been so miserably bad at them that Jane hadn't bothered.

"I don't know," she said, though she longed to try.

Jeffrey was right—how surprised Rosalind would be, and Daddy and Iantha, too. And Ben, why, she could teach Ben everything Jeffrey taught her. "Well, maybe."

"Good. Now blow into it."

She blew and heard music coming out. She blew some more, then sucked in instead of blowing out, and although this was a mistake, music still came out, and it hadn't been a mistake after all. Batty was astonished, and Hound, who had suffered through the older sisters' struggles with music, was even more so.

"Teach me more," she said. "Please."

And right there, with the rushing, crashing waves for accompaniment, Batty had her first-ever music lesson. Jeffrey showed her how to make her mouth smaller to keep from playing lots of notes all at once, and talked a little about the difference between blowing in and out—though Batty didn't get all that right away—and when she had a little more confidence, he started teaching her a song. He played one note at a time on his clarinet, then waited for her to find that same note on her harmonica before he went on to the next. They did that for six whole notes, and then together they played the six notes all in a row, and Batty couldn't have been happier if she'd had an entire orchestra behind her.

"Again?" she asked.

"We need to go back to sleep, but I can show you more tomorrow."

"Yes, please." She stood up and took his hand. "Maybe I'll be a musician when I grow up, just like you."

"I'd like that," Jeffrey said, and took her and Hound inside and put them safely back to bed.

CHAPTER FIVE
An Accident

Even with her head under the pillow, Jane could hear the harmonica. She knew what time it was, and there was no reason for anyone to be playing a harmonica at eight o'clock in the morning. Unless Jeffrey was having an uncontrolled urge to play music, any music. But whoever was playing seemed to be playing the same notes over and over, and Jeffrey wouldn't torture people like that, especially not this early. It couldn't be Skye, because she was still asleep in the cot next to Jane's, and Aunt Claire had never shown interest in harmonicas or any other musical instruments. Which left only one possibility.

Jane came out from under her pillow and shook Skye. "You'd better go see what Batty's doing. I think she's got hold of a harmonica."

"Impossible," mumbled Skye.

"Improbable, but not impossible. Go find out. You're the OAP." Jane went back under her pillow, trying to block not only the harmonica but the thumps and crashes of Skye getting out of bed. Jane needed quiet, because she was working on her book. This was her favorite time to think about writing— while she was still in bed, no longer asleep but not quite awake, or as she put it when she thought about writing her autobiography, while she floated between dreams and reality. She was trying to come up with a good second sentence. She was almost sure she wanted to keep *Once there was a beautiful maiden named Sabrina Starr who had never been in love* as her first sentence. But where to go from there? Last night she'd come up with several possibilities, full of words like *yearn* and *destiny*, but this morning they all sounded ridiculous.

Now it was Skye shaking her. Jane's pillow fell to the floor.

"What?" she asked crossly. If this morning was any indication, she wasn't going to get much writing done in Maine.

"You were right," said Skye. "Batty does have a harmonica. She says that Jeffrey gave it to her in the middle of the night, that he's teaching her to play, and from what I can tell, he's teaching her to play 'Taps.' Aunt Claire's in there with her, looking very patient.

Do you think there could have been a rule against musical instruments on my list?"

Jane listened to the notes still being played in the house. Yes, they did sound like the beginning of "Taps."

"If not, there should have been," she said.

"I agree," said Skye. Crouching, she tossed a shoe under the bamboo room divider. She must have aimed well, because now there came a series of snorts, and finally Jeffrey's indignant voice.

"Why did you do that?"

"'Taps'? On a harmonica?"

The bamboo screen was shoved aside and Jeffrey's head came through. "It was the easiest song I could come up with," he said. "And I think she sounds pretty good."

When Skye picked up another shoe to throw, Jane scooted down under her blanket. A second line had just come to her, and she didn't want to lose it. *Sabrina told herself that she didn't long for love, but this was a lie.* No, that wasn't right at all! Rats! Maybe it would help to choose a name for Sabrina's love. Arnold, Akbar. No. Aidan? No. Bartholomew. Ha. Crispin, no, Carl, no, no, no. Go on to D. But to Jane's annoyance, her brain got stuck on Dexter, and that of course was out of the question.

"What's wrong with me?" she moaned. "Am I washed up as a writer already?"

No one answered, not a helpful muse or even a sister. Jane peeked out from under her blanket. Skye was gone, and Jeffrey's shoes, his hat, and a golf club were on this side of the bamboo curtain. There must have been an exhilarating battle while Jane had gotten exactly nothing done. She twisted her blanket in frustration.

But now Skye was bursting back onto the porch, full of energy and plans. Aunt Claire was sending the two of them and Jeffrey on a walk to that market with the moose in front. For groceries, and also to keep Skye from breaking Batty's harmonica in two and throwing it into the ocean. And also to work on soccer skills. Skye loved working on soccer skills. Jane would have preferred to stay in bed and think—Eamon? Felipe?—but Skye was waving around three fat slices of Churchie's gingerbread, and suddenly Jane was too hungry to worry about Sabrina Starr's love life.

Skye didn't hand over the gingerbread until they were all dressed and outside. It was a gorgeous morning, bright with sunshine while still fresh and cool, and with traces of dew glittering on the grass. Across the street a broad meadow was dotted with wildflowers and, in the middle, one giant oak lording it over all. The pinewood to their left was as dark and secretive as a pinewood should be, and to their right was a long stretch of privacy, broken only by Alec's red house, and that was half hidden by the birches.

"I like it here," said Jeffrey, cramming the last of his gingerbread into his mouth.

"It's idyllic," agreed Jane.

"Enough chatter. Get ready for soccer drills," said Skye. "Taps" had been only a temporary setback. The combination of Jeffrey, gingerbread, and the invigorating ocean air had her nearly giddy with happiness. "Dribble pattern Isosceles."

Isosceles was one of Skye's favorite drills. It needed three people—positioned at the three points of a triangle—and consisted of a complicated pattern of passing, receiving, and switching places in the triangle, while all the time running forward, even when passing backward. Jeffrey and Jane groaned—weren't they on vacation after all?—but Skye was already tossing out two balls, so off they went down Ocean Boulevard. They passed Alec's house and the stretch of rocky coast that separated it and Birches from the rest of Point Mouette.

Then came a large white building, which they'd been too rushed the day before to notice. It turned out to be an inn—Mouette Inn—and was comfortable-looking rather than grand, with cheerful flower gardens and a wide porch full of lounge chairs, and across the road from it was a wooden dock built far out into the ocean, which everyone agreed was full of possibilities.

None of this slowed down the intricate dance of

Isosceles, but when they had to turn off Ocean Boulevard and start up the hill, the triangle had a hard time holding its shape, and as the road got steeper and curvier and there were cars, even Skye knew that the soccer drill was over. Still, she insisted they all run in a straight line, carrying the balls. She wanted them to chant as they went, but while she was trying to decide on a chant, Jane and Jeffrey ganged up on her and said that if they had to chant, they wouldn't run. Even without the chanting, it was grueling work, and they were grateful to reach Moose Market.

Inside, the store had wide-planked wooden floors and leaning shelves, and it smelled delicious, like ripe fruit and new bread. Jeffrey, in charge of Aunt Claire's list, sent them hunting and gathering for groceries, and when they'd finished that, all three ended up staring at the rows of fresh-baked pies in the glass case near the cash register, debating the merits of each, and finally deciding on one lemon meringue and one strawberry-rhubarb. Then Skye grabbed extra cartons of orange juice to drink on the way home, since the run there had made them thirsty, and they were ready to check out and head back.

On the way down the hill, Jane lagged behind the others, laden down with a soccer ball, her orange juice, and both pies. Moose Market had made her think about her book. Maybe she needed to come up with a particularly interesting place for Sabrina to meet her love, like a country store with wooden floors. *Looking up from the pies, Sabrina saw him across the aisle, near the lettuce and celery.* No, that doesn't work, thought Jane. Was it possible that Sabrina Starr simply wasn't ready for romance? And how does somebody become ready for romance, anyway? This was an enigma, one that Jane needed to solve.

"For my art," she said out loud.

Ahead of her, Skye called out, "What did you say?"

"Nothing." Jane knew there was no point in discussing love with Skye, who didn't have what Jane considered to be a romantic soul. Or with Jeffrey, whose head was so stuffed with music that there wasn't room for much else. Like right now—Jane could hear him trying to explain to Skye about something called a diminished seventh chord while Skye was beating him with a roll of paper towels to make him stop.

Jane wished she'd begun thinking about love a week or so ago, when the family was still together. Iantha would have answered her questions. She always did—it was one of the million nice things about her. Rosalind might have, too, though she had said it was none of Jane's business that one time Jane asked what it was like to kiss Tommy. Maybe that hadn't been a good question to start with. Maybe she should work out better questions to ask, and make up a survey for research. Yes, a Love Survey. Jane liked that idea a lot. What she needed was a good first question, one that would get people interested without scaring them away.

"Do you believe in love at first sight?" she asked out loud.

"Jane, what are you talking about?" It was Skye again, but this time she was only a few feet away. Jane had caught up without noticing.

"She wants to know if we believe in love at first sight," said Jeffrey.

"More love," said Skye, now hitting Jane with the paper towels. "As the OAP, I demand you don't mention love for the whole rest of the day."

Jane thought this hardly fair, but before she could launch an argument, everyone was distracted by the rattle and clatter of something rushing down the hill. They turned and saw a boy flying toward them on a skateboard, his arms outstretched. Almost immediately he was upon them and then passing by, at such a speed Jane felt her curls lift. She thought he would keep going, but no, he executed a sharp turn that should have ended in disaster, slid to a dramatic halt, and dismounted with careless grace.

My goodness, thought Jane, staring. He was magnificent, with sunglasses, lots of hair, and the self-confidence of a movie star, or even a prince. Jane cast about in her mind for possible European princes who could be traveling incognito in Maine, but her knowledge of present-day royalty was limited to William and Harry of England, and this boy was certainly neither of them. She would have to hear him speak for a clue—a foreign language or at least an accent—and, look, he *was* about to say something. Jane held her breath.

He said, casually, "My sister might crash into you."

The accent was disappointingly pure American. But what an interesting thing to say, thought Jane, full of possible hidden meanings. Like the opening of a spy conversation, in which one spy said *Looks like fog* and the other spy answered *Or mist,* and then they both knew that it was safe to discuss state secrets. What would be a good response to *My sister might crash into you?*

Jane never got to decide, because other, cooler heads—that is, Skye and Jeffrey—prevailed, pushing Jane out of the path of a bicycle that was wobbling dangerously down the hill. Riding it was a wispy, awkward-looking girl who could barely reach the pedals.

"I don't know how to stop," she called.

"Use the brakes!" shouted Skye and Jeffrey together.

But apparently the girl's cycling lessons had not included brakes, because instead of using them, she decided to launch herself off the bike. She went one way—into the grass beside the road—and the bike went the other, crashing and sliding with lots of wheel spinning. Jane and Skye dropped their groceries and rushed to the girl's aid, but she easily scrambled to her feet, unhurt and not at all embarrassed by her clumsy entry. Meanwhile, Jeffrey picked up her bicycle and set it back upright—and she looked at him as though he were a god.

"I'm Mercedes Orne," she said.

"Jeffrey Tifton." He shook her hand, then straightened her helmet.

In all this activity, the one person who hadn't budged was the boy in the sunglasses. Jane looked at him curiously. Did he care so little about his sister crashing her bicycle? Or maybe he was simply being generous about letting the others be heroes. Yes, it was probably generosity.

Skye, however, seemed to have come to a different conclusion. She was glaring at the boy and was clearly about to scold him. Jane jumped in.

"I'm Jane Penderwick, and this is my sister Skye," she said brightly. "We're staying in Birches, that tiny house at the end of Ocean Boulevard."

"Dominic and I live at Mouette Inn during the summer," said Mercedes. "Our grandparents own it."

So his name was Dominic—Jane thought it a strong name—and he was staying right down the street from them. Maybe they would all get to know each other—that is, if Skye didn't scare Dominic off.

At least she'd stopped glaring, but now she'd turned her back on him and was picking up her groceries, ready to go. Jane sighed. This was not a good beginning. If only Dominic would say something intelligent, maybe Skye could be brought around.

And then he spoke. "Which one of you is the oldest sister?"

"Why?" asked Skye in a tone that offered no hope of brought-aroundness.

He shrugged and did a little move with his skateboard.

"I'm seven, and Dominic's twelve," said Mercedes. "Are you twelve, too, Jeffrey?"

"I will be in August," he said.

Dominic looked sideways at Jeffrey, then back down to his skateboard. "I'm twelve and a half, actually."

"Well, we should go," said Skye.

Which made it clear to Jane that Skye wasn't going to claim being the oldest for Dominic. If Skye didn't want to, could someone else? How exciting to be the oldest for once, and especially the once that included a boy with such flair and swagger. Jane thought quickly. She refused to lie—no boy could be worth that—but there was something she could say, if she was careful.

"Neither of us is the oldest sister, really. That's Rosalind, who's in New Jersey. But we have a little sister, named Batty. You should meet her, Mercedes—she's only five, but advanced for her age. Anyway, Dominic, when it's just me and Batty, I'm the oldest."

Jane didn't dare look at Skye or Jeffrey. She kept her attention on Dominic, who seemed to be trying to work out what she'd just said. It took him a while, but at last he nodded, leaped onto his skateboard, and skated off with the maximum noise and spectacle.

Jane watched him go. "I wonder if he plays soccer."

"No, but I do." Mercedes was struggling to remount her bike, since her brother showed no sign of waiting for her. "That is, I'd like to."

While Jane steadied the bike, Jeffrey helped Mercedes on, then gave her a push in the right direction. She turned to wave and almost crashed but managed to keep going without further injury. When Mercedes was safely out of sight, the threesome set off again, with Skye in the lead and moving quickly. Not so quickly that they might catch up with the Orne siblings—that was the last thing Skye wanted—but just enough to burn off her irritation with Dominic, whose conversational skills hadn't impressed her at all. Why Jane had been so friendly to him was a mystery. Rosalind had wanted them to be polite to people in Maine, but being polite is one thing, and telling people where you live is quite another. Unless Jane hadn't noticed that Dominic was all hair and attitude. No, not even Jane could be that gullible, right? Skye glanced back at Jane but wasn't reassured—Jane was again muttering to herself about love.

Skye groaned. Why, oh why, had she ever agreed to be the OAP?

Then she heard the barking, and Dominic flew out of her mind. It was Hound's barking, the kind that said Trouble Trouble Trouble. Skye threw her share of the groceries at Jeffrey and Jane and took off toward Birches, running, running, and as she got closer, along with Hound's deep barking she could now hear Hoover's yapping. She ran faster. Whatever bad was happening involved Batty—Skye was sure of it. Batty had been blown up, drowned, smashed on the rocks, or some combination of the three. And it was all Skye's fault. She would never get over the guilt, and her father and Rosalind would hate her forever.

Past Alec's house now, and Skye could tell that the barking was coming from behind Birches. Around the house she flew, and suddenly Batty, without any visible wounds, was running toward her.

"You're alive!" said Skye, so relieved her heart hurt.

Ignoring such an obvious statement, Batty grabbed Skye's hand and urgently pulled her across the lawn. At first Skye could see only Alec, standing near the seawall, holding the two dogs, who had finally stopped barking. Then Alec stepped aside, and there on the ground was Aunt Claire, clutching her ankle and trying to look brave.

Skye rushed over. "What happened? Are you all right?"

"I'm okay." Aunt Claire smiled, then winced.

"She fell off the seawall," said Batty.

"It was Hoover's fault," said Alec. "He startled your aunt, and she fell."

Hoover again! Skye turned on Alec. "You can't control him at all!"

"I know. I'm sorry."

Skye was trying hard to loathe the man and his dog, but Alec was making it difficult by being so sincerely remorseful. Meanwhile, Jane and Jeffrey had arrived. Explanations were made all over again, with Alec apologizing several more times while Skye knelt beside her aunt.

"How badly are you hurt?" she asked.

"I think it's just a sprain," said Aunt Claire. "Help me stand."

But when Aunt Claire put weight on the bad ankle, she cried out in pain and had to be lowered onto the seawall.

"She needs to see a doctor," said Jeffrey.

"I'll drive her to the hospital," said Alec. "There's one only about a half hour away."

"We'll all go." Skye was determined that there be

no more tearing apart of the family, especially in emergencies. "Aunt Claire needs people she knows around her for comfort."

"Comfort is good," Alec agreed, "but since your aunt will need to stretch out in the backseat, there won't be room for all of you."

"Even if we can't all go with Aunt Claire, some of us can," said Jeffrey. "I will, if that would make you feel better, Skye."

"I'll go, too," added Batty.

Skye couldn't help noticing Alec's mouth twitching with amusement at the idea of this small girl in her orange life jacket being any kind of help or comfort. He did sort of look nice, she thought—not as respectable and dignified as her father, but who was? Some people might even think him handsome in a grown-up sort of way, with brown hair that didn't seem to want to lie down properly and a splatter of freckles across his nose. It could be just the beard, she thought, that gave him a less-than-dependable look.

"All right, Jeffrey, you go with him," she said.

"Good." Jeffrey grinned at Alec. "And, Skye, I like him, even if he can't control his dog."

"I like him, too," said Jane. "I even like his dog."

"Oh, I don't like his dog," said Skye.

"Stop this right now!" Aunt Claire waved her arms frantically. "Listen to me. I don't need comfort. I just need a ride, which means that Alec will drive me to the hospital, just me, by myself. You four will stay here and have a good time and not worry. Agreed?"

"You can't expect Skye not to worry," said Jane. "She's the OAP."

"Fine. Skye, as long as you do everything else I say, you may worry all you want."

Skye wasn't going to give up altogether without one last gasp of authority. "You need ice for your ankle. Jane, go get the ice. Batty, your job is to keep Hound calm."

"And I'll take Hoover home," said Jeffrey.

So while Jane went inside to fill a plastic bag with ice, and Batty whispered words of comfort into Hound's ear, and Jeffrey set off for Alec's house with the wayward Hoover, Skye and Alec managed to get Aunt Claire to the car without causing her too much more pain.

"Here's the ice," said Jane, running up.

"Thank you, girls. You are my angels," said Aunt Claire. "Now, truly, there's nothing to be concerned about. I'll call you."

Skye and Jane smiled and waved as the car pulled away.

"Nothing to be concerned about," said Skye, her smile gone as soon as the car was out of sight.

Jane and Batty were staring at her like they expected her to know what to do. She'd seen them stare like that before, but always at Rosalind, never at her.

She turned her back on them for a bit of relief, and then, because a tree happened to be in front of her, she kicked it. Pleased with herself, she kicked another tree. Maybe she could escape to the pinewood at the end of the street, where there were hundreds of trees to kick.

She was the OAP, however, and having the OAP respond to a crisis by kicking too many trees would demoralize the troops. She had to think, and quickly. She was certain that neither her father nor Rosalind had given her guidance for what to do in the case of Aunt Claire damaging an ankle. Skye glanced over her shoulder at Jane and Batty huddled together, looking scared. Think! If only she weren't so hungry— the gingerbread was a distant memory—maybe her brain would be working properly. No leader, not Caesar or Napoleon, not Washington himself, could have developed strategy on a stomach this empty. And then Skye realized that there was her answer. In any emergency, food is always an excellent idea.

She turned away from the trees, courageously faced her sisters, and said, "Let's have breakfast."

CHAPTER SIX
Pancakes

JUST AS HUNGRY AS SKYE, Jane rashly volunteered to make pancakes for everyone. She'd watched her father make pancakes from a mix a hundred times and was sure she could do it herself. After all, the directions would be right there on the box. Unfortunately, those directions turned out to be not as clear as she would have liked, starting with the first step. *Heat skillet on medium to low,* it said. But the knob on the stove had numbers, with no indication which number meant medium or low, let alone medium to low. If only Jane had paid attention to the setting her father had used at home—but who cared enough about stoves to notice things like that? She was going to have to experiment, and since experimentation can get messy, Jane didn't want Skye around watching the process. Too stressful. So she wondered loudly why Jeffrey wasn't yet back from taking Hoover home. This worked perfectly—Skye rushed off, certain that Hoover had broken Jeffrey's leg or arm or killed him altogether.

Batty stayed behind, too hungry to run away, even for Jeffrey.

"I'll help," she said. "So will Hound."

"Thank you." Jane lifted Batty onto a chair to make her tall enough for helping. "And we can talk while we work. Do you have any fears or anxieties to discuss?"

"I don't know."

"I mean, was it scary when Aunt Claire got hurt?"

"Yes, but then Skye and Jeffrey came. "

"And me, too."

"Uh-huh." Batty blew the opening notes of "Taps" on her harmonica. "But not Rosalind."

Jane would have liked a more enthusiastic response to her own role in this tale, but she understood that Rosalind would have been preferable. "How many pancakes should we make?"

Once they'd decided on the recipe for twenty-four pancakes, they put together the ingredients. Once again, the directions proved to be vague, calling for two cups of mix and one and a half cups of milk. After some deliberation, Jane decided that a mug was sort of a cup, so she used one with a seagull on the side for measuring. Batty proved to be surprisingly good at breaking eggs without smashing them to bits. Only a few pieces of shell got into the batter, and Hound licked off all the yolk that splattered onto Batty's shirt.

Next came stirring. The directions said to stir with a wire whisk, but since neither of them could find anything that might be called that, they settled on a fork. While they worked, Jane told Batty about meeting Dominic and Mercedes Orne, and about the Love Survey she was putting together to help with research for her book.

"And I'm still looking for a name for Sabrina's true love. Do you like Dylan?" But when Batty vehemently shook her head, Jane remembered. "Sorry. That's the name of the boy who poured glue on you at day care, right?"

"He poured glue on everybody," said Batty darkly.

"What about the other boys?"

"Isaac is nice. He invited me to his birthday party. So did Jaimon and Gabe. Satchel didn't. Also Satchel pushed me off the swings, and Zoe said it was because he likes me, but I don't like him, and if he likes me, he should've invited me to his birthday party. He invited Zoe." Batty frowned. "She got a stuffed animal for a party favor."

"I won't use Satchel, then." Jane gave the batter one last stir. "Let's try a pancake."

The directions said to use less than a quarter cup of batter for each pancake. Jane found that it was harder than it looked to pour batter from a mug into a hot pan, which meant that a lot of batter ended up on the stove and the floor. But the hiss when the batter hit the heat, and the way the batter turned itself into a round cake—all that was quite gratifying.

"We're supposed to turn the pancake over when it starts to bubble," Jane told Batty, and thought seriously of becoming a chef someday, if it should turn out that she was indeed washed up as a writer, which she could be if she never got this book started.

"And don't use Hamish for your book," said Batty. "Hamish is always kissing people."

"You mean like you?"

"Not me. I run faster than him." Batty pointed at the pan. "Bubbles."

With great excitement, Jane slid the spatula under the pancake, lifted it, and flipped it over. It was unevenly browned, but it was a real pancake.

"We did it!" she said, hugging Batty. "Only twenty-three more to go!"

While Skye rushed over to Alec's house, she steeled herself for the grisly sight of Jeffrey felled by a triumphant Hoover, his doggy jaws dripping with gore. She took the back way, racing along the seawall, down the steps, across the beach, up Alec's steps, then onto his rear deck. This was where she stopped, forced to reassess the situation. Someone was playing the piano in Alec's house, and since it couldn't be Hoover, it had to be Jeffrey, which meant he probably wasn't felled or even bleeding after all.

She peered in through the sliding door. Yes, right in front of her, with his back to the door, was Jeffrey, sitting at a baby grand piano, oblivious to the world around him. She'd seen him in this kind of musical swoon before and knew not to startle him. Once when she hadn't been careful, Jeffrey had banged against the keyboard cover, making it fall onto his hands. No serious harm had been done, but Skye had learned her lesson.

Quietly she slid through the door and found herself in what should have been Alec's living room. True, there were a few living-room kinds of things— a couch and some chairs and a table—but mostly the room had been turned into a music studio. Besides the piano, there were saxophones, drums, trumpets, and maybe those were violins tucked away in the corner. There were also shelves upon shelves stuffed with sheet music, and even what Skye thought might be recording equipment. And there was Hoover, peacefully asleep under the piano. Now Skye had two reasons not to make any sudden movements—Jeffrey's hands and not waking up that insane dog. Nevertheless, she had to get Jeffrey to stop playing. He really shouldn't be in the house of an almost stranger using a piano without permission. More important, she was growing ever hungrier by the moment.

"Jeffrey." Skye said it quietly, and waited several moments before saying it again, a little louder. "Jeffrey, what are you doing?"

Only then did Jeffrey realize that he wasn't alone. He stopped playing and swiveled around to face her, his face alight with happiness. "I'm working on Stravinsky's Piano Sonata. My teacher in Boston suggested it—he said I need to take an occasional break from the nineteenth century, because I was spending all that time with Liszt, you know."

"I suppose so," said Skye, though she didn't know anything about either Liszt or Stravinsky. "But what I meant was—why are you playing Alec's piano?"

He looked embarrassed. "I guess I shouldn't have, but the piano was right here—and I couldn't help it. Hoover doesn't seem to mind, anyway."

Skye didn't consider Hoover to be the best judge of right and wrong. At least he was still asleep.

"And Alec must be a real musician, of course. This is his life." Jeffrey said it so simply. "What I wouldn't give for a room like this. And no one to tell me I had to leave it."

Skye knew who Jeffrey meant by "no one"—his mother had never been enthusiastic about his music. "I'd never tell you to leave it—that is, if it were yours. But we should leave this one."

"I know." He turned back to the piano and played

79

one quiet chord, and then another. "Do you think Alec will let me play it again? It's a wonderful piano."

Because already he was slipping back into his swoon, Skye declared loudly that she was about to faint from hunger. Jeffrey jumped up apologetically, and they left, escaping just as Hoover woke up and lunged at Skye, determined to kiss her once again. Now that Skye had Jeffrey safely in tow, it occurred to her that leaving Jane and Batty alone with knives and a stove might not have been the best idea. So the trip back was even faster than the trip over had been. When they arrived, the kitchen was a disaster—flour, eggshells, and melted butter everywhere—and Hound had that all-too-familiar air of having eaten too much food not suited for him. But no one had been slashed, burned, or suffocated, and since Jane and Batty were just sitting down to the table with a huge stack of pancakes, Skye and Jeffrey sat down, too, and the eating began.

"Delicious," said Skye after her first pancake.

"Fantastic," said Jeffrey after his second. "Good job, Jane."

"Thank you." Jane was quite proud of herself. "And Batty helped a lot."

"I cracked the eggs," said Batty, except that no one could understand her because her mouth was full.

Skye knew it was her job to reprimand Batty about table manners, but since her own mouth was full at that moment, she didn't bother. Instead, she took several more pancakes from the stack and slathered them with butter and syrup. That was when the phone rang. Swallowing hastily, Skye grabbed the phone—it would be Aunt Claire!—but when she checked the display, another name was there.

"It's Rosalind," she hissed to the others. "I don't want to talk to her right now."

"I will, I will," crowed Batty.

"You can't say anything about Aunt Claire's ankle. Not until we know more."

"I won't." Batty frantically reached for the still-ringing phone.

"Swear! Rosy might think we should go home for Aunt Claire's sake!"

"I swear, I do, Skye. I do swear, I promise!"

Skye needn't have worried. Once Batty got hold of the phone, a great flow of words came, but not one about Aunt Claire's accident. Batty went on and on about Jeffrey and Hoover, and a letter in the ocean—what the heck was that about?—and the harmonica and the steps to the beach, and then for a while she was just nodding her head and saying uh-huh, and after that she hung up the phone.

"Why did you hang up?" asked Jane, who would have liked to tell Rosalind about the sleeping porch and about how inspirational it would be if only she could start writing again.

"Rosalind said the signal was bad and we might be disconnected, and then we were, so I hung up."

"What else did she say?" asked Skye, to whom the bad signal was good news.

"She said she misses me."

Through all this, Jeffrey had continued to eat, but now he laid down his fork. "Skye, do *you* think we should leave Maine for Aunt Claire's sake? There would be people to take care of her in Cameron."

"I don't know." Skye wondered, once again, how her father could have been so foolish as to let her be the OAP for two whole weeks.

"I don't want to leave." This was, surprisingly, Batty.

"Neither do I," said Jane. "Not at all, not even a little bit."

Jeffrey didn't say anything, but no one needed him to. Leaving Maine for him meant going back to Arundel, Dexter, and loneliness. Thinking about this helped Skye in her struggle to decide. She couldn't have been ungenerous to Aunt Claire for her own sake, but she could for Jeffrey's.

"If Aunt Claire's ankle is really bad and she needs special doctors, we'll have to go home," she said.

"You're right," said Jeffrey bravely.

"And if we stay, you know we're going to have to take care of Aunt Claire for at least a few days, and probably longer."

"That won't be hard. Not like dressing a wound." Though Jane thought that dressing a wound could be rather exciting. "Just giving her aspirin and ice packs."

"And doing all the cooking and cleaning and shopping," Skye said sternly, making certain the others realized what they were taking on.

"We can get everything we need at Moose Market," said Jane. "And this will give me a chance to get better at cooking. Rosalind showed me how to make a tuna noodle casserole once."

"I can cook, too," said Jeffrey. "Some."

This was news. "Like what?"

"Omelets and stuffed green peppers. Churchie's been teaching me."

The sisters had never met a stuffed green pepper, but if Churchie made them, they must be delicious. So they added omelets and stuffed green peppers to Jane's casserole, plus there were always sandwiches that even Skye could make, and spaghetti with sauce from a jar—with all those to choose from, they decided that meals would be no problem.

Their rising confidence was stemmed by another phone call. Since this time it *was* Aunt Claire, Skye took the call and got the news. Aunt Claire's ankle was severely sprained and she would need to be on crutches. This was a blow. But when Skye hung up and looked around at the anxious faces, she decided that if she wanted to be a successful OAP, she needed to rally her troops, not upset them. So she explained that although Aunt Claire had a bad sprain, a broken bone would have been far worse, and that if they were really organized and responsible, maybe Aunt Claire wouldn't need to go home. Inspired, they began being responsible immediately. Jane rearranged the living room so that Aunt Claire would have her choice of comfortable places to rest, then collected wildflowers from the field across the street to put in jars. Jeffrey and Skye tackled the kitchen so energetically that it ended up cleaner than it had been before Jane started cooking. When Batty begged to help, Skye gave her a broom and told her to sweep the living room, and though not very much actual sweeping was done before the whole thing turned into a game of tug-on-the-broomstick with Hound, Jeffrey took over later to do it right while Skye gave the bathroom a quick go-over.

When the house was spotless, everyone had worked so hard that Skye ordered them into their bathing suits for some enthusiastic diving and splashing in the ocean. They were cleaning up from that, and Skye was about to attack Batty's wet curls with a brush, when Alec and Aunt Claire returned. The four children lined up to show off their good work, but as Alec half carried Aunt Claire into Birches, they could see that she wasn't in an observant mood.

"The medicine the doctors gave her for pain has

made her a little goofy," said Alec after he'd gotten her settled on the sofa, with her feet propped up and the crutches beside her.

"'Edelweiss, edelweiss,'" sang Aunt Claire in several different keys, "'every morning you greet me.'"

"Like I said, goofy. She's been singing a lot."

"She never sings," protested Skye. She wasn't ready for this. The crutches and the poor ankle—encased in yards of bandages, tape, *and* a white plastic boot—were bad enough, but if Aunt Claire had lost her mind, she was going to be difficult to care for.

"'Blossom of snow may you bloom and grow, bloom and grow forever.'"

"That's from *The Sound of Music*," said Jane, then started to hum along, in yet another key.

Batty covered her ears and Jeffrey winced.

Skye was less delicate. "Jane, be quiet," she said, and Jane was.

Aunt Claire now moved on to "Do-Re-Mi," which sounded awful enough to make Hound abandon his exploration of the crutches.

"She should fall asleep soon," said Alec. "And then the singing will stop."

Skye hoped so. "Thank you for taking care of her. We'll be grateful forever."

"Well, it was Hoover's fault and Hoover is my responsibility, whether he agrees or not." Alec rubbed his beard worriedly. "So now what should I do for you kids? You can't take care of your aunt all by your-selves. We need to call someone—your father?"

"Call Daddy? You can't do that!" Jane was ap-palled. "You'd wreck his honeymoon in England!"

"And you can't tell Rosalind either." This was Skye, with Jeffrey nodding in agreement.

"Who's Rosalind?"

"Our older sister in New Jersey. If she finds out about Aunt Claire's ankle, she'll try to get up here, and her vacation will be over."

"Her long-due vacation from us," added Jane. "That's what Daddy called it. We can be a lot of trou-ble, especially Batty."

"I'm not," protested Batty. "Anyway, Jeffrey can make stuffed green peppers."

For some reason, that got through to Aunt Claire. She stopped singing and said, "I like stuffed green peppers."

"Plus Skye is good at cleaning," said Jeffrey.

Jane added, "And I'm also going to nurse you, Aunt Claire. Soothe your spirits and bathe your forehead."

They all looked at Aunt Claire to see how inter-ested she was in forehead bathing, but the singing had tired her out, and she was asleep. Alec covered her with a blanket, then led everyone to the other side of the room, where they could talk without waking her up again.

"Okay, I might be crazy, but we'll try this for now,"

he said. "Here are my conditions. For the rest of to-day, your aunt can't be left alone, so one of you older three always has to be here. She has to keep her ankle elevated, and it should be iced every few hours. When she's a little less goofy, she has to get used to the crutches—you can help her with that. In the mean-time, I'm going to be over here a lot, and if anything goes wrong, we're going to call in reinforcements."

Skye opened her mouth to protest, but he cut her off.

"That's nonnegotiable. If all goes well today, we'll talk about it again tomorrow with your aunt, who should be coherent by then. Until then, any help you need or want—anything at all—you must come to me, promise?"

"We promise," said Skye.

Alec nodded, satisfied, and turned to go.

"Actually, there is something," said Skye, nudging Jeffrey, who nudged her back threateningly, shaking his head no, but she pressed on regardless. "When Jef-frey took Hoover to your house, he saw your piano. That is, Jeffrey saw it, and he also played it."

Jeffrey flushed. "I couldn't help it. It's such a good piano."

"Oh, yes, Claire told me you're a musician," said Alec. "Piano, clarinet, and what else?"

"A little cello, and I've just started on the clari-net, really."

"Don't let Jeffrey's modesty fool you," said Jane. "He's a genius."

"I like geniuses." Alec smiled. "Use the piano whenever you want, Jeffrey. I mean that. Come this afternoon, if you'd like."

"Thank you, I will." Jeffrey shook his hand fervently. "Thank you very much."

This time Alec did leave, and Skye sagged with relief. Gaining Alec's trust made her trust herself more. Maybe they really could manage all this on their own.

"'Sol, a needle pulling thread,'" sang Aunt Claire in her sleep.

Or maybe not, thought Skye. Her work had just begun, and she was already worn out and wondered longingly if she dare take a nap. Of course not—what kind of a message would that send to the others? She needed to do something practical and soothing.

"All right, troops," she said. "Let's have lunch."

CHAPTER SEVEN
Another Accident

By THE NEXT MORNING, Aunt Claire had stopped singing and was able to hobble for short distances on her crutches. Even better, she didn't want to leave Point Mouette either.

"But if any of you want to go home, I should be able to drive soon, since it's my left ankle, not my right," she told the children. "Staying here will be harder on you four than it will be on me. My ankle and I will be lolling around while you do all the work."

"We've split it up," said Skye. "Even Batty's helping."

"I can sweep now." Batty got the broom from the kitchen and waved it around to prove her proficiency.

"We really want to stay," said Jane. "Don't we, Jeffrey?"

"Yes, please." Jeffrey was drawing on Aunt Claire's plastic boot with Batty's markers. He didn't have much space—the girls had taken their turns before him—but he was managing a decent picture of Hound playing the piano.

"All right, then it's settled," said Aunt Claire. "We'll stay as long as there are no problems."

"There won't be." Skye crossed her fingers for luck, though in normal times she didn't believe in luck. Just in case it did exist, she figured she could use as much as she could get. She was greatly relieved that Aunt Claire was willing to let her be so completely in charge. That had been her first goal for the morning. Her second goal was to convince Alec to stop fussing. He'd come by half a dozen times the day before, and Skye expected him to appear again soon, making sure that Aunt Claire hadn't died or had her leg amputated during the night.

And moments later, Alec did arrive, bearing many gifts—a pile of books and magazines for Aunt Claire; a plate of warm cinnamon buns that everyone dove into, though breakfast was a very recent memory; and an invitation for them all to have dinner with him that evening.

"A friend of mine will be here who's visiting for several days," he said. "Please come. Feeding all of you is the least I can do since Hoover maimed your primary cook."

"Really, you don't have to," said Aunt Claire. "You've forgotten about Jeffrey's stuffed green peppers."

"But Turron—my friend—would enjoy the company." Alec turned to Jeffrey. "He's a drummer. Maybe the three of us could make some music after we eat."

Jeffrey, in the middle of his second cinnamon bun, made a strangled kind of sound that combined pleasure, humility, and excitement in equal measures.

"That means he wants to, Aunt Claire," said Skye. Taking up Alec's invitation the day before, Jeffrey had spent several hours at the piano and had talked of little else since.

"Then we will accept for Jeffrey's sake," said Aunt Claire. "And so that he doesn't have to make stuffed green peppers."

"Good," said Alec. "Now, what else can I do for you?"

"Nothing, thank you. We're all organized." Skye didn't mind Alec cooking dinner for them, but she could handle things until then. It took a while to convince him they would continue to survive without his help, but finally he was gone.

"I really like him," said Jeffrey.

"We all like him," said Skye, "but we don't need him. Besides, we have chores to do."

The kitchen needed cleaning after breakfast, and because Jeffrey had made omelets and Batty had cracked open all the eggs for him, that meant a lot of cleaning. Skye took that on for herself, since the OAP should always volunteer for the worst. Jeffrey and Batty were assigned sweeping duty because, though it had been done just the day before, somehow Birches was full of sand all over again. That left Jane, who offered to help settle Aunt Claire on the deck, complete with an ice pack for her ankle.

"Would you like me to bathe your forehead?" Jane asked when her aunt was comfortable.

"No, thank you. Just talk to me. How's your new book coming?"

"I'm still doing research." Jane plopped down beside Aunt Claire's chair. "I've thought of putting together questions to ask people. Here's the only one I have so far: Do you believe in love at first sight?"

"That's an interesting question."

"Well, do you?"

Aunt Claire stared out at the ocean, pondering. "I guess I must, since it's happened to me. In high school, there was a French exchange student named Stéphane. I fell for him the very moment he walked into my biology class."

"What happened?" asked Jane, enthralled. She'd never met a real French boy.

"Not much. He ended up dating Marjorie Wright, who broke his heart. But I fell at first sight another time, with Leon, a friend your father brought home from college. And after him was Bill the basketball player. There were a number of Bills, now that I think about it, except not every one of them was love at first sight. Hmm, who was next? I think my art history professor. Oh, and I forgot about Charlie! Mad Charlie. I adored him. Does any of this help, Jane?"

"Yes, keep going!"

"This could take hours."

"Well, then, what happened to them all?"

"Different things. I almost married one—I'll tell you that story when you're older." Aunt Claire stopped to shift her ice pack. "But don't put them all in the past. I'm not too old to keep falling in love, first sight or second or third."

Jane had a thought, interesting and scary at the same time. "Not Alec!"

"No." Aunt Claire shook her head. "I like him, but not to fall in love with."

"But how do you know? How do you learn how to know?"

"So many questions! Let me think—how *do* I know when I've fallen in love? It's hard to explain without sounding silly. Like being struck by lightning, except nice. Or like having your heart sing."

"Singing heart. That's good. May I use it for Sabrina Starr?"

"Use away. I'd be honored."

Skye came out through the sliding door, sponge in one hand and dish towel in the other. A supply run to Moose Market was needed, and since Jane wasn't doing anything important right now—book research didn't count—it was up to her. Jane didn't mind. Aunt Claire had already given her a lot to think about. She set off down Ocean Boulevard with the grocery list in her pocket and her imagination on fire.

> Sabrina Starr was fuming. Her sprained ankle was a disaster. If she didn't rescue the Chinese ambassador from his kidnappers within the next forty-eight hours, discord would spread, countries would fall, and World War III would loom. And here she was stuck in the hospital. "Ms. Starr? I'm Dr. Albert, Ankle Specialist." Sabrina gazed up at the doctor and her heart sang.

No, that wouldn't work, not with Sabrina on crutches and wearing that awkward plastic boot. There could be no dancing by moonlight, for example. In the movies that Jane had seen, people in love were always dancing. But was it like that in real life? That was a good second research question: *Does being in love make you want to dance?* Jane wished she had her notebook with her.

She passed Alec's house and came to the long stretch of rocky coast, with the great piles of boulders guarding the ocean, just as they had for hundreds of years, Jane thought, or maybe thousands or even tens of thousands, all the way back to the dinosaurs or the Ice Age—she never could remember which came first. The idea of treading rocks so ancient was too tempting to pass up. They weren't hard to get to. She just had to slide down a pebbly slope for about five feet, cross a narrow band of coarse sand, and there she was at the rocks, a whole landscape of them, all tumbled together. Jane leaped from one to another until she came close enough to the ocean to feel the spray from the crashing waves.

"Great and powerful Neptune," she said, raising her arms in supplication, "grant me . . ."

But she couldn't think of anything sea-related that she would like to have granted, and Neptune never bothered with anything else, like helping writers with their projects. Mermaids were a possibility, but even if Jane believed it possible to be turned into one, she probably shouldn't bother. In the books she'd read, mermaids were never that bright, worried only about combing their hair and driving sailors mad with passion. Of course, Jane's hair was almost long enough now to be mermaid-like, and that thing about sailors could be a way to learn about love. Jane again raised her arms.

"Great and powerful Neptune," she cried, "let me be a mermaid just long enough to research my book."

Nothing happened—no fishtail or scales—which Jane figured was just as well, since Skye would be annoyed if she didn't return soon with the groceries. She made her way back toward the road, stopping only to pick up a few smooth stones that were the right size for paperweights. But when she reached the slope, she found that going up was more difficult than coming down had been. Her sneakers couldn't get a grip on the pebbles, and the few tufts of weeds she grabbed tore away under her weight. Jane stubbornly persevered, however, and was almost to the top when she heard the rattle of a skateboard. Eagerly she looked up, and yes, there was Dominic, waving regally to her as he sailed by.

"Hello," Jane called to him, and if she'd been content with calling, all would have been well. But she just had to wave back, and what with the paperweight rocks in her left hand and her right hand now flailing around at the rapidly departing skateboarder, Jane lost her balance, teetered for a panicky moment, then was spinning and falling, arms and legs and paperweights flying everywhere.

Her first thought upon landing was that she hoped Dominic hadn't seen her be so clumsy. Her second thought was that someone nearby must be in pain, because that someone kept saying "Ouch," except that it was more like "Ouuuuuch." Jane would have liked to help the person, except that she herself was having difficulty with her nose, mixed up as it was with sand and paperweights and something else that was warm and sticky—and then Jane realized that she was the one making all the noise.

So she stopped. Sabrina Starr never said ouch.

Even with a nose that, Jane realized, hurt as much as any part of her ever had, including the time Skye had accidentally stabbed her with a barbecue fork. At least the damage seemed to be limited to her nose. Jane tested her limbs one at a time. All was well there, which meant she should be able to stand up. But because she was dizzier than she would have liked, it took a while to get upright, and once she was there, the pain got worse.

"Ouch, ouch, ouch, ouch, ouch," she said because she just had to, Sabrina or no Sabrina.

The next task was to climb up to the road. But if it had been tricky before, it was close to impossible now. She kept getting partway up the pebbly slope and sliding backward again. Maybe Jane would have done better if she'd had the use of both hands, but she'd lost most of the paperweights in her fall and wasn't thinking straight enough to throw away the one she had left. Once, twice, three times she tried, and was about to give up and go beg old Neptune for help when a car stopped on the road above her, and soon after that a man was lifting her up as easily as if she were Batty. He gently set her down beside his car.

"I can stand," she said, wobbling.

"Not very well," he said. "Sit."

So Jane let her legs collapse under her, and the man guided her to the ground. A minute later, he was handing her a water bottle.

"Drink," he said.

She drank half the bottle of water, which did nothing for her hurting nose but did ease the dizziness enough to let her focus on her savior. He was a dark man, tall and strong, with kind eyes and no hair at all. Not having hair suited him, Jane thought, and made him look even stronger. No wonder he could lift her so easily.

"Thank you," she said. "You rescued me."

"What happened?"

"I think I smacked my nose with this," she answered, showing him the paperweight rock. "Not on purpose."

"Do you know you're covered with blood?"

Jane looked down at her shirt, which was indeed a mess. "Oh, boy. My sister is going to be furious, especially if my nose is actually broken. Do you think it is?"

"Can you breathe through it?"

"Yes."

"It looks straight, so unless it used to be crooked, I'd say it isn't broken. Come on, I'll drive you to this furious sister of yours." He stopped and frowned. "But of course you don't know anything about me, so you can't get into my car. What a world."

Jane was glad he'd mentioned it first. "Tell me about yourself, then."

"My name is Turron Asabere and—"

"And you're Alec's friend! My family is staying

next door to Alec, and we're having dinner with you tonight."

So Jane, safe now, let Turron help her into the car and drive her back to the house—without the groceries she'd been sent to buy, and with a face that would have looked just right on a heavyweight boxer. But for the moment she wasn't worried about the groceries, her nose, or her bloody shirt, because it had occurred to her that if she could come up with enough questions for her Love Survey, maybe Turron and Alec wouldn't mind being her first real test subjects.

Skye gave the kitchen counter one final polish, then stepped out into the main room and looked around. Not bad. Jeffrey and Batty had done a good job with the sweeping, and if they were now obviously messing around with that stupid harmonica on the sleeping porch, that didn't necessarily mean Skye's authority was being flouted. A good leader knew when to let her people relax from their duties.

"You'd better be finished with your sweeping," she called.

Jeffrey's voice roared back at her. "Sir, yes, sir!"

"Not funny." But it was kind of funny, she thought, and went out onto the deck to check on Aunt Claire.

"Hello, niece of mine," she said.

"Are you ready for another ice pack yet?"

"No, thank you."

"Anything to drink?"

"Nope."

"Am I too bossy with the others?"

"What?"

"Because the true measure of a leader isn't just how she handles herself in a crisis, but how she manages herself in the day-to-day, right?"

Aunt Claire reached out and took Skye's hand. "You're an excellent OAP, Skye Magee Penderwick."

"Thank you." Skye chewed on her lower lip to keep from looking too proud. "I guess I'm doing okay."

She wandered back into Birches, wishing her father could see her right at that moment, calmly adjusting after a disaster and even keeping everyone properly fed. Or Rosalind. If Rosalind called now, Skye would certainly pick up the phone and say that everyone was just fine and everything under control. She did a half dozen celebratory deep knee bends and decided that it was time to have some fun. Like a good round of soccer on the beach when Jane got back from Moose Market, and after that a chapter of *Death by Black Hole*, by which time they would all be hungry again.

Her musing was interrupted by a quiet knock at the front door. Alec again, she thought, though he usually came around the back. But when she opened the door, she found a big, strong-looking bald man who was certainly not Alec.

"Skye?" he asked. "I'm Turron Asabere, a friend of Alec's."

"Oh, the drummer. Nice to meet you." Skye shook his hand. "But if Alec sent you to check on us, please tell him that honest-honest-honest I don't need his help right now."

"I'm sure you don't. But Alec didn't send me. I'm here to make a delivery."

"What kind of delivery?" She noticed now that as large as Turron was, he seemed to be trying to make himself even larger. But not quite successfully, because it was becoming obvious that someone was standing right behind him. "Jane, is that you?"

"Don't be furious, Skye." It was Jane.

"About what?"

"Turron, you'd better let her see."

When Turron shifted to one side of the doorway, revealing Jane in all her blood-soaked glory, Skye shrieked. Then shrieked again and clutched at her sister, searching frantically for the source of all that blood.

"It's just my nose, honest, and I have a perfectly good explanation." Jane held up one of her paperweight rocks and was about to launch into the explanation, but Skye's shriek had brought Jeffrey and Batty running, and then came Aunt Claire, heaving herself along on her crutches, and there were introductions to make for Turron, and damp cloths to be fetched to wipe up Jane's blood, and Hound to force onto the sleeping porch because he was as panicked as Skye herself at a battered Penderwick. So it wasn't until several minutes later that Jane started to tell her story, and by this time Skye had at least started breathing normally, until Jane came to the part about why she fell.

"Wait a minute!" Skye shouted. "All this is Dominic's fault? Did he try to shoot you?"

"Of course not. He skateboarded past me and I wanted to wave but I slipped and I was holding this rock . . ." Jane sheepishly held up the rock.

"Which she hit herself in the nose with," said Turron. "Accidentally."

"I can't stand it. I give up." Skye sank onto the couch.

"And then Turron rescued you, Jane, and brought you home," said Aunt Claire brightly. "That was nice of him."

"Dominic Orne!" This came out of Skye as a kind of growl. She was no longer following the conversation.

Jane glanced uneasily at her OAP. "My nose isn't broken. No special doctors."

"That's good," said Jeffrey.

"Yes, that's excellent," said Aunt Claire. "Jeffrey, could you please show Turron out? And, Turron, thank you so much."

"Anytime." He waved to her and smiled, then was gone.

"All right, then. Forward." Aunt Claire took a

closer look at Jane's nose. "Jane, you go change out of those clothes. Then if Jeffrey could find some bandages and cotton—in the bathroom cabinet, I think—we can get you patched up."

While Jane was being cleaned and repaired, Skye stayed slumped on the couch, brooding. She'd been so confident, the great and powerful leader doing deep knee bends, and all the while a second Penderwick was undergoing serious damage. It was quite clear that she rated about a zero as the OAP. She'd told her father so—she'd warned him. She'd warned them all, and no one had listened, and now the family was being picked off one at a time, one body part at a time. Next it would be Batty blowing up her arm, and then Hound would lose a rib, and then Jeffrey his head. Complete disaster.

Nevertheless, Skye knew she couldn't quit. Not yet. Failing as the OAP was embarrassing, but quitting would be rank humiliation. She sat up straight, took a few deep breaths, and then sprang off the couch and back into the fray. Seconds later, she was bundling Batty into the orange life jacket. Then she was searching out Hound, to tighten his collar and hook up his leash. She went for Jeffrey and Jane next, determined to make them accident-proof, but without more life jackets—or leashes—there was nothing she could do but order them never to go anywhere alone.

"Teams of at least two at all times," she said.

"That's ridiculous," protested Jeffrey.

"Promise!" But Skye was already moving on, insisting that Aunt Claire could no longer move without help.

When she actually tried to lock Aunt Claire's crutches in a closet, a rebellion erupted, followed by a coup. The end result was that Aunt Claire got her crutches back and declared Jeffrey Temporary OAP for as long as it took Skye to get hold of herself.

It took most of the day. Skye wouldn't have managed it even in that time if Jeffrey hadn't worked her so hard. He made her run all the way to Moose Market for the groceries Jane didn't get, and run back again. After that, he put her through two hours of soccer practice, the grueling kind, not at all fun. Lunch came next, at which Skye drank up all the milk while finishing the last of Churchie's gingerbread, so after lunch, Jeffrey sent her back again to the market for more milk. When she returned, Skye told him that she was fine now and not at all nervous, but moments later he caught her once more trying to stuff Batty into the life jacket, though she was nowhere near the ocean. So off Skye was sent again, to run down to the inn and back—five times. That licked her. She was finally too worn out to fear instant catastrophe, and when it was almost time to leave for dinner at Alec's, Jeffrey gladly handed back the reins of OAP-dom.

"I don't like being in charge," he said.

"Neither do I." Skye wearily surveyed her small troop, assembling now for the walk to the red house. While Jeffrey was in great shape, glowing from all the sun and exercise, the rest of them were not at their best. Batty's hair was in a tangle. Hound was hiding under the table, woozy from eating who knew what. Aunt Claire had been forced to slit open the leg of her best jeans to get them on over her plastic boot. And then there was Jane. Her nose was no longer stuffed with bloody wads of cotton, but its swollenness was still covered with a gigantic bandage.

"How do I look?" she asked, making herself cross-eyed by trying to see her own nose.

"Horrendous," said Skye.

"Scary," added Batty.

"Different," teased Jeffrey, "than you used to look."

"My phone is ringing," said Aunt Claire. "It's in my bag, if someone could get it for me."

Everyone went for the phone, but Skye got there first, just in case the display had Rosalind's name on it. Skye snatched it up and, yes, it was the true OAP. Skye's newfound calm evaporated.

"It's Rosy! No one tell her about all the accidents! Please!"

Again taking charge, Jeffrey wrested the phone away from Skye, tossed it to Aunt Claire, then dragged Skye out of the house and sat her down on the seawall.

"You're acting nuts, you know," he said.

"I can't help it. All that work to keep people safe and then Jane smashes her nose because she's waving at Dominic. It kills me."

Jeffrey leaned in to look at her closely. "Are you crying?"

"I never cry."

"Yes, but—"

"I'm just tired," said Skye. "If Aunt Claire doesn't mind, I probably shouldn't go to Alec's for dinner."

"Do you want me to stay with you?"

Skye knew what it took for Jeffrey to offer that. He'd been talking all day about music after dinner with Alec and Turron—that is, whenever he hadn't been torturing her. "Don't be silly. I need you to make sure Batty doesn't drown or blow up."

"Skye, repeat after me. Nobody is going to blow up!"

She refused to say it—not after the day she'd had—until he threatened to shake her, and even then, she'd only muttered the first few words when Jane came out onto the deck to call All Clear. Skye and Jeffrey went back inside.

"Rosalind is fine and reading lots of mysteries, and Anna has a crush on a lifeguard named Serge," said Jane.

"And they rode on a Ferris wheel," said Batty.

"Rosalind and Anna, not Serge," added Aunt Claire. "And though I told Rosy that my ankle was hurt, I may have left her with the impression that it wasn't as bad as it is. There's no point in her worrying."

"And I didn't mention this." Jane pointed at her nose. "It's too embarrassing."

"Good. Thank you," said Skye.

Aunt Claire didn't mind at all if Skye wanted to stay home, as long as Hound stayed with her, in case she had a sudden desire to protect someone from certain danger. Jeffrey offered to send Hoover back to Birches, too, so that Skye could have another potential victim to save, but she declined the offer—and could almost summon the energy to smile at the joke. And then it was time for the dinner contingent to set out for Alec's. Jane and Jeffrey were taking up positions on either side of Aunt Claire and her crutches when Turron unexpectedly appeared at the sliding glass doors.

"Taxi service," he said, and scooped a giggling Aunt Claire into his arms as easily as he'd lifted Jane that afternoon.

"Be careful with her," cried Skye.

"You bet." And he took off, with the others trailing after him.

Skye sank onto the couch and stayed there, too worn out to move, until Hound jumped up to lick her face. When she still didn't move, he gently took her arm in his mouth and tugged.

"I'm all right," she said, taking her arm back. "It's

just that no matter what anyone says, I know that people wouldn't be getting hurt if Rosalind were here. And I can't believe I'm talking to you."

"Woof."

"Right."

She was glad she'd stayed behind. When she got hungry, she could have a sandwich, and until then she'd read *Death by Black Hole,* and when it got dark enough, she could go outside with her binoculars to look at the stars. It would be a peaceful and intellectually satisfying evening, and the first time she'd had to herself since coming to Maine.

But Skye never got to the sandwich, let alone the stars. She managed only to wander out to the sleeping porch and collapse onto her cot with *Death by Black Hole.* After two paragraphs about cosmic plasma, the book slipped from her hands, and Skye was gone, sleeping the sleep of an overtaxed OAP.

CHAPTER EIGHT
Moose

Someone was poking at Skye, trying to wake her up. But because she was determined to stay lost in dreams unburdened with younger sisters, she jammed her fist in the general direction of the poking.

"Ouch!"

She opened her eyes and saw Jeffrey hovering next to her cot, rubbing his stomach.

"What are you doing?" she asked. It was ridiculously early in the morning. "Is somebody else hurt?"

"No, everyone's fine."

"Then I'm going to continue sleeping." Her eyes closed, but before she could escape back into slumber, Jeffrey was shaking her.

"No, you have to get up, because I'm too happy to sleep and I want company."

He moved on to Jane and started poking her. It took a while, but finally Jane rolled over and muttered, "I do adore you, Gary."

"Who's Gary?" Jeffrey asked Skye.

"Probably one of Sabrina Starr's boyfriends," she answered, reluctantly sitting up. "You'd better leave Jane alone if she's in that kind of mood—and go away so I can dress."

"You *are* dressed," he said. "When we came home last night, you were out cold and Hound was standing guard over you."

Skye looked down and saw that she was indeed wearing the clothes she'd fallen asleep in. *Death by Black Hole* was beside her pillow, looking like it had been rolled on. Now she remembered—she'd gone to sleep and hadn't woken up again.

"Then who put Batty to bed?"

Jane suddenly threw out an arm as though to catch at someone. "And I adore you, too, Herschel! Stay with me."

"She did," said Jeffrey.

"Jane?" Skye told herself that Jane was surely capable of putting Batty to bed without help. "Maybe I should just go look . . ."

"I'll meet you outside."

Skye swung out of bed and made her way through the dark to Batty's room. In the pink glow of the night-light, she could see Batty's dark head on the

110

pillow, and next to her Hound, who thumped his tail twice, his way of saying a silent hello. Little green Ellie had tumbled out of bed—Skye picked her up and tucked her in next to Batty, who now stirred and murmured a few words that sounded like "bee" and "sharp." This made no sense to Skye—and then she wondered if Rosalind had ever gone around at night listening to her sisters talking in their sleep. How strange. But Skye had nothing to worry about. She was certain that anything she herself said would be more interesting than boys' names or bees.

She slipped away and found Jeffrey waiting for her in front of Birches. It was that bewitching hour when night has gone but day hasn't arrived, when there are no greens anywhere—not in the grass or in the leaves—but instead only grays and shadowy blues, and the birds are frenziedly singing, encouraging the sun to rise yet one more time. Skye shivered, because it was also chilly.

"Come on," said Jeffrey. "You'll warm up when you start moving."

Skye thought that she would more easily warm up by going back to bed. Still, when Jeffrey took off toward Ocean Boulevard, she followed, sleepily curious about this happiness of his. When he turned left instead of right on the road, she almost balked. There was nothing in that direction but the pinewood, and she saw no reason to explore it so early in the morning. But Jeffrey took her hand and pulled her to the end of Ocean Boulevard and on into the trees. It was another world in there—dark, with the thick branches blocking the faint light of dawn, the ground slippery with fallen needles, and the heady smell of a thousand Christmas trees. Skye couldn't see at all, but Jeffrey led her safely past tree after tree after tree until they spotted a glimmer of light up ahead. A moment later, they were out of the wood and on the edge of yet another world altogether. To their left were the same rocks and ocean they'd left behind, but in front of them and to their right was a great expanse of short grass, broken only by the occasional tree, big patch of sand, or small pole with a numbered flag on it. One of these flags was only yards from where Jeffrey and Skye stood—number twelve.

"It's a golf course." Skye couldn't believe it. "Why are we here? We hate golf. Besides, your clubs are back at the house."

"We're not going to play golf. Alec told me that sometimes if you're out here early enough, you can see moose."

"You dragged me out of bed at dawn to *maybe* see a moose?" But the truth was that she was already hooked. She'd never seen a real moose, only pictures, and of course that statue in front of Moose Market.

So once again she followed Jeffrey. Heading away from the ocean, they kept to the edge of the pine trees and found themselves gradually climbing. They'd seen several of the flags—and Skye had long been warm enough to forget about shivering—when Jeffrey stopped at a large boulder jutting out of the pines. Here the golf course sloped down away from them, and at the bottom was a small lake rimmed with tall marsh grass.

"Alec said that the lake is the best place for moose. We'll wait." Jeffrey sat down and leaned against the rock. "Admit you're glad to be here."

"I won't give you that satisfaction."

"Then I won't tell you why I'm so happy."

"Okay, don't." She knew he would anyway.

"Because of last night and the music. Alec played the sax—Skye, he's so good—and Turron played the drums, of course, and they were fooling around with some jazz, which I know nothing about, but Alec told me to listen and drop in with the piano whenever I could, and I didn't think I'd be able to, but after a bit it started to make sense, and I could follow along a little. Then Alec told me that once I understood the melody, I could work out some chord progressions, and that was hard until all of a sudden it was easy." Jeffrey stopped his rush of words. "You have no idea what I'm talking about, do you?"

"Nope." She yawned and stretched out on the ground. She enjoyed listening to Jeffrey, especially when he didn't care whether or not she understood him. And when he didn't expect her to respond with long speeches about what she herself was thinking. Or feeling—feeling was the worst.

"Never mind about that part, then, but listen to this. The red house belongs to Alec's family—he's been coming here for summers most of his life. His real home is in Boston, though, not very far from my school, and he already said that I could visit him there. And Turron lives in New York City, but he plays in Boston sometimes, so maybe I'll see him, too. Skye, I could learn so much just from hanging around them."

"I know."

"You actually were listening to me, then?"

"Sort of." She grinned up at him. "Want to arm-wrestle?"

"Skye!"

"Oh, come on. The moose isn't here or anything."

With a show of reluctance, Jeffrey lay down opposite Skye and grasped her right hand with his. After a brief struggle, Skye's arm was flat on the ground.

She protested. "You're stronger than I am!"

"No kidding."

"Let's do it with our left hands."

They switched hands and once again Jeffrey won, even more quickly this time.

"Sorry," he said.

"Never mind," Skye answered grouchily. "You'd better go back to talking about music."

"Right. Well, you know how much I want to make music my whole life. Then last night, when Jane was asking Alec and Turron questions about love—"

114

"Please, no." Skye shook her head. "I should have gone after all."

"It was all right, because Aunt Claire didn't let her ask anything too embarrassing. Anyway, Alec and Turron ended up talking about how difficult it is to mix family with music, because of all the travel and uncertainty. They're both divorced and neither of them have any children. Alec's marriage was so bad he won't even talk about it—just that he was young and it lasted only a few months. That's sad, don't you think?" Jeffrey shook his head at the sadness. "I hope I never get divorced."

"You can't even get married for years and years. Why worry about getting divorced? Besides, I'm sure there are plenty of musicians who manage to stay married."

"I guess so," he said, then: "Do you ever wonder if we'll get married?"

"To each other? Good grief." She felt his forehead for a fever. "What's wrong with you? Is Jane getting to you with all her crazy talk?"

Jeffrey laughed. "Maybe."

The sky was brightening now, its pink-edged clouds reflected in the lake below. Skye watched as the grass on the golf course turned from blue to green and tried not to be discouraged about the arm wrestling. But the summer before, at Arundel, she'd been just as strong as Jeffrey, and almost as fast a runner.

"Let's see who can do the most push-ups," she said.

"I already know. I can do twenty-nine."

"Twenty-nine!" Skye could do ten, twelve at the most. "You never told me that."

"I don't tell you *everything.*"

"I thought you did." She stuck out her tongue at him. At least she was still a slightly better soccer player than he was.

"But I should tell you what happened with Batty last night. Alec was showing her a few things on the piano—"

"So that he could avoid Jane's love questions."

"No, Skye, listen. When he showed Batty the difference between major and minor chords, she understood right away. He thinks she might have real musical talent. And you should have seen her listening to us play."

"It's you she adores, not music. What about sit-ups? How many can you do?"

Jeffrey shook his head, warning her. "Hundreds."

"I dare you," she said, and got into position for a sit-up contest. "Ready?"

Maybe Jeffrey could have done hundreds of sit-ups and maybe Skye could have kept up, but before they made it even to thirty, he was grabbing her arm and pointing to the woods on the other side of the lake. What they'd come for was happening—moose were arriving. First came a huge cow moose, pushing her way out of the trees and sauntering casually to the water, dipping her head to drink. A great big brown beast, she was treat enough, but what came next made Skye catch her breath—two young calves, wobbly on their still-spindly legs and playfully bumping each other as they rushed to catch up with their mother.

"Twins?" she asked in a whisper, although the moose were much too far away to hear.

"Yes. Alec told me that we might see twins."

They sat quietly for a long time, watching the family below go about its morning business. Skye had a pang of regret that Batty wasn't there to see them, too, especially when the calves teamed up on one of the golf flag poles and head-butted it until it broke in half. Batty would have loved that. It was just a brief pang, though, and Skye figured she wouldn't have had it at all if she weren't getting hungry for breakfast.

When the moose finally wandered back into the trees, Jeffrey had one last thing to say before leaving for Birches.

"It's just that sometimes I wish we lived closer to each other, Skye. I sometimes sort of miss you. Sometimes."

"I do, too." She cleared her throat. "Sometimes."

Batty was on the little beach, up to her ankles in frigid water. It wasn't enough this morning to just dip her feet into the ocean. No, she needed to keep them there for a long time, trying as hard as she could to be close to Rosalind.

"I wish I could swim," she told Hound. "I'd swim to New Jersey to see her."

Thinking this a terrible idea, Hound grabbed hold of Batty's orange life preserver.

Batty went on. "Rosalind would never go see a moose and her babies without me."

It didn't matter to her that Skye and Jeffrey hadn't been positive they'd find a moose. They shouldn't have even gone looking without her, and once they saw the moose, they should have come to get her, and now she would never see a baby moose in her whole life, let alone two at a time. Hound let go of Batty's life preserver to lick away her tears, but they kept coming, and soon her face was as wet and salty as her feet, though not as cold.

Batty only stopped crying when she noticed the seagulls floating on the water not far from her. They were the same ones that Hoover had chased away the other day—Batty was certain about that—and she was glad they were back and not worried about being eaten by a dog. But, oh, how she wished Ben were there to see the seagulls with her. She missed him terribly and had so much to tell him. Bad things, like not seeing the moose, and good things, too, like how she'd decided to be a musician when she grew up.

She pulled her harmonica out of her pocket and played a few notes of one of the songs Jeffrey had played the night before. The notes sounded good, but not as good as they had on the piano. But that was all right, because Batty had also decided that she wanted her own piano. She would keep it in her bedroom at home, and Ben could sit on the bench beside her and listen while she played.

Hound, who had been patient until now, decided that Batty had been in the freezing water long enough, and he dragged her to higher ground. She submitted because her feet really were awfully cold, and because playing the harmonica had made her feel better. But she felt worse all over again when she looked up at the deck, where Jane was supposed to be watching over Batty, making sure she didn't drown. This is what Jane had promised she would do before Skye and Jeffrey had left for Moose Market.

Not only was Jane paying no attention at all to Batty, she was talking to two people Batty had never seen. She was pretty sure she knew who they were, though, because Jane had described them to her. The boy in the skateboard helmet was Dominic, the one who'd made Jane fall down and hurt her nose, and the girl with him was his sister, Mercedes. Jane had said that maybe Mercedes and Batty could be friends. This had sounded interesting at the time, but with Mercedes right there on the deck, Batty felt that making a new friend was too scary, especially if she had to also meet the new friend's older brother.

Now Jane was pointing down toward the beach,

but before Mercedes or Dominic could turn to look, Batty dropped to all fours and crawled over to the sea-wall, where she would be out of sight of the deck. She hoped that Jane would decide she'd drowned and tell Mercedes to go be friends with someone else. But what Batty hoped the most was that Dominic wouldn't come down to the beach. If he did, maybe she could pretend that she *had* drowned and was too dead to meet anyone. While she was wondering what a drowned person looked like—closing her eyes seemed like a good start—someone said hello to her.

Batty cautiously opened her eyes and saw only one set of feet in front of her. And the feet had on purple sneakers with pink laces, which made Batty think they probably belonged to Mercedes and not Dominic. She looked higher and saw that she was right.

"Hello," she said.

"Hello. I brought you a present," Mercedes said, and when Batty stood up, handed her a small wooden box. "You can keep stuff in it."

Batty had never seen anything like it. Its wood was golden brown, and there were words carved in the lid. She loved it immensely, and loved it even more when she opened it and found that it smelled of faraway forests. "I don't have a present for you."

"That's okay. I'm older than you, and anyway I have lots of these. My grandmother sells them in the gift shop at the inn." She pointed to the lid of the box. "See? 'Mouette Inn.'"

Hound had to sniff the box, too, and then he had to sniff Mercedes all over and make sure she was safe enough to be Batty's friend.

"He's Hound," explained Batty. "I have a cat, too, and also a little brother."

"I wish I had a little brother. I only have Dominic and two more brothers older than him even. They stayed home in California because they have summer jobs."

"If they have jobs, they must be really old."

"They are."

Batty was proud and pleased to have made a friend. Soon Mercedes was showing Batty the treasures of the beach. The small, smooth rocks that were dull gray until dipped into the water, when they turned all sorts of lush blues and greens. There were shells, too, tear-shaped and dark—Batty put one of these into her new box. Best of all were the teeny-weeny snails, each no bigger than a pea, who lived under the seaweed. The girls watched them crawl, oh so slowly, and gave them names. One was Mickey and one was Trish, and Batty loved them dearly. When Mickey and Trish, finally tired of being stared at, retreated into their shells and refused to come out, Batty told Mercedes all about Rosalind and how much she missed her, and about how everyone else was in England, and finally Batty told about her great disappointment over the moose and her babies.

"Maybe the moose are at the lake now," said Mercedes.

"Do you think so?"

"Why not?"

Why not indeed? Batty had visions of the moose and her babies standing in the lake, waiting and waiting for Batty to arrive.

"We could go look for them," said Mercedes. "I know the way."

"I'm not allowed to go by myself. My sisters worry that I'll get lost or drown." She left out blowing up, because it was too confusing to discuss with a brand-new friend.

"Dominic never worries about me. He hardly notices me at all."

This was a strange idea for Batty. She thought that older sisters and brothers taking care of their younger sisters and brothers was a rule, like brushing your teeth. "I'll worry about you, Mercedes, if you want me to."

"Thank you." Mercedes stood on one foot, then the other, to show her appreciation. "I fall off my bike a lot."

Batty took hold of Mercedes's hand, worrying as hard as she could about falling off bikes, then remembered about the moose. She looked up to the deck, where Jane was again alone, staring off into space, her blue notebook open in her lap.

"Come on," Batty told Mercedes. "Maybe Jane will take us to see the moose babies."

So they went up to the deck to see Jane, who was very complimentary about Batty's new box. But when they asked her to take them to the golf course, she said that the moose probably hid during the day to avoid all the golfers. "Besides, I'm working."

"She's writing a book," Batty explained to Mercedes. "A real book like *Ivy + Bean*, but about love."

"I love *Ivy + Bean*!" Mercedes gazed at Jane with ever-growing respect. "Can I read yours?"

"Well, actually, I'm still trying to get started on this one," answered Jane, too gratified not to tell the truth. "I might have writer's block."

"Wow," said Mercedes, impressed but puzzled. "Is that what's wrong with your nose?"

Jane's hand flew to the bandage across her nose. "No, I hit—I mean, Dominic was—oh, never mind. Let's go look for moose."

They left Hound behind, not trusting his reaction to either moose or golfers, then followed the path that Skye and Jeffrey had taken earlier that morning, through the pinewood and up the hill toward the lake. Along the way they saw lots of golfers in brightly colored trousers, but they didn't see moose, not by the lake or anywhere else. It wasn't a wasted trip, though, because of the golf balls. Mercedes found the first one nestled next to a pinecone. As soon as she showed it to Batty, Batty found another ball half buried under a fallen branch.

"Can we keep them?" Batty asked Jane.

"I think so." Jane found another. "They've been lost and abandoned, poor things."

Once the three girls started looking, they found golf balls everywhere. They walked up and down the pinewood until all pockets were full to overflowing. Then Jane discovered that balls stuffed down Batty's life preserver stayed there if Batty didn't wriggle too much, and they walked more and found more. When even the life preserver was full, and it was time to head back to the house, one last ball suddenly appeared, rolling right up to Batty. She and Mercedes crouched down to look but didn't touch, because maybe a golfer was following along behind it. And a few minutes later, one did arrive, wearing a green skirt and a worried expression.

"Oh, is that my ball?" she cried when she saw them. "Is it a Dunlop?"

There was a word on the golf ball. Mercedes spelled it out for the lady. "D-U-N-L-O-P."

"Yes, Dunlop! Thank you so much. It's my first day and I've already lost four balls. My husband is getting annoyed."

Batty didn't care about the lady's husband, but when Jane started emptying her pockets, Mercedes did, too, and then Batty was shamed into generosity, so she wriggled and wriggled until another fifteen golf balls fell out of her life preserver. Quite pleased, the woman found four more Dunlops.

"How much do I owe you?" she asked, pulling a slim wallet out of a green pocket.

"We don't need money," said Jane. "They're just balls we found."

"No, no, you must take something. You saved me." The lady handed a five-dollar bill to Batty, and hurried back to the course and her husband before Jane could insist on returning the money.

The sudden acquisition of money can startle, and for a while none of the girls knew what to say. Then Batty, remembering that she'd already had one gift that day, gave the money to Mercedes, who, horrified at the idea of taking it for herself, handed it to Jane. Though Jane was tempted—five dollars would buy her a new blue notebook—she was embarrassed to be more grasping than the others, so she gave it back to Batty.

"Keep it in your new wooden box," she said. "We'll figure out what to do with it later."

Batty would still have preferred the golf balls. "Maybe we can look for more another day."

"Sure," said Jane, gathering up the scattered balls and stuffing them back into pockets and the life preserver. "Jeffrey will help."

"So will I," added Mercedes. "I'll help you, Batty, and you can keep them all."

"Thank you, and maybe Alec and Turron will help, too." Batty didn't think there could be too many people finding golf balls for her. She imagined piles and piles of them. It would be her own collection to take home and share with Ben, who would enjoy golf balls as much as she did—she just knew it.

CHAPTER NINE
Burning Wishes

JANE STILL HADN'T BEGUN her Sabrina Starr book. She had, however, written a new sentence in her blue notebook, just after Dominic stopped by and while Batty and Mercedes were looking for tiny snails. *I will meet Dominic in French Park after lunch.* Jane thought it an enthralling sentence, brimming with possibilities. That it was a true sentence—written down because Dominic himself had told her to meet him—made it even better, though until now Jane had never been as interested in true stories as in made-up ones.

Because Dominic had told her where the park was—on Ocean Boulevard, just past the road that led to Moose Market—getting there would be no problem, but Jane wasn't so sure about the *after lunch.*

When she'd asked Dominic what time that meant exactly, he'd brushed her off, as though exact times weren't of any importance. This had seemed impressively sophisticated to Jane, but later, while she was eating lunch, she wished she'd pushed harder for details. She didn't want to be late and miss him.

"Why are you eating so fast?" asked Skye.

"I'm not," said Jane, though her whole sandwich was gone and everyone else was still on their first half. "Jeffrey, can I switch cleanup with you? I'll do dinner if you do lunch."

"Sure. Are you going to eat those potato chips?"

Jane passed Jeffrey her potato chips. "May I be excused, Aunt Claire? I'm taking a walk."

"Sure, honey."

Feeling a twinge of conscience, Jane told the whole truth. "That is, I'm taking a walk to meet Dominic. He invited me when he was here this morning."

"Yes, I saw him when he was talking to you on the deck," said Aunt Claire. "He looks like a nice boy."

"Nicely dull," said Skye. "Not worthy of a Penderwick. Certainly not worthy of a Penderwick almost breaking her nose."

"You barely know him, Skye," protested Jane. "I believe he has hidden depths."

Jeffrey stuffed a potato chip into Skye's mouth to keep her from commenting on Dominic's depths.

"I could go with you, Jane," he said.

"If Jeffrey goes, I will, too," said Batty.

Skye swallowed her potato chip. "I will go, because I am the OAP."

A crowd at the park was not what Jane had imagined, especially a crowd of people—mainly Skye—who didn't much like Dominic. Aunt Claire must have agreed.

"Noble though everyone's sentiments be," she said, "because only Jane was invited by Dominic, only she should go."

"Thank you, Aunt Claire," said Jane.

She gratefully left the table and headed for the bathroom for a new bandage, though it managed to do nothing more than the old bandage to hide the scratched and swollen mess of her nose. For a moment, Jane considered adding another bandage, or three or four, but she talked herself out of such vanity. Her poor nose had been on full display for Dominic that morning. There was no reason to try to hide it now.

So Jane grabbed her blue notebook and set off, wondering why Dominic wanted to meet her at the park. He hadn't explained—he'd said only two sentences altogether. "Meet me in French Park after lunch" was one sentence. "It's on Ocean Boulevard, past the road to Moose Market" was the other one. Though Jane would have liked him to say more, she was pleased with the mysteriousness of him saying less. This was what she'd meant by hidden depths. Jane had occasionally tried to develop her own hidden depths, but she never could decide what to hide and how far down.

If she didn't know why Dominic wanted to meet her, Jane certainly knew why she wanted to meet Dominic. She was going to ask him questions from her Love Survey. If he gave her intriguing answers, maybe she would finally get started on her Sabrina Starr book. The answers from Alec and Turron the night before had been very . . . grown-up. And not especially interesting, except perhaps for Alec's brief and terrible early marriage. Jane would love to hear more about that someday, but not for this book. This book was to be about exciting true love, not heartbreak.

Then there was also Dominic's smile, which Jane very much wanted to see again. When she'd met him the first time, he was so serious, and he'd been the same again that morning until right after he told her to meet him at the park. That was when he'd smiled, and after all that seriousness, his smile was a revelation, like a rainbow after a storm, like spring after winter, like dawn after the darkest night.

She stopped, opened her notebook, and wrote that down.

His smile was a revelation, like a rainbow after a storm, like spring after winter, like dawn after the darkest night. She read it out loud as she wrote. "I like that. I'll use it to describe the smile of Sabrina's true love."

Closing her notebook, Jane set off again and soon found French Park, where Dominic had said she would, though she would have found it anyway by following the now-familiar sound of skateboard wheels on asphalt. The park was not a large one—just a simple square of grass with a bench, several rosebushes, a memorial plaque, and a path that went around and through it all in a kind of figure eight. It was this path that Dominic was traveling along noisily, and with such great concentration that he didn't seem to notice Jane's arrival, not even when she enthusiastically waved at him.

Undeterred, Jane looked first at the rosebushes, which were in bloom and smelled like heaven, then at the plaque. It dedicated the park to CAPTAIN ATHERTON W. FRENCH, WHO WASHED FROM THE WRECK OF THE SCHOONER MARY ALICE IN 1869. Feeling very bad for Captain French, and even worse for his sorrowing family, who'd had to think about him being washed from his wreck, Jane went back to the roses to cheer up again. After that, she sat on the bench and watched Dominic while he skateboarded, and though it was nice to watch him, she thought it even nicer when he stopped and came over to sit next to her on the bench. Now the conversation would begin.

But, oh, it was hard going! Jane asked Dominic about his family, his school, and his hobbies, but Dominic could hardly stir himself to give answers. So she told him about playing soccer and writing the Sabrina Starr books. Nothing. At this rate, she didn't dare bring up the Love Survey. Discouraged, Jane stopped talking at all, and they both just sat, staring at the view. Jane watched a sailboat as it came into sight—she decided that if it went away again before Dominic said anything, she would say good-bye and leave. She was starting to think that Dominic wasn't at all mysterious—he was just a terrible conversationalist.

Suddenly he cleared his throat, and Jane turned expectantly toward him. Was he about to explain why he'd invited her here?

"That's—" He cleared his throat again, then pointed out across the ocean, to a dark blurry hump caught between the blue sky and the bluer water. "That's Gandy Island. It's got a little house on the other side."

Jane was much encouraged by what was for Dominic a vast number of words. Maybe finally this was a topic they could converse on. She forged onward.

"When I grow up, maybe I'll live on an island. Writers need lots of solitude." She stopped and held her breath, hoping he would go on.

He did. "I don't want to wait until I'm grown up. I'd like to live there now, all by myself. I'd catch rainwater in barrels and boil it for drinking, and to get clean I'd swim in the ocean, even in the winter. And I'd build skateboard ramps all over the island and practice all the time."

"That sounds nice," said Jane, though she thought the ramps would be out of place on a pretty island.

"And I wouldn't bother with furniture."

"Except a bed, right?"

Scornfully, he plucked a rose from a nearby bush and squashed it into nothing. "A hammock."

This seemed brave and strong to Jane. She herself would need at least a cot—a hammock might make her seasick. And she'd want a table and chair for when she wrote. She wouldn't mind sitting on the floor when she ate, but writing was different.

"And you could have a woodstove for cooking," she said.

"I wouldn't bother with a stove either. I'd cook over an open fire on the beach."

Now Jane was really impressed. She could see it—Dominic crouched over the fire, keeping it alive at night, the wary eyes of wild animals just outside the ring of light. She hoped Dominic would expand on this intoxicating picture, but once again he'd lapsed into silence. This silence, however, was different from the earlier one, more relaxed and friendly. Jane felt that she could even launch into her research if she started with an easy question, like—oh, like whether he believed that love was more a matter of head or heart. She took a deep breath, but before she could get a word out, Dominic abruptly leaped off the bench, landing with one foot on his skateboard.

"See you later," he said.

Jane stood up, startled. "When?"

"I'll come get you." With that, he flashed his magnificent smile, then was off and away on his skateboard, not looking back even once.

When Jane returned from French Park, Skye was behind Birches with a soccer ball, shooting at the seawall, trying to hit the same spot each time. She was glad to see Jane back so soon and without blood all over her. At least this time Dominic's presence hadn't made her smash herself with a rock.

"Where's everyone else?" asked Jane.

"Aunt Claire's inside doing a jigsaw puzzle Turron brought for her. Jeffrey's at the red house with Alec, playing the piano. And Batty and Hound are over there with him." Skye steadied the ball. "Jane, do you think Batty has musical talent?"

"Of course not."

"That's what I told Jeffrey." Relieved—because Batty had gone so willingly, so enthusiastically to Alec's—Skye passed the ball to Jane. The next half hour was a most satisfying workout that ranged from the grass to the deck to the beach, the sisters battling fiercely for mastery over the ball and each other. When at last they collapsed, neither could claim victory, which was how they always liked it best.

"You're getting better," said Jane, who had more talent.

"You are, too," replied Skye, who worked harder. "So how are Dominic's depths?"

Jane threw a handful of sand at her sister. "Let's cook dinner over an open fire out here tonight."

"We can barely cook dinner on a real stove."

"Well, maybe we won't cook the whole dinner. What about— Oh, I've got it! What about roasted marshmallows? They'll be our dessert."

"I don't know. There could have been something on the list about Batty and fire."

"Forget the list for once," cried Jane. "What are we, men or mice?"

Skye was stung. This was a question she'd asked her sisters dozens of times, but never before had any of them asked it of her. As if to increase her humiliation, the incoming tide chose that moment to drench her sneakers.

"All right," she said. "We'll roast marshmallows for dessert."

"We'll roast them over an open fire that we've built ourselves," said Jane. "We'll be Robinson Crusoe or cowboys in the Old West or Jill and Eustace in *The Silver Chair.*"

There was a problem, though, which Crusoe and cowboys had never faced. Because Skye had been tossed out of Brownies at age eight for refusing to wear the hat, and Jane had quit out of loyalty to Skye, neither had learned even the basics of fire building. So they went inside to ask Aunt Claire, who was indeed working on a jigsaw puzzle that showed a scene of Paris. While they helped her find pieces of couples strolling along the Seine, she admitted that she'd made it all the way through the first year of Girl Scouts, although she'd hated the hats, too—Jane decided it must be in their blood—and could tell them what to do.

"You need to collect lots of dry wood, small stuff for kindling and logs to keep the fire going. Oh, and some straight sticks to hold the marshmallows—you can whittle them to make them sharp enough. Then you dig a shallow pit in the sand and surround it with rocks. I wish I could help." Aunt Claire looked daggers at her still-bound-and-booted ankle. "But I *am* known as an expert stick whittler."

Skye and Jane promised to let Aunt Claire whittle the sticks and set off on their hunt for wood. Jane suggested they start by looking for driftwood, but an hour of combing the rocks all the way down to the dock, and then another quarter mile past that, yielded only one soggy plank with *Jarrett loves Gina* scrawled on it in Magic Marker. Disgusted, Skye threw the plank into the ocean and said that it was time to try the pinewood. They had better luck there, picking up plenty of small branches for kindling and marshmallow sticks, and along the way Jane found another six golf balls for Batty's collection. But the only possibility for logs came in the form of a fallen tree.

"We need an ax," said Jane, looking around as if axes lived in pinewoods.

"Holy bananas, Jane. Do you really think we could chop apart a whole tree without cutting off one or several of our body parts? And do *not* ask me about men and mice again."

"Then what do you suggest we use for wood?"

"We could burn Dominic's skateboard."

The sisters glared at each other. They were hot, the branches they'd collected were scratching their arms, and a family of mosquitoes had just arrived.

"Should we forget about the fire?" Jane didn't want to at all.

"No," said Skye reluctantly. "Not yet."

Friends again, they trudged back to the house, where they found Jeffrey and Batty in the backyard, perched on a pile of neatly cut firewood.

"Aunt Claire told us about the marshmallows," cried Batty when she saw them, "and I know about octaves now!"

"That's nice," said Skye, dumping her kindling.

"Where did you get that firewood?" asked Jane. "We've been searching everywhere."

"Alec gave it to us. He's going to help with the fire," said Batty. "Skye, if we go over there, I can show you octaves on his piano."

"No, thank you."

"Alec has a woodstove for winter, which is why he had wood to give us," said Jeffrey. "Can you imagine how great it would be to come up here in the winter, with no one around and the snow falling into the ocean? Alec says he just plays music for days on end."

"I would like that." Batty mimed playing the piano.

Skye was seriously considering killing both of them, or at least whacking them with a piece of kindling.

"Enough about winter," said Jane brightly, because she could always tell when Skye was thinking murderous thoughts. "We have a lot more to do for this marshmallow roast. Right, Skye? What do we do next?"

Skye took a deep breath. "Find rocks."

"Rocks it is." Jeffrey slid off the woodpile, then lifted Batty down. "At your command, OAP. Lead on."

After dinner, Turron carried Aunt Claire over to Alec's deck, where they could oversee the marshmallow roast from afar. With them went Hound, because no one trusted him or Hoover—especially Hoover—near an open fire. The others were about to head for the beach, where the fire was all ready to go, when the phone rang. Batty rushed to pick it up, as she always did, in case it was Rosalind.

"If it's Rosalind," said Skye, "don't tell her about the bonfire and marshmallows."

"Or Dominic," added Jane.

"Hold on a minute, please," said Batty into the phone, then turned to her sisters. "What *can* I tell her?"

Jeffrey laughed. "Tell her about my stuffed green peppers."

Batty went back to Rosalind. "Jeffrey made stuffed

green peppers for dinner and they were delicious, but we didn't have dessert, because— I can't tell you why."

Jane snatched the phone from her and managed to steer the conversation away from dessert—roasted marshmallows—or anything else that might cause Rosalind concern, by asking questions. After the connection failed, as usual, Jane filled in the others while they all walked down to the beach.

"Rosy and Anna met some girls from Philadelphia to play volleyball with, and some girls from Pittsburgh to do yoga with on the beach. I think I got that right. It could be the other way around. It might be yoga with the Philadelphia girls."

"It doesn't matter," said Skye.

"Also, they're riding bikes on the boardwalk every morning, except when they sleep in too late."

Skye couldn't remember what it was like to sleep in late. Or what it was like not to fret all the time about younger sisters. And now that they'd reached the beach, she couldn't remember what had made her agree to go through with this fire thing. Everything was ready—the pit dug, the stones in place, the kindling laid, the marshmallows standing by, Alec up on his deck waiting to be summoned as supervisor—but Skye was ready to back out, more mouse than man.

"Maybe we shouldn't light it," she said.

"It's impossible to roast marshmallows over an unlit fire," said Jeffrey calmly.

"Then maybe Batty shouldn't stay."

Batty moved closer to Jane for protection. She'd already endured much to be here, and she had no intention of leaving now. First was the afternoon nap she'd been forced to take because she was going to be up past her bedtime. And then, much worse, there was the rope Skye had tied to her orange life preserver. The rope was supposed to be for pulling her out of the fire or the ocean, whichever might be needed, but so far it had only been used by Hound, who'd thought it was a leash and dragged Batty around accordingly.

"Batty will be fine," said Jane, also calmly. Earlier she and Jeffrey had worked out this strategy, just in case Skye lost her nerve.

"We'll all be fine," said Jeffrey.

Skye looked suspiciously at him, then at Jane, and they smiled reassuringly back at her. Unconvinced, she shifted a piece of kindling to what looked like a safer spot, then shifted it back to where it had been.

"Are you ready for Alec yet?" called Aunt Claire from above.

"We're waiting for sunset," Jeffrey shouted back.

"It *is* sunset," said Batty plaintively.

She was right. The horizon was glowing pink and orange, and the clouds had turned dark blue. The moon was already gleaming faintly, and soon the sun would be gone altogether and night would come.

"We did decide on sunset, Skye," said Jane.

"Though we could wait a few more minutes if you want."

"We're sure Alec knows his way around fire?" Skye shook her head. "I'm being an idiot, aren't I?"

"Sort of." Jeffrey waved his arms at the deck—*now* they were ready for Alec.

He arrived with a box full of long wooden matches, let Batty select one, and took it back from her.

"Before I light up, should we have some theme music?" he asked. "How about Springsteen's 'I'm on Fire'?"

"No!" said Skye, snatching up Batty's rope and pulling her close.

"Sondheim's 'City on Fire' doesn't really fit, and we don't have a soprano for Ravel's 'Fire' aria. Jeffrey, help me."

"The '1812 Overture' has cannon fire in it. Does that count?"

"Close enough." Alec held up the match like a conductor's baton. "Everyone, we'll start with the French horns playing 'The Marseillaise,' a minute or so before the first cannon shot. Got it?"

Naturally, only Jeffrey had any idea what he was talking about, but between the two of them they managed half the orchestra—Alec was particularly good at being French horns—and they could have made it all the way through if Jeffrey hadn't fallen over laughing when they got to the crashing booms of the cannons. By then, everybody else was laughing, too, and it took a while for them to get calmed down and ready for business.

"Shall I do it?" asked Alec.

"Yes," they all answered.

He ceremoniously lit the match, then held the tiny flame to the smallest pieces of kindling, mere twigs. At first nothing seemed to be happening, but then all at once several of the twigs were glowing red. Alec blew gently on them, encouraging the fire to spread to the rest of the kindling, and suddenly—a blaze! Cheers went up, echoed by the adults on the deck, and Jane and Batty did a celebration dance, being Robinson Crusoe and cowboys all at once. After Alec fed the fire with two larger pieces of wood, Jeffrey pulled Skye to her feet and made her dance, too, swooping and whooping and, for now at least, not worried about anything at all.

Then it was time for marshmallows.

Roasting marshmallows over an open fire is an art. The marshmallow should be evenly toasted all around until it's a golden brown. A slight puckering of the skin is all right, and some people like that the best. The inside should be hot all the way through and softened, but not melted into messy gooeyness. Not one of the marshmallows roasted that night came even close. Many were burned black at least on one side, and the ones that weren't were barely roasted. No one cared. They gobbled them up, declaring them delicious, and not remembering about sharing with the missing grown-ups until Turron roared down at them. After that, Jeffrey and Skye took turns running marshmallows up to the deck, where Turron and Aunt Claire devoured them as greedily as the others had, and a few of the blackest were slipped to Hoover and Hound as compensation for not being on the beach.

When the marshmallows were all gone, and the fire was burning low, Alec joined the other grown-ups on his deck, and the four children were alone on the beach, sated and happy. For a long time, they sat, staring into the flames and listening to the soft slapping of the waves. The breeze off the ocean was cool now, the ocean was as dark as the sky, and the stars were arriving, dozens, then hundreds, then thousands of them, blinking and glowing overhead.

"We should make wishes," whispered Jane. "Wishes to the Firegod."

"I wish for more golf balls, and to see the moose and her babies," said Batty, drowsily leaning against Jeffrey. "And I wish for a piano."

Skye groaned. "What would you do with a piano?"

Jane went on, warming to her idea. "The wishes must be silent and secret, Batty. And to increase their power, we should each throw something of ourselves into the fire."

"Nail clippings," said Jeffrey.

"Excellent idea, but I've got a better one," exclaimed Jane. She dashed off to Birches and was soon back with a pair of scissors. "Hair!"

"We're not cutting our hair," said Skye. "And anyway, this is ridiculous. Wishes!"

"But I've got one," said Jeffrey. "A good one."

"What is it?"

"The wishes must be silent and secret." Jeffrey imitated Jane perfectly.

"Thank you, Jeffrey," said Jane. "And we only need tiny bits of hair."

"I'll go first," said Batty.

"One minute, please. I must call up the magic with an ancient spell. Which I haven't made up yet." Jane thought for a minute, then chanted:

"Fire, Moon, Sand, and Sea,
  Listen now and hear my plea.
  Humbly do I ask of thee,
  Please bring what I wish to me."

She cut off a tip of one of Batty's curls and threw it onto the fire.

"I wish for a piano!" Batty jumped up and down with excitement.

"Silent wishes, please," admonished Jane, then took her own turn, with a particularly dramatic reci-

144

tation of the chant and a properly silent and secret wish.

Jeffrey went next, and only Skye was left. She couldn't think what to wish for. She so barely believed in wishes that she hadn't wished even on her birthday candles since she was seven. But it did seem a waste not to, now that they'd gone to all the trouble to build the fire, so she thought and thought, and hemmed and hawed, until Alec called down to them that he was on his way to help put out the fire.

"Hurry, Skye," said Jeffrey.

"Okay, I'm ready. Do your chanty thing, Jane."

"Fire, Moon, Sand, and Sea,
    Listen now and hear my plea.
    Humbly do I ask of thee,
    Please bring what I wish to me."

Skye tossed her bit of hair just as Alec arrived. She wished that all the others' wishes would come true. Except for Batty's piano.

CHAPTER TEN
Seals, and a Kiss

As a future astrophysicist, Skye didn't believe even the slightest bit in a Firegod who could grant wishes. Nevertheless, when no piano magically appeared over the next few days, she was glad she'd countermanded Batty's request for one. There would have been no room for it in Birches, and besides, she was sure that Batty would soon forget about pianos and go back to wanting only stuffed animals and Rosalind.

As for Batty, it was possible that someday she would forget about pianos, but it wasn't going to happen soon. Because now Jeffrey and Alec were teaching her how to play. A little here and a little there, and when they weren't teaching her, she was watching and listening while they played, and when she grew restless from sitting too long, Turron took over and made up games with his drums to teach her about whole, half, quarter, and eighth notes; and three-four time and four-four time; and even syncopation. It was Turron, too, who had the idea of Batty and Jeffrey giving a concert for the others on the last night of their stay, although he himself was leaving before then and so wouldn't be there to see it, and soon Jeffrey and Alec had picked out the perfect song for them to perform and started working on an arrangement. Batty blissfully soaked it all up and didn't tell anyone in her family what she was doing, not Aunt Claire or Jane, or even Rosalind when she called, and especially not Skye. She did talk to her new friend Mercedes about it, because Mercedes would never say that Batty was too little for music or that she couldn't be a musician because Penderwicks never were. Mercedes only said that she wished she could learn to play the piano, too, so Batty told her about wishing to the Firegod, but when she couldn't remember Jane's chant, Mercedes gave up on the piano and went back to trying to ride her bike without falling down.

As a future—and current, though not recent—writer of novels, Jane was able to believe just a little bit in a Firegod who granted wishes. And perhaps she was right, because for the same few days that the piano wasn't appearing, Jane's wish was coming true. Her wish? To finally have enough research material for her

Sabrina Starr book. She hadn't suggested how this should happen, but the Firegod was no dummy. He used the most direct method, having Jane herself fall in love—and with the most logical candidate. When she went to sleep the night of the marshmallow roast, Dominic wasn't much more than a skateboarder with a dazzling smile. When she woke up the next morning, he was the love of her life. And as time went on, her adoration for Dominic grew and grew, all without the slightest encouragement from him.

Occasionally he zipped by on his skateboard, and once he slowed down enough to hand Jane a wooden Popsicle stick, still damp from the cherry Popsicle he'd just finished, and once he told her that she looked better now with her bandage gone and her nose almost back to normal, but that was obvious, and there were no love notes, gifts, or flowers, and no more meetings at French Park. Jane didn't need any of it. Thinking about Dominic, dreaming about Dominic—this was enough to keep Jane in raptures, in fact too much so to risk talking about her feelings to anyone, and especially not to Skye.

Nevertheless, Skye knew that something was odd about Jane. Her giddily high spirits and the way she always seemed to be gazing off into the distance with an enigmatic smile—these were clues. And now when Jane talked in her sleep, Dominic's name popped up among the usual Sabrina Starr wanderings. Although concerned, Skye held off asking Jane about it all, because she believed in privacy, and also because she couldn't stand the idea of hearing about how much Jane liked Dominic. But then came the Popsicle-stick incident. Not the actual receiving of it—Skye had been there for that, and though she saw Jane blush and tuck the stick into her pocket, that wasn't too bad. Maybe Jane didn't want to litter. No, it was much worse than that. One evening Skye walked into their portion of the screened porch and caught Jane *dancing* with the Popsicle stick, dancing and humming, and even murmuring to it. Skye heard only one word, which was, naturally, "Dominic."

"What are you *doing*?" she barked, horrified that a Penderwick would sink so low.

Jane dropped the stick and casually covered it with her foot. "Nothing," she said. "Just dancing."

"Dancing with—" Skye couldn't bring herself to say it out loud.

Jane burst out with more humming, swaying back and forth. "Isn't life just wonderful, Skye? Magnificently wonderful. Fabulously and wonderfully magnificent."

"Not right this minute it isn't. Jane, I know what you're standing on."

"You do?"

"And I have to say that you seem a little wacko to me. I mean, maybe if that stick had belonged to, say, Einstein, but . . ." Skye let her voice trail off. No one got crushes on Einstein. Even she knew that much. "I wish Rosalind were here. I don't know what I'm doing."

"Oh, no, Skye, you're a brilliant OAP! Glorious and wonderfully fabulous!"

"But, Jane—"

"Don't fuss over me, Skye. I'm just happy!" Jane picked up her Popsicle stick and beamed. "Someday it'll happen to you, too, when you meet the right boy, and then you'll understand."

Skye managed to get off the porch and outside without punching Jane in the nose and making it swollen all over again, and she was quite proud of that, at least. But now she was really concerned. How could she protect Jane from this idiocy? Wondering what Caesar or Napoleon would do in this situation was worthless. Skye needed a tree to kick, now, immediately. Poor patient birch trees—this wasn't the treatment they deserved. But kicking them calmed Skye down a little, enough to help her realize that she did after all have someone she could talk to about boys, crushes, and dancing with Popsicle sticks. Aunt Claire, of course. Skye apologized to the birch trees and began to plot how to broach these painful subjects without giving away Jane's secrets.

The next morning, Skye waited until Aunt Claire was alone in Birches, working on yet another jigsaw puzzle from Turron. This one showed the Grand Canal in Venice, and Aunt Claire was trying to find one final piece of a gondola.

"Help me," she said when she noticed Skye lurking.

150

"I don't know if I can't find it or if Hound ate it. He was looking guilty earlier."

Skye found the puzzle piece under the couch, and indeed it was a little wet, as though it had been sucked on and spit out by a certain dog.

"You're lucky he didn't swallow it, for once," said Skye, sticking the piece into its rightful place. "Aunt Claire, may I ask you a question?"

"Ask away, young Jedi."

"When you were young and—"

Aunt Claire interrupted. "I am not yet old."

"Sorry, younger. When you were younger, did you ever keep stuff that boys had given you? Weird stuff?"

"You're not writing a book about love, too, are you?"

"No!"

"That's a relief." Aunt Claire poked around the jigsaw pieces, looking for the gondolier's hat. "When I was in college, a really cute ice hockey player gave me one of his shin guards. Is that weird enough? I kept it until—probably until I started dating Micah, the chemistry major. You wouldn't think a chemist would be the jealous type, but he hated that shin guard."

"Did you ever talk to it?"

"Talk to what?"

"The shin guard."

Aunt Claire squinted at Skye as though trying to recognize her. "What's this about?"

"Nothing, really. Just a hypothetical."

"You're sure? Then no, I don't remember talking to the shin guard."

"Or dancing with it?"

"Honestly, Skye, you have to give me more to go on here. Should I be concerned? I can't even imagine you dancing, let alone with weird stuff from a boy."

"I'm not!" Stung that anyone could think she'd be so foolish, Skye was still too loyal to tell Jane's secrets. "Never mind. This is all just something I've been wondering about. I shouldn't have said anything."

"So you're all right?"

"Fine." Skye wandered over to the refrigerator and bent down to look at the postcards of England and New Jersey. She bet no one in either of those places had ever dreamed of dancing with Popsicle sticks.

"I did know a girl in middle school who made hand puppets from her boyfriends' socks," said Aunt Claire. "I don't know if she talked to the puppets, but she did make the puppets talk to her. Does that help?"

"A little bit." And it did, because that poor girl had been much worse even than Jane. "If I ever do anything that idiotic, lock me up. Promise?"

"I promise. Penderwick Family Honor."

Making hand puppets from boys' socks! Horrified, Skye went outside and glared at the ocean. She was starting middle school that September. If she discovered that kind of nonsense going on, she would drop out and go live on a mountaintop all by herself.

There was a great deal of raucous noise coming from the beach—what sounded like a circus. That wasn't what was supposed to be happening. What was supposed to be happening was soccer drills. Jane had announced them, Jeffrey had agreed to take some time away from the piano to join her, and since Jeffrey was going, so was Batty, and wherever Batty went these days, there went Mercedes.

Normally Skye would run down and throw herself into the fray, but only if there was actual soccer going on. She dropped down and slithered across the lawn until she could peek over and see what was happening without being seen. Yup, a circus. Jane, Batty, and Mercedes were leaping, spinning, shouting, and kicking the ball only when it occurred to them. Adding to the mayhem were Hound and Hoover, their leashes tied together, which turned them into a kind of manic ball-hungry Cerberus. Only Jeffrey was attempting to maintain some order, but Skye could tell that his endless patience was being tried. Skye knew she should go down to the beach to liberate him, but hardening her heart, she instead crawled back to the house, grabbed *Death by Black Hole,* and found a shady spot in the grass where she could stretch out and read.

She'd reached the section called "When the Universe Goes Bad" and was finding it most soothing. Killer asteroids, a frozen Earth, the end to humanity— all this was much easier to handle than a besotted sister.

Down she dove into exploding stars and stray comets, and there she stayed, happily reading on and on until she was distracted by one of the last things she wanted right then, a bag full of golf balls floating above her.

"For Batty's collection," said Turron, the person at the other end of the bag.

"More golf balls!" said Skye, pushing them aside and sitting up. Lately everyone except Aunt Claire and Skye herself had been hunting golf balls for Batty. "What is she doing with them all?"

"No one knows," said Alec, who was there, too.

"We just find them for her. We are her humble servants." Turron winked at Skye.

She couldn't help winking back—Turron had that effect on people.

"The golf balls aren't why we're here, Skye," said Alec. "My friend is letting me borrow his boat today. Are you ready for that boat ride now?"

Skye knew all about this boat—how fast it was, and how it had plenty of room for passengers. When Alec had mentioned the possibility of a ride a few days ago, she hadn't been sure they should go. She'd managed to keep Batty from drowning so far. Why risk taking her out onto the ocean in a small boat? But now perhaps the risk would be worth it, just to put as much distance as possible between Jane and Dominic. Even he couldn't ride a skateboard on water.

Alec went on. "Mercedes's grandmother has said that Mercedes can go, and Turron is kindly going to keep Claire company at Birches."

"Because I'm terrified of boats," added Turron.

"You weren't supposed to say that, moron," protested Alec. "Skye is very safety-conscious."

"Right," said Turron, grinning. "I'm staying with Claire because I'm leaving Maine tomorrow and would rather spend my last day with her than with any of you."

"I promise the boat won't blow up, Skye," said Alec. "Batty will be safe."

And Jane would be safe, too, with all that open water between her and Dominic. "Okay," she said. "A boat ride would be great."

"Good. Meet me at the dock in a half hour. Make sure Jeffrey remembers his clarinet, and don't ask me why. It's a surprise."

Thirty minutes later, four Penderwicks (including Hound), one Tifton, and one Orne ran down Ocean Boulevard to the dock across from Mouette Inn. It was a long dock, stretching out into the ocean, with fat seagulls perched along the railings like an honor guard. Skye led the way onto it, and with the creak of the dock's wooden planks under her feet, the seagulls comically flapping away two at a time, and the vast blue sea ahead, her burden of responsibility started to lift. By the time they'd reached the end of the dock and run down a ramp to where boats could tie up, Skye was almost as carefree as the others. And when Alec and Hoover arrived in the speedboat, she was the first to jump on board.

The boat was called the *Bernadette,* and it was silver, with green racing stripes, an impressive set of controls and dials, and a Maine state flag fluttering on a pole. There were also enough orange life jackets for everyone, which Alec insisted they wear, thrilling Batty—at last she wasn't the only person dressed like a pumpkin. Jeffrey stowed his clarinet case, then sat up front beside Alec; the four girls settled along the wide bench at the back; and the dogs claimed the space in between, with Hound exploring a million unfamiliar smells and Hoover licking the face of anyone who couldn't avoid him.

Alec started the engine and Jeffrey pushed off. The *Bernadette* moved out slowly, picking up speed after they cleared the dock, and then more speed and more, and soon they were flying across the ocean, everyone's nose pointing into the wind, the thrum of the engine beneath them, the salty spray flaring out behind them. It was glorious, and when Jane shouted nonsense about trimming mainsails and hauling jibs, the others shouted along with her, even Alec, even Skye.

They were heading northeast, which took them past Gandy Island. Alec slowed down to show them the island's one little house, lonely on its patch of green lawn. No one cared much except for Jane, who stood up to stare at it and kept staring until they were long past and the house and then the island were just specks in the distance. And still Jane hadn't had enough—she muttered something about Dominic and a hammock and tried to climb onto the bench to stare some more, but Skye yanked her down and kept a good hold on her. By now, they were in open water, and the *Bernadette* raced on and on for a wonderfully long time, until another island came into view. Larger than Gandy Island, it was all gray rocks and pines, with no small houses or any other signs of people.

Alec cut the boat's engine. "Everyone keep your eyes open."

"For what?" Skye asked.

"Just look," he said.

Jeffrey already knew what they should be keeping their eyes open for, but the girls had a wide range of places to look, scanning the island and the horizon, gazing deep into the sea, squinting up into the sky, all the while throwing out a clamor of questions and comments. It was Batty who finally noticed that some of the smaller gray rocks on the island were oddly shaped—like gigantic sausages that narrowed and came to a point at one end. Then Batty shrieked, Hound and Hoover barked, and one of the giant sausages was shaking its pointy end and sliding off the rocks and into the water.

"Seals!" shouted Mercedes. "They're seals, Batty!"

Seals they were indeed, a few dozen big fat ones, calmly sunning themselves on rocks just as gray and fat as they were.

"We won't go in any closer, out of respect," said Alec. "But Jeffrey and I do have something special planned just for them. This is one of my family's traditions—a McGrath tradition—that my brothers and I started back when we were teenagers, anytime we could get hold of a boat."

While Alec talked, Jeffrey had been removing his clarinet from its case and putting it together. Now Alec reached down and pulled out a larger case that no one had noticed before and took out his saxophone.

"Ladies and dogs," said Jeffrey, "we are about to perform 'Fanfare for the Uncommon Seal.'"

"With apologies to Aaron Copland," added Alec, locking eyes with Jeffrey, who put his clarinet to his lips. Together they nodded out the count—one, two, three, four . . .

From Jeffrey's clarinet poured a haunting, stirring melody, a soaring string of notes that floated out over the ocean. All alone Jeffrey played, his eyes closed in concentration, until it seemed that the song was ending. But then Alec's saxophone joined the clarinet, and together the man and the boy again played the heart-stopping tune, note for note. The girls clung to each other, each one feeling as though she'd never really heard music before, and although the splendor of the music was almost too much, the players began yet once more, this time in rich harmony, finally ending with a flourish so thrilling that when the music stopped, it seemed for a moment as though the world had to stop along with it. No one knew what to say. Skye helplessly turned to Jane, but Jane shook her head, for once without words.

Mercedes broke the spell. "I wish I could play an instrument," she said with great despair.

This made everyone laugh, but kindly, because who wouldn't feel the same way? Jane gave Mercedes a sympathetic hug, and Batty handed over the harmonica so that she could at least try to play. Mercedes dedicated her few notes to the seals, but they paid no more attention to the squawking harmonica than they had to the sweet-toned clarinet and saxophone.

Then Alec announced that it was time for lunch and produced a big cooler that turned out to be full of cheese-and-tomato sandwiches, fresh strawberries, and gallons of lemonade, the perfect lunch to eat in the middle of the ocean. It didn't take long for seagulls to find them—seagulls never can resist free snacks—and Skye and Jeffrey had a contest to see who could throw scraps of sandwich the highest, but the birds were better at swooping low to catch food— even with a frenzied Hoover leaping at them—than

Skye and Jeffrey were at throwing it high, so neither could claim victory.

Too soon it was time to leave. The boat needed to be restored to its owner, and Mercedes to her grand-mother. Everyone waved good-bye to the seals, who continued to stoically ignore them, and Alec turned the boat and headed back to shore.

"Deliriously and deliciously delightful," murmured Jane, leaning into the wind, her hair streaming out be-hind her. "Magnificently wonderful, and fabulously and wonderfully magnificent."

Skye started to protest, but didn't. Certainly there had been delight on Jeffrey's face while he and Alec were playing, a look that had been mirrored back to him from Alec. And now, Skye noticed, Batty was cheerfully humming the "Fanfare" melody while Mer-cedes snuggled peacefully against Jane. The two dogs, exhausted by the thrill of their shared adventure, slept side by side. All was well on the *Bernadette*.

"I'm happy, too," Skye told Jane.

Skye was indeed happy. And so relaxed that when they reached the dock and Batty begged to stay on board while Alec returned the boat, Skye agreed and didn't even insist that Batty put on an extra life jacket or two. Since Jeffrey was staying on board, and Hoover and Hound, too, naturally, only Skye, Jane, and Mercedes needed to disembark. They climbed up onto the dock after thanking Alec over and over, then watched the boat pull away, Batty boldly alone on the back bench, waving and waving. Only then did Skye turn toward land, and she saw that the seagulls were again lined up along the dock's railings, pretending they'd been waiting all along, and taking no responsibility for the scavenger seagulls that had been so greedy out at sea.

There was someone else who seemed to be waiting, too, at the far end of the dock.

And all of Skye's responsibilities and worries came back, like a bowling ball dropping on her head.

"Your brother's here, Mercedes. He must be looking for you," she said, willing it to be true.

"Maybe." Mercedes sounded doubtful. "He hardly ever does look for me."

"It's possible," said Jane, already moving away, "that Dominic is looking for me."

"Jane, don't go," said Skye.

But she was already gone, gliding—Skye didn't know how—like a movie princess in a long ball gown. All the way down the dock Jane glided until she reached Dominic. She stopped, they talked briefly, and then off they went together, away from Birches, toward French Park.

"I don't understand," said Skye helplessly. "Why is she doing that?"

"Lots of girls act that way around my brother," said Mercedes simply. "At home they stand in front of the house crying if he won't talk to them, and I can't play outside because they ask me questions about him."

"I'd certainly never cry over Dominic."

"Really?" Mercedes was so impressed with this show of independence that she slipped her hand into Skye's.

"Really," said Skye, and didn't let go, at least not for a while.

Jane knew she was gliding, graceful and proud, like a maiden on her way to meet Peter Pevensie, High King of Narnia. And since that was how she looked, she was also thinking maidenly thoughts. About how much she loved this boy, Dominic, and how this would be their first real time together since the love for him had captured her, enveloped her, devoured her. And how she hadn't been able to write a word since she'd fallen—no, that wasn't a maidenly thought. What was art when compared to love, anyway? And who could write when every waking minute was taken up with wondering where Dominic was, what he was doing, what he was thinking, if he'd fallen off his skateboard, and if so, what Jane could say to comfort him while she held his bloodied head in her lap. Now *those* were maidenly thoughts.

And now she'd reached the end of the dock and she was with him, her beloved, and they headed to French Park, where she knew they would sit and share their love, and she would tell him so many things, like about seeing Gandy Island from the *Bernadette*, and how she'd been thinking of him all the time, and how he had to promise that if he fell off his skateboard, to do it when she was around so that she could hold his bloodied head. In fact, Jane had so much to tell Dominic that she didn't want to wait for French Park. She wanted to begin immediately while they walked together. Except that they weren't walking together, because Dominic wasn't walking at all, really—he was on his skateboard, either ahead of her or behind, or making large circles around her. She didn't care, not really, trying to thrust away the suspicion that Peter Pevensie would never make circles around a maiden. You're being disloyal, she scolded herself, and anyway, there weren't any skateboards in Narnia. Besides, soon they reached French Park, and Jane was able to sit down on the bench, and although Dominic continued to ride in circles for a while, she could now close her eyes to better picture him as a noble presence worthy of her love, and by the time he sat down beside her, she was feeling steadier.

"I have many things to tell you, Dominic," she said.

"Yeah." Dominic shuffled his feet. "Me too. I mean, I have something to ask you."

"You do?" This was a surprise. Until now, asking personal questions had not been one of Dominic's skills. "You go first, then."

"No, that's okay."

"Please?"

"Okay, here's my question." Dominic shuffled his feet again, then cleared his throat. "Can I kiss you?"

"Excuse me?" Jane was so surprised, she jumped off the bench. Did he love her, too? She hadn't hoped for as much.

"It will be a short, little kiss." He looked sternly out to sea. "Hardly a kiss at all."

She sat down again. "Oh, Dominic, love has no measure."

"What?"

"I mean, yes, please kiss me."

She turned expectantly to him, and he turned to her, too, tilting his head first this way, then that, to accommodate both noses, before moving in for the finale. He'd been honest—it was a short, little kiss, hardly a kiss at all, and immediately afterward he was gone—back on his skateboard and flying out of French Park.

Was it over already? So quickly here and gone? But Jane didn't mind. Not that he was gone, or that she hadn't told him about Gandy Island or about holding his bloodied head. Jane didn't think she'd ever mind anything again. She'd been kissed by the object of her adoration, and now she was beyond bliss and all the way to—what was beyond bliss?

Paradise.

Late that night, Skye was reluctantly dragged out of a deliciously deep slumber. Her first thought was that

164

she was really tired of people waking her up all the time. Her second thought was that Jane was talking in her sleep again.

"*Snare, wear, pear, lair, solitaire*—maybe," said Jane. "And *dare* and *care*. They're good ones."

"Wake up, Jane," said Skye wearily. "Or if you have to talk in your sleep, could you please be more interesting?"

"I'm not asleep. Sorry—I'll be quieter." Jane dropped her voice to a whisper. "*While, dial, mile, file, guile. Style!* No, that doesn't help. *Rile?*"

Skye sat up and saw that her sister was hiding under her sheet with a flashlight. "Come out of there."

Jane's head popped out. "As long as you're awake, maybe you can help me with my ode."

"What ode? Never mind, don't tell me." If Jane was writing an ode for Dominic, Skye didn't want to know about it. Though of course that was what Jane was doing. Ever since she'd returned from French Park, she'd been so goofily strange that her previous behavior seemed almost normal.

"What rhymes with *smile?*"

"*Bile*, as in *Your smile makes me want to throw up.*"

A sleepy voice came from the other side of the bamboo curtain. "How about *denial?*"

"*That I adore your smile, there can be no denial,*" said Jane with delight. "Thank you, Jeffrey!"

"You're welcome. I like your smile, too."

"Now I need a rhyme for *skateboard*," said Jane.

Skye dove across the porch and wrenched the flash-light away from Jane. "No more rhymes. I mean it."

Jane sighed loudly and tossed and turned for a while. Skye was about to lose her temper in a most un-OAP fashion when that sleepy voice spoke again.

"*And it can't be ignored that I also like your skate-board.*"

"Jeffrey, you're brilliant!" exclaimed Jane.

Skye contented herself with throwing a sneaker at each of them, and then at last all was quiet on the sleeping porch.

CHAPTER ELEVEN
Haircuts

IT WAS TIME FOR TURRON to leave Point Mouette, and no one wanted him to go. Even Hoover and Hound were uneasy and kept tangling him in their leashes.

"Stay for just a few more days," said Jeffrey. "Skye, tell him."

"Why not, Turron?" she asked.

"Yes, why not?" Aunt Claire swung on her crutches. "Who will do jigsaw puzzles with me when you're gone?"

Turron didn't want to leave either. "Unfortunately, I have to get back to work. A recording session."

"An important one," added Alec, "that might lead to more work."

167

"Actually, I'd leave for that, too," said Jeffrey.

"Me too," said Batty.

Skye shook her head at her littlest sister. "Do you even know what a recording session is?"

"Sure she does," Turron said, and crouched down to say good-bye to Batty. "I'll see you sometime, kiddo. Keep up your music, and good luck with you-know-what. Break a leg."

Batty knew that you-know-what was a secret code for the concert she and Jeffrey were working on, and Turron was using code because it was going to be a surprise concert. She wasn't sure, though, why he'd said that about breaking her leg, and she glanced nervously at Skye, who was so sensitive these days about people getting broken or blowing up. But Skye hadn't heard. She was too busy observing Jane, whose behavior had changed once more. Last night she'd been rapturously writing odes. Now she was a mess, jiggling around like a bobble doll, her head turning this way and that, watching for someone who had to be Dominic. Skye wished him at the bottom of the ocean.

"Jane," she said, "you haven't even pretended to say good-bye to Turron."

"I'm sorry." Jane gave Turron an enthusiastic hug. "Good-bye, Turron, and thanks for rescuing me when I hurt my nose and for being funny and kind and an excellent drummer and I hope you find happiness in your life and that every minute is wonderful and perfect and that the light of love shines on you and—"

Aunt Claire cut her off, smiling apologetically at Turron. "We all hope the best for you."

"Thanks." And he smiled back. "It's been a pleasure to meet you. All of you. Jeffrey, you've got my phone number. Let me know when you want to visit me in New York, where the best music is made."

"Ahem," said Alec. "Jeffrey doesn't need New York. He's going to be busy making music with me in Boston, right?"

Jeffrey shook his head, too overwhelmed at the offered riches to joke about it. And now it really was time for Turron to go. As Batty played a mournful tune on her harmonica, he got into his car, and out again because he'd forgotten to give Batty a few final golf balls he'd found for her, and then Hoover tried to knock him over in one last attempt to keep him there forever, but it didn't work, and Turron drove away and left them all behind.

Despite being sad about Turron leaving, Batty was pleased with the new golf balls, not just because she loved them, but because they also gave her an excuse to go off by herself. The surprise concert wasn't her only secret; she also knew why Jane was acting so screwy. Jane had told her all about it early that morning—how she'd dropped a node off at the inn for Dominic, that she hoped that he'd like the node enough to come see her, and how she thought she might die of grief if he didn't. Batty had asked Jane what a node was, and Jane said never mind, but just don't tell anyone else, especially Skye. Batty hadn't told and wouldn't, but it was easier not to tell when she didn't have to see Skye staring anxiously at Jane. Plus she didn't like thinking about Jane dying. It was too sad.

So Batty and Hound slipped back to Birches with the new golf balls, and went into Batty's room, where she'd hidden her collection under the bed. There had been so many searches for lost balls, with so many people helping, that Batty figured she must have almost a million by now. She crawled under the bed and pushed aside the big floppy plastic duck that Hound had hidden the first night in Maine. And there was her treasure trove—three whole buckets full of golf balls. Jeffrey had bought the buckets for her at Moose Market. One was red, one yellow, and one purple, and there were three empty blue buckets, too, which Batty was sure she'd fill soon, since golfers weren't very good at holding on to their belongings.

Using both hands, she tugged the yellow bucket, heavy with its load, out from under the bed and compared the balls Turron had given her to what she already had. What she liked most about the golf balls were all their different marks—the words on them, and the grass stains and little gouges where they'd been hit with clubs. She tried to show a few of the most interesting to Hound, but he believed that once you'd seen one golf ball, you'd seen them all. Batty decided to change games. Since the boat trip the day before, the two of them had spent a lot of time playing seals on an island, and neither of them was tired of it yet.

"Hound, let's play seals." With a great heave, she managed to get the yellow bucket onto the bed. "The balls can be the rocks, and my stuffed animals can be the seals."

Maybe Hound thought that there were real seals up there on the bed, because his leap onto it was so enthusiastic that the yellow bucket flew up into the air, did a somersault, and fell to the floor, its contents clattering and banging all around it. The noise was horrific, and Batty did the only thing she could think of—yank the blanket off her bed, throw it onto the floor to hide the bucket and golf balls, and hope no one had heard.

While Batty was trying to get Hound interested in her golf balls, Skye was spying on Jane.

"Not spying exactly. More like watching over her," she explained to Jeffrey.

"Because she can see us, too," he said. "If we want to spy, we should be hidden."

That was true. Skye and Jeffrey were sitting on the deck and Jane wasn't far away at all. She was leaning against one of the birch trees, gazing fervently out at Ocean Boulevard, on the lookout for anyone who might be skateboarding along it.

"You're not taking this seriously, Jeffrey. I'm afraid

contact with Dominic has destroyed Jane's brain," said Skye. "What are you humming?"

"It's a song Alec and Turron were messing around with the other night." Jeffrey hummed another line, then quoted the lyrics. "'There's nothing sadder than a one-man woman, looking for the man that got away.'"

"You're a big help."

Then came the crash that Batty was hoping no one would hear. Skye leaped up in a panic.

"Hound's not barking, so it can't be too bad," said Jeffrey. "I'll go see what happened, and you stay here, watching over Jane."

Skye knew he was teasing her about Jane, but she let him go anyway. And she also knew that she *was* being a little silly. She should probably just ask Jane face to face why she was acting like such a goofball, and Jane would give her some logical answer—but here Skye's line of reasoning fell apart, because she knew that Jane's answer wouldn't be logical. It would again be all about love and Dominic and what Skye might experience someday when she met the right boy; and if Skye could keep herself from tossing Jane over the seawall and onto the rocks below, she still wouldn't be any further ahead in understanding. If only, Skye thought, oh, if only she had no younger sisters, she would be on the beach right now with her soccer ball, happy and carefree and working on her left-foot dexterity, which had never been as good as her right.

"Instead of spying on Jane like a noodle-brain," she said, and calmed herself down with calf-stretching exercises until Jeffrey returned.

"You know those golf balls Batty's been collecting—she spilled some of them," he said. "She tried to hide them with a blanket, but I am much too intelligent to be fooled by a mere blanket."

"That loud noise was just some of her golf balls? How many does she have?"

"She says about a million. Now don't look so disgusted."

"I don't."

"Yes, you do. But I already worked it out with her. She wants to take a few home to Ben, and we're going to have a golf ball sale tomorrow to get rid of the rest—she told me about a lady in a green skirt who gave her five dollars for some balls—and I'm donating my golf clubs."

"Your golf clubs?" Skye was appalled. "Your mother and Dexter will be furious."

"Maybe, but I could always stay with Alec until they calm down." Jeffrey looked quite cheerful at the thought. "Besides, they're my golf clubs to give away, and I promised Batty that she can save all the money we get from the sale for a piano. We're going to the pinewood right now to collect more. Do you want to come with us?"

"No to everything—going to the pinewood, the sale tomorrow, the piano, especially the piano."

"Skye."

"And don't look so trying-to-be-patient-with-Skye."

"I don't." Though he really did and knew it, so he wriggled his eyebrows at her.

Skye turned her back on him. Any minute now he was going to make her lose her temper or start laughing, and she didn't want to do either.

"I'll make you a deal," he said. "You come to the pinewood now, and afterward we'll play soccer on the beach."

She pointed to Jane, who still hadn't moved. "What about her?"

"I'll ask if she wants to come with us." But Jeffrey was soon back, and without Jane. "She says she needs to stay where she is for now, and you can stop spying on her because she's fine."

"So she says." But Skye was wavering. The sun was bright, there was a soft breeze off the ocean, and the tide was low. Perfect for soccer on the beach. "You mean real soccer, with no crazy stuff like dogs and Mercedes, right?"

"Right."

Then Hound arrived, carrying one empty bucket in his mouth, and Batty came after him with another two, and without exactly agreeing to anything, Skye found herself taking one of the buckets and setting off for the pinewood to collect more stupid golf balls. She allowed herself one final glance over her shoulder at Jane, then told herself not to be ridiculous. They wouldn't be gone longer than a half hour. What could happen to Jane in a half hour?

It was an excellent question, and one that would eventually become a Penderwick family joke, a teasing shorthand for "You haven't thought this through properly," and no one would laugh at it more than Skye, except for Jane. But for Skye on that morning in Maine, halfway up a pine tree and reaching into a bird nest for a golf ball pretending to be an egg, it was suddenly a very real question. Off in the distance, someone was shouting her name.

"Did you hear that?" She slid and jumped her way down the tree.

Jeffrey straightened up, his hands full of balls he'd found hiding under pine needles. "Is it Jane?"

The voice came again. "Skye, Skye, where are you?"

"It's Mercedes," said Batty.

Skye knew immediately that something had happened to Jane. She tossed aside the golf balls that had lured her away from her duty and sprinted off in the direction of the voice, her head full of horrifying visions of Jane broken on the rocks, bitten by sharks, hand in hand with Dominic. Down through the pinewood she dashed, ignoring the branches that whipped at her, mocking her, and slowing down only when she found Mercedes stumbling through the trees.

"Where's Jane?" cried Skye.

"On the beach. Oh, Skye—"

But Skye was already running again, too impatient to wait for any explanations. The distress on Mercedes's face had been enough to intensify Skye's fears. Jane was now dead on the rocks, eaten by sharks, or eloped with Dominic, each fate worse than the others, and all of them Skye's fault for leaving Jane alone.

And now Skye reached Birches and was throwing herself down the stone steps, and now she was on the beach, skidding to a stop beside Jane, who wasn't dead or even dying, but upright and without any visible bloodstains. Nor was Dominic anywhere to be seen. It was a bit odd that Jane was staring fixedly into the marshmallow-fire pit while fussing with a pair of scissors, opening and closing them, snip, snip, snip, snip, but certainly that couldn't be enough to throw Mercedes into a tizzy, right? Silly Skye, she told herself, for not bothering to ask Mercedes what was happening. Good leaders don't jump to conclusions.

She leaned down, hands on her knees, to catch her breath. "Hello, Jane."

"Hello," said Jane, though still not looking at her sister. "Please don't be furious."

Skye straightened up so quickly she almost went over backward. The last time Jane had told her not to be furious was when she'd just smashed her nose to pieces.

"What's going on, Jane? What are you doing with the scissors?"

"Not much, just making more wishes."

With a jerky abruptness, Jane turned to face Skye. The curls on her left side had been chopped off almost to her ear.

Skye shrieked, just as she had with the nose, and stomped around in the sand like an enraged bear. What could happen to Jane in a half hour? What *could* happen to Jane in a half hour? Other than losing her mind and giving herself a haircut worthy of a two-year-old?

The others were arriving now—Mercedes panting and frantic, Jeffrey with Batty bouncing along on his back, and Hound barking TROUBLE TROUBLE because he'd heard Skye's shriek and knew what it meant.

"What's wrong? Who did that to Jane's hair?" Jeffrey asked Skye, who was trying to stop stomping.

Jane answered him. "It was me. I lost my temper. Skye, you would have been impressed."

"You got mad at your hair?" asked Batty, sliding down from Jeffrey's back. This she understood, much better than dying for nodes.

"Not exactly." Swiftly, before anyone could think to stop her, Jane cut off another piece of hair and tossed it into the circle of rocks, and now everyone noticed the pile of curls already there, limp and dark on the sand.

"Oh, no, we're back to the Firegod," said Jeffrey, because Jane was chanting:

> "Fire, Sun, Sand, and Sea,
>   Listen now and hear my plea.
>   Humbly do I ask of thee,
>   Please bring what I wish to me."

"That's what she keeps doing," said Mercedes. "I tried to stop her, but she wouldn't listen."

"Has she gone crazy?" asked Batty, holding on to Hound for moral support.

"Yes," answered Skye bleakly, "and it's all my fault. Jane, hand over the scissors."

"No." But before she could use them again, Jeffrey had snatched them away.

"No more cutting," he said. "And, Skye, it's my fault. I shouldn't have convinced you to leave her alone."

"I shouldn't have listened to you. It was my responsibility."

"I am my own responsibility, thank you. And if you won't let me cut any more hair, I'll make do with what I have." Jane took a box of matches from her pocket. "You should be pleased that I didn't light the fire while I was alone, Skye. So responsible of me, right? But now that we're all here, I'll do it, just a little fire—and then my wishes will be official."

"No fire," said Skye, and Jeffrey took away the matches, too.

Jane made a feeble attempt to get them back, but it was clear that her heart wasn't in it, for the anger was quickly leaking away, and soon she'd sunk into Jeffrey's arms, beaten, with tears pouring down her miserable face with its fringe of butchered hair. Batty and Hound circled protectively, and Skye turned to Mercedes.

"Now. Tell me what happened, quickly."

"Dominic told me to give Jane back that poem she'd written—"

"Dominic! I knew it," growled Skye.

Mercedes hung her head. "I'm ashamed to be an Orne."

"Never mind that part. Tell me about the ode—the poem."

"So I came over and gave it to Jane, and I didn't know it, I swear, but Dominic had written a note on the back. When Jane read his note, she was really quiet for a while. Then she said that we should make wishes to the Firegod, and she went to get the scissors and matches and she explained to me what to do, and I cut off a tiny bit of my hair and wished—um, Jane said I wasn't supposed to tell anyone what I wished, but it was to stop falling off my bike." Mercedes glanced at Batty, who nodded. That was a good wish.

"Go on," said Skye.

"Jane took the scissors and cut up her poem and

threw it into the rocks, and she cut off a big chunk of her hair and threw that in, too, and she was sort of yelling, and when she did it again, I went to find you." Mercedes stopped to gaze mournfully at Jane, still sagging in Jeffrey's arms. "I think her heart is broken."

"Not my heart," sobbed Jane. "It's my pride that's broken. I am a fool and a chump. A dupe and a ninny and—"

Jeffrey cut in. "That's enough of that. Can you stand up by yourself?"

"Of course I can." And she did, with as much dignity as one can muster in such a situation. "How bad does my hair look?"

"Awful," said Batty.

"We just need to even it out a little," said Skye. "Well, a lot."

Jane tentatively poked at what was remaining of her curls, and a few more tears rolled down her face. "Give me back the scissors and I'll do it."

"Not now. Good grief."

What Skye wanted most in the world right then— wanted it so much she thought about wishing to the Firegod—was to knock down Dominic Orne and make him crawl and beg for forgiveness. And after the crawling and begging, he'd have to perform some specific act of contrition. Like cutting off his own hair. That was it! Skye's fingers itched to grab the scissors and go hunt him down.

"Concentrate," said Jeffrey warningly.

He was right, as usual. She would have to wait for revenge. Her job now was to get Jane safely to Aunt Claire. Aunt Claire knew more about hearts and hair than Skye ever would. So she and Jeffrey helped Jane away from the beach and up to Birches, where Aunt Claire was just coming out onto the deck.

"Aunt Claire, we've had an incident," said Skye, following up with a series of violent faces that meant *Please don't react too much to what you're about to see, namely Jane.*

Miraculously, Aunt Claire did understand, and other than fumbling with a crutch and swaying dangerously until Jeffrey caught her and lowered her into a chair, she managed to stay calm.

"An incident," she repeated, her voice only a little higher than usual. "Yes, I see."

"I chopped off my hair," said Jane. "My one beauty."

"Your hair's not your only beauty, but I don't understand—" Aunt Claire stopped and looked around at the others. "Did anyone else cut their hair? Hound, even?"

"Just Jane," said Batty, and patted Hound to reassure him that they wouldn't cut his hair.

"And it was my fault," added Mercedes. "Because I'm an Orne."

Jane shook her head. "It was no one's fault but my

own. Skye tried to warn me, but I wouldn't listen. I was a nincompoop. A moron. A block—"

"Don't," said Jeffrey.

"—head." She started to cry again.

Aunt Claire held out her arms. "Jane, come sit on my lap, sweetheart. Tell me what you've been a nincompoop about."

Jane went to her, sobbing, and kept sobbing until Aunt Claire looked up to Skye for a hint.

Skye made a few awkward dance moves and said, "Shin guard."

Somehow Aunt Claire understood that, too—at which Skye decided she was the most brilliant aunt who had ever lived—and stroked Jane's hair and murmured to her.

"Honey, do you remember all those Bills I told you about? The ones I fell in love with? What I didn't tell you was how badly one of them hurt me."

Jane's sobbing slowed down a little. "I thought my heart was singing, Aunt Claire, I really did. But it was humming, or maybe it was just speaking. And all the time that treacherous Dominic . . . Oh, I can't stand it!"

"You know what's best for this kind of situation, Jane, is to tell the story from the beginning. Like one of your books." Aunt Claire looked up at Skye and cocked her head toward the seawall.

This time it was Skye who understood. Jane would more easily tell her tale if they weren't all there, hovering. She led Hound and the others off the deck and to the seawall, where they perched in a row, thinking various unhappy thoughts. Occasionally a spurt of talking would break out—like when Batty asked Jeffrey about nodes and he tried to explain, and when Jeffrey asked about the dancing shin guard and Skye tried to explain, but mostly there was pained silence. So it was a relief when Alec arrived, because he wasn't miserable, and because he was inviting them over for a movie that evening—which sounded pleasantly normal, not at all like when people chopped at their own hair. But after they'd thanked him about the movie, he couldn't help noticing Jane and Aunt Claire in a huddle on the deck. He asked what was wrong, and Skye and Jeffrey gave him a brief explanation, leaving out the ode, only hinting at Dominic's role, and shushing Mercedes and Batty whenever they tried to add anything.

"How bad is Jane's hair now?" asked Alec when they finished.

"Nightmare bad, like she lost a fight with a lawn mower," said Skye. "It should look better after we even it out."

"Do you know how to cut hair?" asked Alec. "Or does your aunt?"

"Not exactly."

"Because it just so happens that I need a haircut myself. I could take Jane along for repairs."

"To a real hair salon?" This seemed like an

183

excellent idea to Skye. "But you don't actually need a haircut."

"No?" Alec ran his hand over his hair, which looked fine.

"No," said Jeffrey.

"Then I'll get my beard shaved off. I've been meaning to."

"Good," said Batty. "I don't like beards."

Alec laughed. "There, it's settled."

Much cheered, Skye waited until she was certain that Jane had finished telling Aunt Claire the whole gruesome tale, then ran up to the deck to tell them about Alec's offer. Aunt Claire gratefully accepted, and Skye bundled Jane into a big hat, plus a pair of sunglasses for added moral support.

"I'm sorry," Jane said to Skye from under her disguise. "I haven't been much of a backup OAP."

"That's okay." It was true that since Jane had fallen for Dominic, she had been about the worst backup OAP imaginable. But that didn't let Skye off the hook. She should have stayed with Jane, not deserted her in her hour of need. No good leader would. Would Caesar have gone off looking for golf balls when his soldiers were at their breaking point? No.

And neither would he let a wounded soldier be carried off the field alone.

"Funny," she told Jane. "I'm suddenly in the mood for a haircut myself."

"No, Skye, you don't have to."

But Skye did have to—it was the very least she could do, she realized—and it turned out that Batty and Mercedes were suddenly in the mood for haircuts, too. While everyone agreed about Batty, especially those who'd tried to brush her hair lately, they explained to Mercedes that she couldn't just get a haircut without permission, so she called her grandmother, who said yes. After making certain that Jeffrey and Aunt Claire didn't need haircuts, too, Alec herded the four girls over to his house and into his car.

As they drove away, Jane whispered to Skye, "Promise me you won't do anything crazy like beat up Dominic."

"May I cut off his hair?"

"No, please, no. Promise you'll leave him alone. I'm humiliated enough without that."

Although Skye reluctantly promised, just thinking about humiliation made Jane start crying again, and she cried all the way to the hair salon.

CHAPTER TWELVE
The Thunderstorm

BY DINNERTIME, Jane had gone two entire hours without crying. Then she made it through dinner, too, despite her tuna noodle casserole—she'd insisted on taking her turn at cooking, although everyone offered to do it for her—which was mysteriously soggy in some places, burned in others, and boringly bland overall. After cleanup, she thought she might have a relapse when Aunt Claire, Jeffrey, and Skye got ready to leave for movie night at Alec's house, with a rented movie and lots of popcorn, but Jane managed to hold back her tears. After all, she told herself sternly, it was her own choice to stay back with Batty and Mercedes. They were having their first sleepover together and were practically expiring from the thrill of it.

"Jane, are you sure?" asked Skye, lingering after Jeffrey helped Aunt Claire and her crutches out the door.

"Yes," she answered nobly, trying to ignore the hysterical laughter coming from Batty's room.

"There's a thunderstorm coming. You won't let anyone get struck by lightning, right?"

"No." It was a ridiculous question, but Jane knew she deserved to be treated as a near imbecile after all the havoc she'd caused that day.

"Or blown up, right?"

But even in her current mood of deep humility and penance, this was too much for Jane. "Skye, no one except you believes in the possibility of Batty blowing up."

"You saw it on the list," said Skye. "It was right there."

"Just go watch the movie and have fun. We'll survive." Jane pushed Skye out of the house and shut the door behind her.

Now that Jane was alone, would she cry again? She blinked experimentally and, when no tears came, decided she might be safe for at least a few more hours. Maybe if she could make it through the whole evening without crying, she would be safe altogether. As long as she didn't think too much about Dominic or that he'd sent back her precious "Ode to a Kiss"—that was the title she'd given it after much deliberation—or mostly if she didn't think too much about the note he'd scribbled on the back of the ode.

There! Already she was thinking about it. To distract herself, she decided to visit Batty and Mercedes. She could pretend it was an official visit.

"Any trouble in here?" she asked brightly, swinging open the door.

"No," said Batty. "We don't need you."

"We're making signs for the sale tomorrow," added Mercedes more politely, showing Jane a large piece of paper with GOLF BALLS scrawled across it. "And Batty's been telling me about how Jeffrey is going to show her the moose babies someday and how he's going to marry her when they grow up."

"Batty, how do you know you want to marry Jeffrey?" asked Jane, snatching a red marker out of Hound's mouth just before he bit it in half.

"I just know."

Her certainty dug into Jane's unhappiness. "I should have given *you* my Love Survey."

Batty ignored her, but Mercedes's sensitive heart reached out. "I'm sorry about my brother," she said. "But your hair looks beautiful, Jane."

"Thank you, Mercedes. Yours looks beautiful, too." Jane left them alone and went outside onto the deck, to breathe in the salty air and not think about Dominic.

She had no illusions about beauty, for either her or Mercedes, but Jane was pleased with her new haircut.

Alec had taken them to a salon called Marilyn's, where the actual Marilyn gave Jane the best haircut of her life, a soft mop of curls that framed her face. Everyone liked it so much, they ordered up exactly the same for Batty—and then Skye got her own version, one more suitable for straight hair. And last, while Alec's beard was being shaved off, Mercedes was given a cut identical to Skye's. Hairwise, the day ended triumphantly, with everyone improved, especially Alec, who they all agreed looked quite handsome without his beard. A few of them also thought that he reminded them of someone they'd seen before, but after Jane came up with a lot of movie stars as possibilities, Alec told them to please stop before his ego exploded.

So the haircuts were a good result of the treachery of Domi—the person Jane couldn't think about. Nevertheless, they could barely balance out the bad results. For example, Sabrina Starr. What Jane now knew about love—that it was all a sham, or at least it was if you fell in love with a skateboarder who cared nothing for you—wasn't anything she wanted to write down. *Sabrina Starr Has Her Heart Broken?* No. That book wasn't going to take its place beside *Sabrina Starr Rescues a Boy* and *Sabrina Starr Rescues an Archaeologist*. But a book had to be written. Jane would feel like a failure if she went back home without a new Sabrina Starr book. This was past writer's block.

"Writer's boulder. Writer's skyscraper. Writer's

Great Wall of China," she said, and was exasperated to find herself crying again.

The storm that Skye had predicted was beginning to show itself. No thunder or lightning yet, but the wind had already picked up, tossing the trees and blowing away the day's heat, and huge clouds, black giants, were sailing in from the horizon. Jane was pleased—there was nothing like a glorious thunderstorm to make you stop crying and realize how silly you were being. She climbed onto the seawall, drinking in the intoxicating smell of the coming rain. And now a distant foghorn was blowing, reminding Jane of battered ships and drowned sailors.

"In the old days," she told the wind, "women walked the shoreline, fearful for the men who were struggling through the storm in frail wooden boats, buffeted by powerful and angry waves. Rats, this isn't cheering me up."

She forced her imagination to go in a different direction and started over.

"I am the opposite of Samson—when my hair was cut today, my strength returned." This was better. Pleased with herself, Jane raised her hands high, commanding the elements. "I am the All-Powerful Jane Letitia Penderwick, Queen of the Storm. Bow down before me!"

A rumble of thunder greeted her, which Jane thought a nice touch. The black clouds were coming fast now, racing toward the setting sun. For a last few moments, pale gleams of light picked out sea froth; then even that light was obliterated and the ocean became a seething gray mass. A bright stab of lightning flickered across the clouds, the thunder rumbled again, closer this time, and the first fat drops of rain splattered down. Several of them landed on the nose of the Queen of the Storm.

"Jane, Jane, come inside! You're going to get struck by lightning!"

Batty and Mercedes were at the screen door, wide-eyed and fearful, with Hound adding his barks to their shouts.

"For heaven's sake," said Jane, but the rain was coming faster now, and even the Queen of the Storm wasn't in the mood to get soaked. She gave a final imperial wave to the sea, then ran back inside.

"Close the door!" cried Batty.

Jane shut the sliding glass door against the rain, then shook the water from her curls. "Why are you upset, Batty? We have plenty of thunderstorms at home."

"Home is not beside the ocean."

"It's just as safe here," said Mercedes bravely.

"What about New Jersey?" Batty asked. "Is it safe where Rosalind is?"

"Yes, of course," said Jane.

"Then we should be in New Jersey." Batty was

pulling Hound to shelter behind the couch. "Besides, I'm scared for the seals."

"She thinks they might drown," added Mercedes.

Instinctively, Jane turned to stare outside at what was becoming a tempest of wind, waves, and driving rain. It certainly wasn't going to be a pleasant night for the seals.

"But they won't drown," she said.

"How do you know?"

"Because they're sea creatures. Sea creatures don't drown!"

Jane knew she wasn't convincing anyone. Batty had that stubborn expression she got when determined to be right against all logic, and Mercedes looked as off-balance as when she rode her bicycle. It was time for a different tactic, Jane told herself, or they would start crying, and there'd already been too much crying for one day.

"Let's play seals on the island," she said, "having fun in the storm."

Without waiting for an answer, Jane started pushing furniture into the center of the room, creating an island out of chairs and the table and couch. It didn't take long for Batty and Mercedes to join in, and before long there was an impressive pile to clamber onto, which they did, and so did Hound, who loved being on furniture, island or no island.

"I am Janilopilis the seal," said Jane encouragingly.

Batty and Mercedes crouched on the rocks—also known as chairs—and waggled their elbows like flippers.

"I am Mercedilopilis," said Mercedes.

"I am Battilopilis," said Batty.

Hound barked and knocked a cushion onto the floor.

"We sea creatures love rain and thunder and lightning." Jane was warming to being a seal. "The Queen of the Storm would never let us come to harm. So say we all."

"So say we all," repeated Batty.

"I think I see a face at the window," said Mercedes, then screamed, "I *do* see a face at the window!"

She was pointing at a small window on the side of the room. By the time Jane looked, there was no face or anything else, but Batty had caught Mercedes's panic, and the two of them and Hound were scrabbling off the island and falling into the deadly sea.

"He's over there!" shouted Batty, pointing to the sliding glass door, and this time when Jane looked, she did see a face.

And while it wasn't at all a scary face, Jane's stomach turned over inside her and she wished she could hide behind the island with the others. Instead, putting on her best Queen of the Storm attitude, she climbed down as gracefully as she could and slid open the door.

"Hello, Dominic." He was soaking wet, and Jane could think of no earthly reason for him to be at Birches. "What do you want?"

He handed her a toothbrush. "Mercedes forgot this."

"Mercedes, it's just Dominic and he's brought your toothbrush," Jane said over her shoulder.

"Thank you." This came from behind the couch.

Jane thought that Dominic would leave, but he just stood there in the rain, staring at her.

"You look different somehow," he said after a while.

"So do you." It was true. He didn't look like a prince anymore. "Well, good night."

"I could come inside."

They'd been happy without him, and he would only upset her all over again. Jane knew this but wavered—it was raining so hard, and he was so wet, and maybe she should let him come in. Would Sabrina Starr let him in? No. But I'm not a hero, Jane thought desperately, and it would be only polite to rescue him from the storm.

"Maybe you can . . ." But, wait, something was happening—something extraordinarily wonderful—Jane's writer's block was shattering into a billion pieces. Hallelujah and glorious days. A miracle had come, and finally she knew how to write her book.

"Now you really look different," said Dominic.

"Dominic, now I really am different. Thank you

and good night." She shut the door in his face and turned back to the living room. "Time for bed, you two! I have a book to write!"

Next door at Alec's, the movie had turned out to be scary indeed. The very real thunderstorm, with its crashing and flashing, had added to the atmosphere of fear, and Skye wasn't the only one to cling helplessly to whoever was sitting nearest her—even if it was Hoover—especially during the scenes with the sheep inhabited by evil spirits. Skye had never realized how frightening sheep could be, and she was glad that Batty wasn't there to see them.

But now the movie was over, the lights were back on, and evil sheep seemed much less likely. Alec and Jeffrey were already at the piano, playing out bits of the movie soundtrack and arguing over when it had and hadn't overwhelmed the plot, which led somehow— Skye stopped paying attention for a few minutes—into a demonstration of the elegantly simple melody line for "The Best Is Yet to Come," which seemed to be about to lead into something else that Skye didn't understand.

"I should go see how Jane is doing," she murmured to Aunt Claire.

"What?" Aunt Claire was listening to all the music talk. "Oh, good idea. Make sure everyone still has the same hairstyle they had when we left."

The thunderstorm was over and gone, with nothing

left to show but fresh seaweed tossed up from the depths by the rough surf and, above, wisps of clouds scudding across the moon and stars. Skye gazed up, found Arcturus, then Spica, and wondered how many black holes were lurking unseen between the two. But even so interesting a conjecture couldn't keep her lingering long. She was too anxious about what she'd find when she got back to Birches. Obviously it hadn't burned down, but Skye fully expected Jane still to be crying, and that was bad enough.

Here is what she found instead: all the furniture in the middle of the room, and Jane lying on the floor, writing in her blue notebook. Skye was glad that Jane wasn't crying, but it was hard to be glad about the furniture.

"What happened?" she asked.

"I've finally figured out how to write my book. Listen: *Here was a terrible moral dilemma. Should Sabrina Starr rescue the loathsome boy who had stomped on, mutilated, wrecked so many hearts? Or should she leave him to the brutal fate his own actions had brought on?*" Jane scribbled a few more words and looked up. "Do you think *mutilated* is too heavy-handed?"

"Yes, but I meant what happened to the room?"

Jane seemed just now to notice the furniture. "We were playing seals on an island. I'll move it back."

She popped up and began shoving things back where they belonged, while Skye peeked into Batty's room. Never had she seen a bed so jam-packed. Batty, Mercedes, Hound, and Funty and Ellie the elephants were all jumbled together—along with several sheets of cardboard with SALE and GOLF written on them, plus one that said TIGHTWAD, a word that Batty had learned from *Ivy + Bean*. The desire to tidy up the mess was strong, but Skye controlled herself. The little girls were peacefully asleep, despite the crowding. She quietly closed the door and helped Jane with the last few chairs; then the two of them sat on the couch. It was nice to spend time together with no one being heartbroken or frantic.

"I'm sorry about earlier," said Jane, "and about the last few days. I can't believe you didn't get furious when I said that about someday you'd fall in love and understand."

"I did get furious."

"Well, I'm all better now. No more crying, at least over Dominic. Maybe not ever again over a boy. I could be cured."

"Good," said Skye, then laughed.

"I *could* be." Jane didn't seem to believe it either. "Oh, Skye, he kissed me yesterday. I didn't want to tell you, but he did, and then I wrote that 'Ode to a Kiss' and he gave it back to me, and guess what he wrote on it, the scum. He wrote: *It didn't mean anything*. My first kiss didn't mean anything to the person I kissed! A major life marker ruined!"

"But it wasn't your first kiss. Didn't you kiss Deane Balogh in second grade?" Skye counted off on her fingers. "And then Walter Li in fourth grade. And who was that kid who followed you around last year—Artie somebody?"

"They don't count. I was young then."

"You're young now."

"I don't feel young." Jane sighed. "Do you ever think about kissing?"

"No."

"And you haven't, right? I mean, except for Ron Hagey."

Skye let herself dwell on memories of Ron Hagey. It had been his sixth birthday party, and out of all the girls he'd picked her as the one to kiss. She still didn't know why. "I kissed Pearson last December. I told you that."

"You did not tell me!"

"I thought I did. It was that time I gave him a bloody nose, even better than the one you gave yourself last week."

"Did you kiss him before or after the bloody nose?"

"Before. He promised he'd finally stop asking me out if I kissed him just once. So I kissed him, then punched him. He didn't seem to mind."

"I wish I had your clarity of vision," said Jane. "I just hope I'm not doomed to a life of falling for the wrong boys, drifting, alone, never settled. Though probably I shouldn't get married anyway. A writer has to be able to concentrate on her work without distractions. What about you—do you think you'll get married?"

Skye frowned. "Why is everybody talking about marriage? First Jeffrey, now you."

"Who is Jeffrey talking about marrying? You, right? Do you want to marry him?"

"I don't know! I'm only *twelve*!"

"Calm down. You're going to have a heart attack or something. Should I try to hypnotize you again?"

"Don't you dare." Skye held up a pillow for protection.

"You know, maybe Jeffrey talks about marrying you because we're his family now and he's afraid of losing us. Because his actual family is an awful mother and a stepfather who hates him and a real father who's either dead or never bothered to meet him, and who knows which is worse?"

"Maybe," said Skye.

"What do you mean *maybe*? I know of what I speak. After all, I'm a writer, and thus understand human emotions."

"Unless they're yours."

"*Touché*." Jane stuck out her tongue at her sister. "Besides, Batty wants to marry Jeffrey, which could solve your problem. Say *touché* back."

"*Touché* back."

Wearily peaceful after the day's traumas, the sisters rested quietly, enjoying the night breeze coming through the windows. Once, faintly, a hint of music blew in with it—a blend of saxophone and piano wafting across the beach from next door. Skye tried to picture the scene over there, with the two of them playing, but she got stuck at Alec, all shaven now. She was one of those who thought he looked like someone else without his beard, and it was still puzzling her.

"Jane, are you sure Alec doesn't remind you of anyone? And no movie stars this time."

"Let me think. *Now that Sabrina Starr had cast off the specter of an unfulfilling romance, her mind was once again clear and sharp.* One of our teachers from Wildwood, maybe?"

Skye concentrated—and thought she had it. "The gym teacher."

"The muscle-bound one with the ponytail?" Jane shook her head decisively. "No."

"Well, it's someone, I'm sure of it."

"I'll tell myself a magic charm before I go to sleep."

"For heaven's sake, no more magic charms or wishes for the rest of the vacation. Please."

"All right, grumpy." Jane picked up her blue notebook. "Shall I read you more of my book? I'll start at the beginning."

Skye yawned. "Sure."

"It's called *Sabrina Starr Rescues the Heartbreaker.*

200

Chapter One. *Sabrina Starr had met him once—this incorrigible heartbreaker—in New York City during her mission to rescue the Chinese ambassador and thus preserve world peace.* Nice beginning, right? Skye? Skye, are you awake?"

But Skye, that overworked OAP, had fallen asleep even before the Chinese ambassador. Wisely not taking this as criticism of her writing, Jane covered her sister with a blanket and went back to work.

CHAPTER THIRTEEN
Questions

THERE WAS MUCH DISCUSSION the next morning about where to hold the golf ball sale. For Batty, who had already met enough new people for any one vacation, the pinewood seemed like the right place—maybe the lady in the green skirt would come back and buy everything, all million balls and every one of Jeffrey's golf clubs. Jane, however, had grandiose visions of hawking their wares on the golf course itself, maybe from one of those fun little carts. Skye, who was still hoping the whole thing would be forgotten, said they should set up in front of Birches, and if no buyers showed up, that would be the end of it. Finally, when the discussion became too heated, Aunt Claire sent Jeffrey next door to ask Alec for his opinion. Alec's answer was so logical—the best place for a sale was the entrance to the golf course—that everyone stopped arguing and packed up to go. Even then, a skirmish with Hound delayed them—he was as insistent that he go with them as they were that he didn't. Once again Alec was consulted, and once again he solved their problem, this time by sending back with Jeffrey a red rubbery thing stuffed full of peanut butter, which so entranced Hound that he barely noticed when the sales team left for the golf course entrance.

To get there, they had to walk halfway up the hill toward Moose Market, then go left on Pomante Street, right on Cross Street, left on Pullem Street, and, finally, right on Greene Street. They set off, carrying among them five buckets of golf balls, ten signs that Batty and Mercedes had made the night before, a blanket to sit on, snacks and water, and the Mouette Inn box to keep money in. Then there was the big heavy bag of clubs, which Jeffrey insisted on lugging all by himself. He said that he relished the agony, knowing the clubs would soon be out of his life forever. It was a long walk to be carrying so much, and they had to make several rest stops, the most pleasant one on Pullem Street, in front of a house where a potbellied pig named Frederica was sunning herself in the yard. Batty and Mercedes were so overwhelmed with the pig's splendor that Skye again let herself hope the sale would be abandoned, but too soon Frederica's owner took her inside, and everyone reshouldered their burdens and trudged onward.

The entrance to the golf course was more imposing than they'd expected, with a wooden arch that said POINTED FIRS in ornate gold letters, fat wooden pillars on either side of the driveway, and around the pillars rigidly straight rows of plants that looked as though they blossomed on command. Jane was sent past the sign and the pillars to search for a possible site for their sale but came back with the information that the grounds got only more imposing farther in, so they decided to set up right there, in front of the arch. Skye spread the blanket, Jeffrey let his heavy bag of clubs crash to the ground, and the others set out the buckets of balls in what they hoped was an inviting display. The signs were a problem, because no one had thought to bring anything to hang them up with, nor was there anywhere to hang them anyway, except on the arch, and they had no doubt that was forbidden. So Mercedes picked up one sign—CLUBS, TOO—and Batty picked up another—BALLS—and they stood beside the blanket holding them high. A car passed them by, and then another car, and then another.

"This isn't going to work," muttered Skye.

"Patience," said Jeffrey.

The fourth car stopped, and the woman inside rolled down the window.

"Is that you, Mercedes Orne?" she asked. "Did you get your hair cut?"

"Yes, Mrs. Domergue." Mercedes stepped forward

eagerly, saying over her shoulder to the others, "She's staying at the inn."

"Your brother isn't going to appear out of nowhere and startle me with his skateboard, is he?"

"No, ma'am," called Jane.

"Then I'll get out of my car and see what's going on." Mrs. Domergue did just that, and she ended up buying six golf balls.

Mercedes was so excited at this success and her part in it that she jumped around like a crazed kangaroo, trying to flag down the next car that arrived, which would have been all right if she hadn't gotten too close to it. Jeffrey pulled her out of the way and gave her a time-out on the blanket, but except for that small trouble, Mrs. Domergue had gotten them rolling, and car after car stopped, and soon two whole buckets of balls were gone and a man had bought what he called the three wood out of Jeffrey's golf bag, after explaining why a club made of metal was called a wood, even though no one cared at all until he gave them much more money than they'd dared ask for, but it was too late to ask him to explain it again, so they simply said good-bye and thank you.

"Do we have enough for my piano now?" asked Batty.

"No," said Skye.

"Not yet," added Jeffrey.

"Here comes our lady!" Jane pointed at a little blue car that had stopped. Out of it climbed the green-skirt lady from the pinewood, except today she was wearing an orange skirt. A man came out of the passenger side, a very tall man who wasn't as pleased to see them as the lady was.

"Brian, here are those children I told you about," she said. "The ones who found my Dunlops."

"Don't forget we're teeing off soon," he said, looking pointedly at his watch.

"We have plenty of time." She smiled at them all, remembering which she'd met before and which she hadn't, and asked everyone's names, and if they'd found any more of her Dunlops, and while they tipped over buckets and started a search, she strolled over to Jeffrey's golf bag. "Is all this for sale, too?"

"Carolyn!" said tall Brian. "We don't have to buy used golf clubs from children."

"But I need clubs, and these look very nice."

"They are nice, and I've hardly used them," Jeffrey told her, then lowered his voice so that Brian couldn't hear. "I hate golf."

"I don't like it much either," Carolyn whispered back. "But since I have to play, I might as well have my own clubs, don't you think?"

Jeffrey did think so, and so did Jane, Batty, Mercedes, and—with less enthusiasm—Skye. Even with all six of them in agreement, it was quite a struggle to convince Brian. However, in the end, seven clubs called irons, plus a putter and a sand wedge, *and* half a bucket of Dunlops were all loaded into the blue car, and kind Carolyn and her husband drove away. She'd been even more generous about the clubs than the first man, and now the Mouette Inn box was so impressively full of money that Batty almost worked herself into a fit about a piano, and maybe would have if Skye hadn't dumped a bottle of water on her head. The day was hot enough that Batty enjoyed the drenching, so everyone else decided they wanted water dumped on their heads, too. At the end, they were all wet and laughing, but now there was no water left to drink.

"We'll do rock-paper-scissors for who goes back for more," said Jeffrey.

"Never mind—I'll go." Skye scooped up the empty water bottles and went, glad for an excuse to get away from all the talk of pianos and golf. She'd run down Greene Street and had already turned onto Pullem when Jane came puffing up.

"Mercedes just fell into the bag of food and got grapes smashed all over her, so you'd better bring back some napkins, too," she said. "Jeffrey said to ask Alec for napkins if we're out."

"Water *and* napkins," said Skye, jogging on.

But Jane was calling out to her. "Hey, and that reminds me. I figured out last night who Alec looks like."

"Who?"

"Jeffrey."

Skye reversed direction and ran back to Jane. "You think Alec looks like Jeffrey? That's ridiculous."

"Not if you imagine what Jeffrey will look like in ten or fifteen years. You should do that anyway, as insurance, in case you marry him."

"I'm not going to marry— Never mind. Was this brilliant revelation a result of a wish or charm?"

"Make fun if you like," said Jane breezily. "I know I'm right. *Sabrina Starr's instincts were impeccable.*"

Skye shook her head and ran off again, wishing— not for the first time—that Sabrina Starr didn't have to be quite so cocky. Jeffrey! Ha! Jane was obviously going to be no more help in figuring out this puzzle. Skye bent her mind to it, going back to the Wildwood gym teacher. If he weren't so full of muscles . . . and then she turned onto Cross Street and saw trouble coming—on a skateboard. Instinctively, Skye ran her fingers through her shorn hair. She really didn't mind having it short, but that didn't mean Dominic Orne shouldn't pay for what he'd done to Jane and all of them. Still, she'd promised Jane that she wouldn't take revenge. And she meant to keep that promise. She meant it as Dominic came closer and closer, and she still meant it up until the very last second, when she abruptly dodged into his path, a move that would be sure to topple him from his skateboard.

Rats! Not only did he easily maneuver around her, but he also managed to pass off a note while he was doing it.

"For Jane," he said, "telling her to meet me at French Park tomorrow after lunch."

"No!" she barked, her loathing for him increased tenfold. "No, no! Believe me, Jane wouldn't meet you at French Park or any other park if it were the last park in the world!"

But he'd already ridden off, leaving Skye furious with herself. She'd both broken her promise to Jane and failed to get revenge all in one stupid move. Oh, that wretched Dominic! For the rest of her run back to Ocean Boulevard, Skye entertained herself with glorious fantasies of true retribution that actually worked. As she got closer to Birches and picked up the sound of a barking dog—Hoover, not Hound, thank goodness—the fantasies became about shutting Dominic and Hoover into a small closet and letting Hoover lick Dominic to death. So pleased was Skye with this idea that when she spotted Hoover in the field across the street from Birches, she thought she could manage to say hello to him. He was bouncing up and down under the big oak tree like he was on springs, yelping with each bounce, with Alec holding his leash and looking resigned. Skye picked her way through the grass and wildflowers to get to them.

"Hello!" Alec seemed glad for the company. "How's the sale going?"

"Good. We sold a bunch of the clubs, and now I need more water." Hoover paid no attention to her, continuing the trampoline act. "What's he doing?"

"Trying to catch the squirrel at the top of the tree."

Skye squinted up—the tree was at least fifty feet tall, and if a squirrel was at the top, it was hidden by the leaves. She looked back down at Hoover, who showed no signs of flagging. "How long can he keep doing that?"

"I don't know. I always get bored before he wears out." Alec grinned, and Skye felt an eerie shiver of recognition go through her, just like the first time she'd seen him without his beard. Who the heck did he remind her of?

"Smile again," she said.

"Why?" he asked, smiling, then laughing, because it's almost impossible to smile and say "Why" at the same time.

Skye shook her head. It was gone again, whatever it was. "I still can't figure out who you look like without your beard. Jane says it's Jeffrey, but she's nuts."

"That's funny—" Alec was cut off when Hoover, having decided that his squirrel had changed positions high in the tree, rushed around to the other side of it, taking Alec and Skye with him.

"What's funny?" asked Skye after Hoover resumed bouncing.

"What? Oh—what Jane said. Turron said the same thing when he first met Jeffrey."

"That you look like him?"

"That he looks like me."

"I don't know." Skye stared at Alec for a while, trying different angles. "It's hard to tell because you're so much older."

"Ancient, in fact."

Hoover's barking suddenly changed, sounding less rhythmic and more like a broken and demented drum machine. Looking up, Skye and Alec saw the reason why. Several curious seagulls were now circling the tree, whether to give moral support to the squirrel or just to bedevil Hoover, it wasn't clear.

"That's it. Heart-attack time." Alec scooped up Hoover and cradled him like a baby, an insane, barking baby. "Let's go, Skye. You can fill those water bottles at my house."

She followed them, keeping her distance from Hoover's tongue, and promising herself she would stick with big, goofy dogs like Hound for the rest of her life. By the time they reached the red house, Hoover had finally worn himself out, and Alec was able to tumble him gently onto the couch, where he immediately started snoring. Skye went to the kitchen sink to rinse out and refill the bottles. She was almost done when Alec interrupted her.

"Look what I've found," he said, showing her an old shoe box. "Old family pictures. I thought there might be some around. Let's check out this Jeffrey theory."

Skye dried her hands and went with him to sit on the piano bench. Alec was already sorting through the box, muttering at some of the photos, laughing and shaking his head at others. Then he stopped to stare intently at one particular picture before handing it over to Skye.

"What do you think?" he asked.

It was Jeffrey and yet not Jeffrey, because the hair was too long and the clothes were from a different time. Skye turned over the photograph and looked at the back. Someone had written in pencil: Alec, age 12.

"Wow," said Skye. "Jane was right."

"Yeah." Alec took it back and stared some more. "Weird, isn't it? I wonder if we're distant cousins. Wouldn't that be great—though I've never heard of any Tiftons in our family."

Skye shook her head. "Tifton isn't Jeffrey's real name. I mean, it is his real name, but it isn't his mother's or father's real name."

"He was adopted?"

"No." This had all been explained to Skye by Rosalind, who'd heard it from Churchie, who knew more about Jeffrey than anyone. "Jeffrey's mother married when she was really young, and the marriage was such a mistake that she got divorced before Jeffrey was even born. Her father—Jeffrey's grandfather—who was kind of a tyrant, didn't want her to keep her married name, and since she didn't want to go back to her maiden name, they compromised on Tifton, an old family name. So Jeffrey was born a Tifton, and he's never been told his father's last name, or where he is, or even if he's alive. His grandfather died when he was little, his grandmother died before that even, and his mother just won't tell him anything."

"That's sad."

"It's even sadder because she's so awful, and her new husband, Dexter, is just as awful, or worse. Last summer they almost sent Jeffrey to a horrible military school to get him ready to follow in the footsteps of his grandfather—you know, the tyrant—old General Framley."

Two things—no, three—happened then. The first was the box of photographs falling from Alec's lap to the floor, loosing a flood of snapshots. The second was Alec turning so pale that Skye could count every freckle on his face. And the third was Skye abruptly remembering what Jeffrey had told her the morning they saw the moose. That Alec was divorced. What had Jeffrey said exactly? *Alec's marriage was so bad he won't even talk about it—just that he was young and it lasted only a few months.*

Skye knew she was pale herself. She sat very still and quiet, as though by doing so she could stop time and keep them all safe. And she watched Alec. He was leaning over, hiding his face from her and pushing the fallen photos around, aimlessly around and around. After a while, he said, "Jeffrey's grandfather was General Framley?"

213

"Yes."

"And is Jeffrey's mother— What is Jeffrey's mother's name?"

He raised his face to Skye now, and she was shocked at the mingled pain and longing there. She stood up. Whatever was happening was too much for her. "Alec, let's go talk to Aunt Claire."

He didn't seem to have heard her. "Jeffrey's mother is Brenda Framley. Am I right? Brenda Framley of Arundel."

"I think so," she whispered, bewildered and frightened. "I mean, yes."

He stood up now and crossed over to the window, and with his back to Skye he said, "Jeffrey is eleven now—he told me that. When will he turn twelve?"

"Next month. August eighth."

"August. Yes, that works." Alec reeled, and for a moment Skye was afraid he'd crash over.

"Are you all right? Because I don't understand—"

"I never thought—she didn't tell me—I need to see him. Is he still at the golf course? No, no, that's not right. It's not fair to say anything to him until I'm sure. I'll have to go ask Brenda. That's what I'll do. Skye, is she at Arundel now?"

"I think so, but Alec—"

"Then I'll go to Arundel and make her tell me the truth." He was already looking around for his car keys.

"It's hours and hours away!" She grabbed Alec's

arm—he looked barely capable of walking, let alone driving all the way across New England. "And even if you find her, she's really difficult to talk to."

"You think I don't know that? I was married to her." He gently pulled away and found his car keys on the piano. "Tell Jeffrey—and your aunt and sisters—that I had to leave because of a family emergency. That's even the truth. I'm sorry to ask you to keep secrets. Can you?"

"I—I guess so," she stammered, barely knowing what she was agreeing to.

"Good." He took Hoover's leash down from its hook. "Hoover, we're going for a long ride, buddy."

Skye ran to the couch, grabbed Hoover's collar, and held on to it, desperate to save someone from the coming conflagration, even if it was just this dog who drove her bonkers. "You can't take him with you to Arundel. Mrs. T-D doesn't like dogs. She doesn't like dogs or rabbits or anything. Please let Hoover stay here. I'll take care of him."

"Naturally she doesn't like dogs. What was I thinking?" said Alec, and tried to smile but managed only a painful grimace. "All right, Skye, you keep Hoover for me. I shouldn't be gone long, twenty-four hours at the most."

He walked out of the house—but came right back in.

"Make sure you tell Jeffrey he's welcome to the

piano while I'm gone." He waved his arm around the room full of music. "He's welcome to all of it."

"I'll tell him."

Alec left again, and again he came back. "You shouldn't have to do this alone, Skye. I'll stop by your house and explain to Claire what I'm doing."

"Thank you."

Once more he left, and Skye and Hoover—united in feelings for the first time ever—waited hopefully for him to return. When it was clear that this time he was gone for good, Hoover crept under the piano, whimpering, and how Skye wished she could crawl under there with him and hide from her fears, her doubts and confusions. Only fifteen minutes ago she'd been at the oak tree, laughing with Alec at Hoover's antics, and now Alec was gone—off on a wild chase to Arundel, looking for a truth that Skye was still too overwhelmed to contemplate. She shivered and would have given anything for her father to appear, and Rosalind, and Iantha and Ben, and for life to go back to normal. No being the OAP, no responsibility, no blabbing about who looked like whom and letting loose chaos on the people she cared about the most.

But none of that was going to happen, and Skye was on her own. What to do first? Hide the evidence. Working quickly, she scooped all the photographs back into their shoe box and crammed it behind a pile of sheet music on the shelf. She even checked the sheet music—it was for saxophone, which meant Jeffrey wouldn't be poking around here. And now? She should finish filling the water bottles and take them back to the others at the golf course, with some funny story of why she'd been away so long. But Skye couldn't think of any funny stories, and she wasn't a good liar anyway, not for important things.

"But I can't stay here all day, hiding," she told Hoover, still in his safe haven under the piano. "I'd better go see Aunt Claire. You ready to go?"

He answered with a sad little moan, his ridiculous squashed face more wrinkled than ever. Which gave Skye the perfect excuse to crawl under the piano with him after all, and even hug him for a while—it helped that he didn't lick her face, for once—until they'd both gathered enough courage to crawl out again and set off for Birches and whatever new terrifying information awaited them there.

They'd gotten halfway across the beach when Skye spotted her aunt tottering down Birches' steps, on her way to find her missing niece. Seconds later, crutches were flying this way and that, and Skye was enveloped in a hug almost big enough to squash out all the awfulness. But not quite.

"Oh, Aunt Claire, what have I done?"

Aunt Claire stroked her hair. "You haven't done anything wrong. Do you think you've done something wrong?"

"I'm not sure." She pulled back to see her aunt's face. "I just don't understand. Does Alec think he's Jeffrey's father?"

"Yes, and he's gone to Arundel to find out for certain."

Cold crept up Skye's spine. "But if he is, how could he not know? None of this makes sense."

"When he and Jeffrey's mother split up, she might not even have known she was pregnant."

"But then she should have told him when she found out, right?"

"Theoretically yes, but we won't know the whole story until Alec talks to her. There could be another explanation. Jeffrey could have a different father, or he could be adopted, or—I don't know. There could be two Brenda Framleys, even."

"No, no, no." One was much too awful. There couldn't be two.

Skye helped Aunt Claire back up to the deck and sent Hoover into the house to see Hound, all the while thinking furiously of matters she didn't want to think about, not for years and years. Rosalind wouldn't shrink from all this. Rosalind would know exactly what to do. But Skye knew nothing, nothing. No, that wasn't true. She did know one thing very well—that she couldn't keep this secret for twenty-four hours.

"Aunt Claire, I'm going to tell Jeffrey what's going on."

"You can't, honey. That's not right."

"None of this is *right*. And even if Alec isn't his father, he was married to Jeffrey's mother. I can't pretend I don't know that."

"Yes, you can, because you have to. It's not fair to Jeffrey to give him half the story, then leave him hanging. You'll have to be brave and patient."

"Patient!" Skye had never felt less patient in her life.

"And it's only fair to let Alec tell his own story. You know that." Aunt Claire brushed Skye's hair off her forehead, just like she had years ago when Skye was small. "We'll manage this together. I'll make sure Jeffrey and Batty spend most of their time with Alec's piano, and if Jane starts getting curious, distract her by asking about Sabrina Starr."

Inside the house, Hound was starting to bark, and it wasn't his Hoover-is-here bark. No, this bark meant that Batty had been away from him for too long and was now on her way back.

"They're coming!" said Skye. "The sale must be over already."

Aunt Claire lowered herself onto a chair and picked up a book. Seeing her, Skye would have thought that nothing out of the ordinary had happened for hours, for days, for weeks. I can do this, too, she thought, sitting down in another chair with what she hoped was languid nonchalance.

"How do I look?" she asked Aunt Claire.

219

"Like a bomb that's about to go off."

"I can't do it," wailed Skye, straightening up again.

"Yes, you can. Think about prime numbers, or those black holes you love so much. Think about black holes!"

Black holes, thought Skye, black holes, black holes, and here came Batty running around the house, waving the Mouette Inn box and shouting about a piano, and then came Mercedes, Jane, and Jeffrey, with empty buckets and no golf clubs or even a bag left—and Skye's battle had begun.

CHAPTER FOURTEEN
Answers, and More Questions

By MIDNIGHT, most of Birches was asleep—Jane and Jeffrey in their beds on the sleeping porch, and Batty, Hound, and Hoover all piled happily into Batty's bed. Only Skye and Aunt Claire were still awake, fever-ishly working on yet another jigsaw puzzle. It had been a good-bye gift from Turron, but instead of Paris or Venice, this one showed a close-up of a dog that looked just like Hoover.

"I'm sorry," said Aunt Claire when Skye complained for the tenth time about staring at Hoover's face. "Turron said it was the only puzzle left in the store."

"Turron was teasing you."

"Probably. Here's a piece of dog leg."

"No, that's an ear, I think." Skye yawned hugely, knocking several pieces of Hoover onto the floor.

"Go to bed, Skye."

"Not until Alec calls. I can't sleep until I know the truth about you-know-what."

Not that she wasn't worn out, wrung out, tired through and through. Never in her life had Skye spent so many hours acting calm and carefree, while all the time her brain was spinning like an out-of-control merry-go-round. Was Alec truly Jeffrey's father? No, it was too bizarre to be true. But that photograph—how alike they were! So then Alec *was* his father—he had to be. No, no, even Mrs. T-D couldn't be that selfish, to keep a boy from his father. Well, then, who *was* Jeffrey's father? Would Mrs. T-D tell Alec that? Probably not. She wouldn't tell him anything unless he himself was Jeffrey's father. So was he? And on and on Skye's brain would spin.

Alec had called once already, after dinner. While Skye created a diversion by tickling Batty, which made her shriek and Hound and Hoover bark, Aunt Claire was able to slip off to talk to him without anyone noticing. She'd told Skye later what Alec had said—he was an hour away from Arundel, nervous out of his mind, and he'd call them again after he'd talked to Jeffrey's mother. And how was Jeffrey, he'd asked three or four times, even though each time Aunt Claire told him that Jeffrey was doing great and spending most of his time playing the piano.

Since then it had been as though an evil genie had gotten into the phone line. All evening it rang. One person looking for Rieke, whoever she was, one man asking for donations to a political party that Aunt Claire despised, and two calls from Turron, to whom Alec had told everything and was now as on edge and looking for news as Skye and Aunt Claire. Rosalind had called, too, and chatted with Aunt Claire about wind surfing and saltwater taffy. Of all the calls, this had been the hardest on Skye. For almost two weeks, she'd avoided Rosalind because of stupid pride and wanting to manage all by herself, and now that she would have given anything to talk with her about Jeffrey and Alec, she couldn't because it was secret. How sick Skye was of secrets. And being the OAP. And telephone calls with people who weren't Alec on the other end.

"Is this his eye or his tooth?" asked Aunt Claire, waving around another puzzle piece.

"Tooth, I guess. My, what big teeth you have, Hoover." Skye, who in her right mind would have scorned such an infantile joke, was convulsed with giggles and knocked even more of Hoover to the floor.

"Only the better to eat—"

The phone was ringing. Aunt and niece stopped laughing and stared at each other, neither ready to answer the phone. This time it had to be Alec.

"Do you want to talk to him?" Aunt Claire asked Skye after the third ring.

223

"No. You do it."

So Aunt Claire answered and Skye watched as she went pale, then red, then pale again, as she nodded and listened. By the time she hung up, Skye knew the truth. But still she had to ask.

"Alec really is Jeffrey's father, isn't he?"

"Yes."

It was a strange experience for Skye to cry that much. She hadn't done so for a long time, longer than she could remember. It helped that Aunt Claire was doing it, too. They clung together and cried and cried—for relief and worry and exhaustion, and for that boy asleep on the porch whose past and future had been tossed into the air and juggled around, with no one knowing what would happen when it all fell down again.

But even in times so burdened, tears eventually dry up, and after a lot of tissues had been used to clean noses and eyes, Aunt Claire filled Skye in on the details. Mrs. T-D had admitted everything to Alec— that she had kept their son a secret from him for all these years and would have kept that secret forever if she'd had her way.

"But why? Why would she do such a thing?"

Aunt Claire pushed doggish puzzle pieces around for a long moment. "It seems that she didn't want to share Jeffrey. She wanted him all to herself."

"That's horrible!"

"Yes."

As for right now, Aunt Claire went on, Alec was in a hotel in Massachusetts somewhere, too drained to make it all the way back to Maine that night. But he would be there in the morning as soon as he possibly could—and would call a few minutes before he arrived—and he asked them to please, if they could, keep his secret until then, so that he could tell Jeffrey himself. And then he'd hung up.

After all that, Skye and Aunt Claire felt even less like sleeping than they had before. And because crying is hard and hungry work, they each had a piece of strawberry-rhubarb pie from Moose Market, plus big glasses of milk, and while they ate, they talked quietly of this, that, and anything but terrible mothers, until the conversation drifted to good mothers, and soon Aunt Claire was telling Skye stories about Skye's very own mother, Elizabeth Penderwick, or Lizzy, or Mommy. Most of the stories Skye had heard before, but not the asparagus one from when she was three. Aunt Claire couldn't remember why the asparagus had caused such a problem but suspected that Jane was somehow involved. What she did remember was how Skye had screamed until her face turned purple, at which point Lizzy, desperate, stuck the asparagus up her own nose, and Skye had been so surprised that she stopped screaming and had loved asparagus ever since.

"I never screamed that much," said Skye, doubled over with laughter. "And I don't *love* asparagus."

"Every word I say is the truth. Believe me, you were a screamer," replied Aunt Claire. "And I've seen you eat asparagus plenty of times—you adore it."

It felt so good to laugh! But Jeffrey showed up then, woken by their hilarity, and at the sight of his untroubled face, Skye's laughter was gone, her sorrow back, and she was afraid it would be days before she had another chance to laugh like that.

"Why are you both staring at me?" he asked. "Do I have toothpaste on my face?"

"No, you're perfect," answered Aunt Claire.

"Right." He yawned. "Is all the pie gone?"

"Yes—go back to bed," said Skye, and watched him stumble off. "I can't stand it, Aunt Claire."

"You have to. We both have to." Aunt Claire rubbed her eyes. "We should get some sleep now, too, honey. Big day tomorrow."

After one last long hug, each went off to her bed to collapse into a troubled sleep . . . and too soon it was morning.

Getting sucked into a black hole is a spectacular way to die. The author of *Death by Black Hole*, Neil deGrasse Tyson, had explained the process clearly, which Skye appreciated, since the chances of her ever getting close enough to a black hole to watch any *thing* fall into it—she wasn't so bloodthirsty as to want to see an actual person fall into a black hole—were pretty slim. It was intriguing to think about, though, especially for someone who desperately needed to continue holding on to a ten-ton burden of a secret. Alec hadn't yet come back, and Skye, clinging for her life to black holes, had come up with this scenario:

She and Tyson were on a spaceship thousands of light-years from Earth and just far enough away from a black hole to escape its lethal pull. They were about to launch tons of space waste—mostly broken-down satellites—at the black hole, giving them the opportunity to observe sucked-into-black-hole behavior while also being ecologically responsible.

SKYE: "Ready for launch, Captain Tyson?"

TYSON: "Just a few last-minute calculations, Lieutenant Penderwick."

SKYE: "Making sure the addition of space waste to the black star doesn't increase its size enough to suck us into it, too? And obliterate us?"

TYSON: "The leader of the heartbroken girls spoke: He had only one request before we stranded him on the island—that we inform you he was out there, just in case you were willing to rescue him. Not that we want you to rescue him, but we're not cruel."

SKYE: "Excuse me, sir?"

TYSON: "Sabrina Starr was appalled that the Heartbreaker thought she'd rescue so low a lowlife.

After making a mockery of the love and poetry of perfectly wonderful girls, and also teaching them never again to fall for an empty shell of a boy who cared only for his skateboard and stealing kisses. Sabrina scorned him! Let him rot on his island!"

SKYE: "Jane!"

She slammed *Death by Black Hole* shut and glowered at her sister. They were in side-by-side chairs on the deck, and Skye was finding that the only way she could talk to Jane was rudely. Because keeping Alec's secret from Jane was almost worse than keeping it from Jeffrey. Lying to Jane was like being mean to a puppy. No one deserved it less.

So Skye had to be as mean as possible. She glowered even more fiercely.

"What?" Jane asked.

"Do you have to talk out loud while you write?"

"I guess not. Why are you so grouchy?"

"Sorry. My head hurts."

Skye's head did hurt. Her head and her heart, and her thumb where she'd chewed the nail down past the quick, though she'd stopped chewing her nails years ago. And she was exhausted, beyond exhausted. Her short sleep had been full of dreams she didn't want to remember. Now Jane was saying something about foreheads.

"What?" Skye asked.

"Do you want me to bathe your forehead, you know, because of your aching head?"

"No! I mean, no, thank you."

"You're welcome. And, Skye, you're absolutely positive that I shouldn't answer that note Dominic passed to you yesterday? About meeting him at French Park? What if he wants to apologize to me? Is it dishonorable not to give him that opportunity?"

Skye now gave Jane a look so evil that her earlier glower seemed beatific. "Here is what I'm positive about," she spit out. "If you ask me that one more time, or even mention Dominic's name, I will throw you and your blue notebook into the ocean."

"Okay," answered Jane. "Be that way."

Skye leaned back in her chair—relieved that she'd managed to keep the secret for another few minutes—and prepared to launch herself back into space with Captain Tyson.

SKYE: "Making sure the addition of space waste to the black star doesn't increase its size enough to suck us into it, too? And obliterate us?"

TYSON: "That's right, Lieutenant. Obliteration is so final these days."

SKYE: "Aye, aye, sir."

TYSON: "Calculations complete. Release space waste on my count, and brace yourself, Lieutenant. Three—two—"

Inside, the phone was ringing again. Skye froze, trying to stick with Tyson and his black holes, but moments later, Aunt Claire was at the sliding door, quietly asking her to come inside. So this was it. With her head about to explode, along with all the rest of her, Skye dragged herself out of her deck chair and into Birches.

"Is Alec coming?" she asked her aunt.

"He'll be here in about ten minutes and wants to talk to Jeffrey right away. I said that he's already next door, playing the piano."

"Not knowing what's about to hit him. Oh, Aunt Claire, I feel sick."

"I do, too, but we have to bear it. Batty's with Jeffrey, right? Send her back to me, and I'll explain to her and Jane what's going on."

"And I saw Mercedes heading over there a while ago. What should I do with her?"

"Mercedes seems to have adopted us, for better or worse. She can hear what's going on, too." Aunt Claire gently poked at Skye with a crutch. "Now go to Jeffrey."

Skye needed most of those ten minutes, first to shove Jane inside, then to run next door, pry Batty off the piano bench, Mercedes off the couch, and Hound from his spot next to Hoover under the piano, and send the three of them scurrying back to Birches and Aunt Claire. But at last they were gone, and Skye was left—with no memory of what excuse she'd used to get rid of them—alone with Jeffrey. Through it all, he'd stayed at the piano bench, where he'd been teaching Batty about harmonic intervals.

"You're a little strange today," he said, his fingers

still running over the keys. "Unless you're just desperate to get me alone."

"That's it." She sat down beside him. "Anyway, we won't be alone long. Alec is coming home any minute."

"Great! I've been working on a song I want to ask him about. I've transposed it into a different key, which shouldn't make any difference, but it doesn't feel quite right. Listen."

He launched into a melody full of loneliness and despair, diving so deeply that he didn't hear the front door open, or even Hoover's ecstatic yaps as he flew across the room to his master. Alec held the dog close, whispering soft greetings, but he had eyes only for the boy at the piano, devouring him. Skye saw that he wasn't at all impatient to interrupt Jeffrey, to be noticed, to start explaining, and she could also see how scared he was. She wanted to soothe Alec, to tell him it would all be fine. But she wasn't sure it would be, and besides, her first loyalty was to the son, not the father. She put her arm around Jeffrey's shoulder—a gesture unusual enough to make him stop playing and look up.

"Alec, you're back!" he said, then grinned at Skye. "You're *very* strange today."

"Hello, Jeffrey," said Alec quietly. "How are you?"

"I'm . . ." Jeffrey stopped, struck by Alec's hesitation and his obvious exhaustion. "You look terrible."

"Yes, I know," he said, and looked at Skye, who shook her head no—she hadn't given up his secret.

231

"It's been a long twenty-four hours. I've missed you, Jeffrey."

"We've missed you, too." Jeffrey's hands started wandering the piano keys again, picking out nervous spurts of notes. "And now you're both being strange."

"I know. I'm sorry," said Alec, coming closer to the piano. "I have something important to tell you, and I don't know where to begin."

"Do you want me to leave?" Skye asked Alec.

"No." They said it together, the man and the boy, then looked at each other, one pleading, one wary.

"All right," she said, pulling Jeffrey in tighter. "Then Alec, maybe you can begin with the photograph."

So Alec began with the photograph, and then went on to his trip to Arundel, and why he needed to go there, and all the while Jeffrey kept playing the piano, his head down, until Skye wasn't sure that he was even listening. But when Alec came to the part about confronting his ex-wife, Jeffrey carefully closed the piano lid, folded his hands like a small schoolchild, and interrupted.

"You're not making any sense," he said.

"I know it sounds crazy," said Alec sadly. "I'll start again."

He started again but this time went all the way back to being a young musician in Boston who fell in love with and married a beautiful college student, and how happy they were for a few months, until they discovered that they had nothing in common but love, and the arguments and sulks began and then got worse, until one day the beautiful wife was suddenly gone, fled back to her home in the Berkshires. And how Alec tried to go after her, but her father—an ex–army man, a general—wouldn't let him see her, and insisted they get divorced.

"And I never saw her again," finished Alec. "But what I didn't know, Jeffrey, was that when she left me, she was pregnant. Even she didn't know it, and then when she found out, she decided not to tell me."

Jeffrey sat very still. Only his fingers moved, convulsively, as if they were trying to get to the piano keys under the lid. At last he shook off Skye's arm.

"He's saying that he's my father," he said to her.

"I know."

"And you helped him figure that out? Why didn't you tell me?"

"Because I asked her not to," said Alec. "I had to see Brenda first, to be absolutely certain."

"My mother," he said reprovingly, as though Alec shouldn't be bandying about her first name.

Skye put her arm around him again. "Jeffrey, Alec was married to her. Don't you understand?"

Now Alec was taking a letter out of his wallet. "I met Churchie, too, Jeffrey. She gave me this letter for you."

He handed over the letter, which Jeffrey took, careful to keep from touching Alec.

"Is there anything from my mother?"

"She was too upset—she couldn't—no, she didn't send anything." Alec shook his head. "I'm sorry."

"Stop that," said Jeffrey sharply. "I don't want your sympathy."

He stood abruptly and pushed his way out onto the deck, where he stood, his shoulders hunched, reading Churchie's letter. Skye felt more helpless than she'd ever felt before, and wanted to get angry, and cry and rage, but she kept it under control, for friendship, because she was the OAP, but mostly because she was afraid that if she started raging, she wouldn't be able to stop.

After a while, Jeffrey came back inside, tucking the letter into his pocket. "Skye, remember the night we made wishes on the bonfire? My wish was that if I ever found my father, he'd be just like Alec. Do you think this is the Firegod's idea of a bad joke?"

"Jeffrey, no."

He waved off her concern and turned to Alec. "I don't care that my mother didn't tell you about me. You should have asked. You should have *known*."

"You're right. I should have. I was a fool."

"Yes, you were a fool. I think I'll leave now." But instead he advanced, with a fierce scowl Skye had never seen before. "Do I have grandparents?"

"Yes, and two uncles, and three cousins."

"Any brothers or sisters?"

"No."

"Are you sure?"

"I deserve that," said Alec. "Jeffrey, I promise I'll do anything I can to make this up to you."

"At least now I understand why Mother hates my music. It's because of you. How can you make that up to me?" He beat his fists against his thighs. "All those years!"

"I don't know, but I'll try. Jeffrey, listen to me, please. Don't you realize that I let myself wish I had a son like you? Almost from the first day we met."

Jeffrey turned his back on Alec and then asked, very quietly, "What do you want from me?"

"To let me love you. Love you and help keep you safe."

"No." Jeffrey shook his head, again and again. "Too late for that."

And now he did leave, slipping through the door, and before Skye could react, he'd leaped off the deck and was gone.

"What should I do?" she gasped at Alec.

"Go after Jeffrey. I'll tell your aunt what happened."

"But what about you?"

"Go! He's the most important—just go."

Jeffrey was already running down Ocean Boulevard at top speed. Skye tore off after him, determined to keep him in sight, because if he disappeared, she might never have the chance to tell him how sorry she was. And how she should have kept this from happening, and how she should have paid more attention, and . . . that she was sorry.

Before Jeffrey reached the dock, he abruptly veered off the side of the road, jumped, and vanished from Skye's view. "No, you don't," she muttered, picking up speed, and seconds later was also plunging down a pebbly slope, falling and getting up again, then continuing to track Jeffrey as he leaped out onto the great boulders, from one to another and another. Skye let up her chase only when he finally collapsed, facing out to sea.

Now that he was no longer moving and had nowhere farther to go, she stopped, teetering on slippery rock. And watched him for a while, and tried to get her thoughts in order. But the wild merry-go-round was back in her brain, and the only words that flew off it were *sorry, sorry, sorry.* So that is what she would tell him, she decided, and quietly, carefully, crept across the remaining rocks between them.

Jeffrey heard her coming. "Leave me alone, Skye," he said without turning around.

"Jeffrey, I—"

"Really, I can't talk now. Go away."

"All right, but I can't leave you out here all by yourself. You wouldn't leave me, and you know it. I'll be back near the road if you change your mind."

For several painful moments, Skye waited, hoping he'd say something, anything at all that would help her help him, but when he resolutely stayed silent, she headed back the way she'd come. At the base of the pebbly slope was a wide strip of rough sand—here she sat down, a sad and weary sentry at the beginning of her watch. The scene before her did nothing to raise her spirits. Rocks and more rocks, a wall of clouds advancing across the sky, and, too far away, a huddled and wretched boy. It was a small relief when Jane arrived a few minutes later, sent by Aunt Claire to make sure the runaways hadn't disappeared altogether.

"Is Jeffrey all right?" she asked, making her way down the slope.

"I don't know. He doesn't want to talk," answered Skye. "So I'm guarding him. Has Aunt Claire told you everything?"

"Yes." Jane looked as strained and unhappy as Skye felt. "But it doesn't seem real yet. I keep remembering last summer—when he talked about how one day he'd see his father somewhere and they'd just automatically recognize each other. And then it happened, and they didn't."

"They kind of did, though, when you think about it. Besides, they had you to figure it out."

"I guess so, but I can't decide if maybe I shouldn't have."

No one could decide that, Skye thought, without going crazy. Because craziness would be just as big a problem as rage, she sent Jane away, back to Birches to report that no one had drowned or run away to Canada. Alone again, Skye wrapped her arms around her knees and settled in for a long wait. She would think about . . . She knew better what *not* to think about. Jeffrey's words of reproach, *And you helped him figure that out? Why didn't you tell me?* Alec's anguished cry, *Go! He's the most important—just go.* No, she wouldn't think about those things or any of the others that had happened in the last half hour. *Leave me alone, Skye. Go away.* Instead, she would recite the prime numbers in order, up to 1,249, which was as far as she'd memorized.

She began, "Two, three, five, seven, eleven, thirteen, seventeen, nineteen . . ."

The wall of clouds reached the sun, covered it, and marched onward. The sky and the sea turned from blue to blue-gray to gray, and curious seagulls circled the motionless boy on the rocks, trying to identify this addition to their territory. Skye reached the end of her prime numbers and began over again, and again and again, and when Jeffrey still hadn't moved, she worked out the next few primes after 1,249—1,259, 1,277, and 1,279—but doing it in her head was so laborious that she went back to reciting the ones she knew. Once she thought she heard

238

snatches of music—the faint cry of a saxophone—but Jeffrey stayed where he was, and the tide came almost to his sneakers and retreated again.

Pebbles and sand were raining down on Skye, and words, too, including "whoops," "whoa," and "help." Jane was back again, this time loaded down with a heavy, bulging bag, plus a clarinet case. Skye jumped up and helped with the precarious descent down the slope. When both sisters were on solid ground, she peered into the bag. It was stuffed full of food—sandwiches, several bottles of lemonade, and an entire pie.

Jane set down her burdens and shook out her aching arms. "Aunt Claire sent me to Moose Market for the pie. Chocolate crème. Very decadent."

"I'm not hungry," said Skye before realizing that she was desperately hungry. "How long have I been out here?"

"Almost two hours, and the food is mostly for Jeffrey, anyway. Aunt Claire said that he doesn't have to talk, but he has to eat—and she sends her love to him, too. Mercedes helped me with the sandwiches, so they might be messy, but we put in lots of napkins. The clarinet was Batty's idea. She was sure he'd want it."

"I don't want to bother him, Jane. He said to leave him alone."

"And Aunt Claire made me promise the food

would get to him because no one can mourn on an empty stomach."

That was true, and Skye knew that being a mouse or a man counted with friendship, too. She would go out to Jeffrey, but not quite yet. "How is Alec doing?"

"Aunt Claire went next door to see him and came back five minutes later. He doesn't want to talk either."

"And how's Batty?"

"Upset and having trouble with some of the basic concepts. You should hear her and Mercedes asking Aunt Claire why Alec didn't know that daddies are a part of making babies."

Skye almost smiled. "Poor Aunt Claire. And you?"

"I'm doing better since I called down revenge and curses upon Mrs. T-D, just like Rosalind told us not to. I added in some for Dexter, and one or two for Dominic while I was at it. But I said it all to my pillow on the porch, to keep it private. I didn't think Aunt Claire would approve of all that revenge."

"We should have made voodoo dolls after all."

"We should have. But, Skye, are you stalling? Because if you don't want to see Jeffrey, I'm going out there onto the rocks myself."

"No, I'll do it." She had to. "Go back and get Batty and Mercedes, then watch through the binoculars. I'll signal you if it's okay to come."

"Make sure he eats some of that pie." Jane scrambled up the slope and was gone.

Sick of Caesar and Napoleon, Skye called instead on her gentle father for inspiration. And realized that Jeffrey could do nothing worse than accuse her of bothering him—thus failing him all over again—but she'd live through that. Picking up the clarinet and the unwieldy food bag, she set off on the journey to her friend.

He'd been sitting there for such a long time without speaking or moving that the seagulls had decided he was just another boulder, or maybe an odd mound of seaweed. This, then, was what Skye saw as she carefully picked her way—a somber world of pale gray sky and ocean, dark gray rocks, gray-green seaweed, and proud and foolish gulls marching around their newfound boulder. Or was he seaweed? He, at least, added a spot of color, but only with the blue of his shorts and shirt—the rest of him was blanched with sadness and worry—and Skye hoped more than anything that he would be ready to talk to her.

The seagulls saw her coming and stuck to their discovery as long as they could, but when it was clear that the new arrival was heading straight to him, they reluctantly flew away. Only the bravest of them waited until the very end, which came when the mound of seaweed turned back into a boy and spoke.

"Hello, Skye," he said.

She was so relieved at that simple "Hello" that a few tears escaped down her cheeks, and she was so embarrassed to be crying in front of Jeffrey that she forgot how off-balance she was with that heavy bag. Swaying dangerously, she yelped, and Jeffrey was immediately on his feet.

"Don't cry, please don't cry," he said, steadying her.

"I'm not, I mean, I've stopped. But, Jeffrey, I'm sorry for not telling you about Alec going to Arundel. I should have warned you."

"You couldn't."

"No, I couldn't. But I hated not being able to."

"I know you did."

"And I'm also sorry about—"

"Shh." He took the bag from her. "What's all this?"

"Nourishment," she said. "Jane and Mercedes made the sandwiches, and Batty sent your clarinet, and Aunt Claire sent love."

"She's not mad at me?"

"Aunt Claire? Good grief, why would she be?" said Skye. "She just wants what's best for you."

"And—Alec? Is he mad at me?"

"No one is angry at you, I promise. Come on, eat something. They made about a dozen sandwiches."

Her silly tears flown away, Skye was hungrier than ever. Still, she waited and fussed until Jeffrey had sat back down and eaten a sandwich. When his color started coming back, she pressed another on him and only then allowed herself to dig in. Jane had been right—the sandwiches were messy, but oh so delicious.

"I've been out here thinking about my mother," said Jeffrey after finishing the second, and then a third. "Did she really hate Alec so much that she had to keep me from him? And if I'm so much like him, does she . . . ?"

"No." Skye was certain of this, if not much else. "Your mother doesn't hate you, Jeffrey Tifton."

"Or whatever my name is." He tried to laugh, but it was enough like a sob to make Skye pull out the chocolate crème pie. When together they'd polished off several slices, plus most of the lemonade, Jeffrey told her what Churchie's letter said—that she liked Alec but loved Jeffrey and would always love him, no matter what happened. And that she hoped he was eating plenty of vegetables.

"Good old Churchie," said Skye.

"Yes," said Jeffrey, spinning a lemonade bottle round and round. "So, what should I do?"

"I don't know," said Skye.

"Really? No advice from the most opinionated person I know?"

"Very funny." She went to punch his arm, but he was too quick for her, dodging away, eluding her. This pleased her immeasurably. "Really, I don't know. It's too hard to imagine not knowing Daddy from the beginning. Although I wonder if he would have liked us

243

before he knew we were his daughters, as much as Alec liked you before he knew you were his son."

"He did like me, didn't he?"

"He still does."

"I guess so." Jeffrey shrugged his shoulders and opened his clarinet case. He was done with talking and ready for music.

As he put together the clarinet, Skye stood and waved her arms in the general direction of Birches, knowing that Jane would be watching and ready. By the time Jeffrey was beginning to play, he had a full audience—four girls to listen to him, cherish him, and wish they could keep him there forever, safe from the perilous world of grown-ups.

CHAPTER FIFTEEN
An Unwelcome Visitor

ONCE AGAIN JANE WAS TALKING in her sleep. This time, however, Skye was so worn out from the day before that nothing could wake her. Jeffrey, on the other side of the bamboo curtain, would have been next, but he was even more worn out than Skye. In the end, Jane had no one to wake up but herself.

"Sabrina Starr held the helicopter steady over the rock island and tossed out the rope ladder. 'You'll have to climb,' she shouted to the pathetic figure huddled on the rocks below her. 'I'm your only hope of rescue.'" Jane's eyes flew open. "Who said that?"

By the time Jane figured out that she was the only person who would babble about Sabrina Starr, she was wide awake, and another line from her new book was working its way into her consciousness. *She still wasn't sure that the Heartbreaker shouldn't be left to suffer. . . .* She needed more. How about this? *He should be left to suffer, alone with his guilty memories.* Excellent, thought Jane. She was going to have to write this stuff down before she forgot it.

Quietly she climbed out of bed, pulled on her clothes, and took her blue notebook outside. The sun was just barely above the horizon, the last of dawn's pinkness was fading, and Jane had the ocean, the sky, and the wheeling seagulls all to herself. She blew a good morning toward England, and another toward New Jersey, and a third to a place much closer than those—the red house next door, where she worried that Alec was slowly eating his heart out for Jeffrey. She knew that she shouldn't have an opinion about what was best for Jeffrey, but everything in her hoped that he would reconcile with Alec.

In the meantime, Jane was very glad to have her book to work on, since whatever problems Sabrina Starr had were nothing compared to those of the real world. She opened her notebook and escaped happily to the island where the Heartbreaker had been stranded by all the girls whose lives he'd wrecked. A sudden inspiration had her adding Batty's seals to the island, and they, too, would spurn the luckless anti-hero. Happily crushing him into the lowest misery before letting him be rescued, Jane wrote and wrote, so engrossed that she didn't hear the approaching foot-steps. It wasn't until a shadow was cast across her notebook that she realized she wasn't alone. She looked up and recoiled. Standing in front of her was Jeffrey's stepfather, the dreadful, the loathed, the vile and mustachioed Dexter Dupree.

"You!" Frantically Jane tried to remember what re-vengeful curses she'd rained down upon the pillow, out on the porch the day before. Had she somehow drawn Dexter out of Massachusetts and up to Point Mouette?

"Hello, Skye," he said.

She watched him narrowly. This was disturbing behavior. Not the part about him calling her Skye—he never had figured out which sister was which—but that he was acting polite. He'd never been polite before.

"How did you get here?" she asked. "That is, have you come of your own volition?"

"I drove, if that's what you mean." He rubbed his face and yawned. "All night—I drove all night. You don't happen to have any coffee, do you?"

"No." Aunt Claire was a tea drinker.

"Figures." Now he sat down uninvited, which Jane didn't think was polite. This was more like the Dexter she knew.

"Mrs. T-D isn't with you? That is, of course you think of her as Mrs. Dupree. She's in good health?" Now all of Jane's threats to the pillow were coming back to her. "Not having problems with mysterious outside influences or anything?"

"No, she was too upset to make the trip." He glowered at Jane. "Don't pretend you don't know why she's upset. Yesterday some friend of your family shows up out of nowhere claiming to be Jeffrey's father—"

Jane interrupted. "Alec *is* Jeffrey's father. And he's not out of nowhere. He's next door."

"Great. That figures, too. And after he left, my wife cries for hours until I promise I'll drive to Maine and get Jeffrey for her." Dexter stopped, embarrassed at having been so open with a despised Penderwick. "So, if you could go tell the kid to pack, we'll be on our way."

Much was now clear, so clear that Jane was ashamed of herself for wasting time thinking about that pillow. Of course Dexter had come to take Jeffrey away. That was what he and Jeffrey's mother were best at—taking Jeffrey away. They'd managed to steal him from the Penderwicks early one morning the summer before, but this time would be different. Jane was determined not to let go of Jeffrey until he had the chance to make up with Alec. But to keep Jeffrey safe, she had to plan carefully. First thing was to keep him away from Dexter for as long as possible. Second thing was to keep Aunt Claire out of it, since as a responsible adult, she might have to let Dexter talk to Jeffrey. After all, a stepfather, even an awful one, probably had more rights than the aunt of a friend.

But did a newly found father that the son wouldn't talk to have more rights than either of those? For a moment, Jane wished that she'd spent less time writing about Sabrina Starr and more time studying law, but after a quick glance at Dexter—he was getting impatient—she pushed legal questions out of the way and went back to thinking things through.

What she needed was Skye. Jane had no illusions when it came to bravery—Skye was by far the most courageous of the sisters and the best at confronting wicked grown-ups, and she would have no problem in subduing Dexter. But Jane couldn't get Skye without leaving Dexter alone, and that was too dangerous. She had to keep him from wandering off and discovering Jeffrey on the sleeping porch. She had only one solution until Skye—or any reinforcements at all—appeared. She would stall.

"You want Jeffrey to pack?" Jane asked, gaily innocent. "Heavens, I'm sure he's still asleep at this time of the morning, and you don't want me to wake him up. Boys need their rest."

Dexter squeezed his eyes shut, opened them again, and seemed disappointed that she was still there. "You're kidding, right?"

Jane prattled on. "While we're waiting, why don't you give me all the news from Arundel? How are the gardens? And the bull that lives next door—have you seen him lately? No? Then I could tell you how my writing is going. You remember that I'm a writer, don't you? Last fall I wrote a play called *Sisters and Sacrifice*, though it was really my sister's homework assignment, and then I wrote another Sabrina Starr—goodness, look who's here!"

Somehow Dominic had snuck up on them. Dismayed, Jane asked herself how it was possible. And then she realized—he hadn't come on his noisy skateboard.

"I don't know," said Dexter. "Who is he?"

"He's Dominic Orne, and Dominic, this is Dexter Dupree, who's Jeffrey's stepfather. Dexter, Dominic is . . ." She wasn't sure how to define Dominic, so she dropped it and went on to what most concerned her. "Dominic, how did you get here? That is, did you come of your own volition?"

"I walked, if that's what you mean," he answered. "My skateboard has a loose wheel."

"Oh!" Jane remembered her angry rant about Dominic the day before. Could that have affected his skateboard? Thank goodness she hadn't gone so far as voodoo. Who knows what would have happened?

"Skye, this is all very chummy, but I really need to get Jeffrey back to his mother," said Dexter.

"She's Jane," said Dominic.

"Who is?"

"I am," said Jane with more irritation than she'd meant to show. Dominic was not the reinforcement she'd wanted. "Dominic, what are you doing here, anyway?"

"You didn't come to the park yesterday or even answer my note."

"Of course I didn't. Not after you made a mockery of my love and poetry and everything I hold dear and true, and also taught me never again to fall for an empty shell of a boy who cares only for his skateboard and stealing kisses."

Dominic's face puckered in confusion. It looked as though he were trying to form a question, but Dexter was too quick for him, cutting in sharply.

"Skye—Jane—whatever your name is—oh, no, here comes another one."

It was Mercedes, who also wasn't Jane's choice for backup, especially not as she was teetering toward them on the bicycle she still hadn't learned to control. But even Mercedes was better than being alone with Dexter and Dominic. So Jane waved to her, and Mercedes joined them by crashing her bike into the deck and jumping off before it fell over.

"I don't remember her," said Dexter. "Is she the one who always wore wings?"

"You're thinking of Batty," answered Jane. "Mercedes isn't a Penderwick."

"Does he think I am?" Mercedes looked kindly upon Dexter. "Wow, thanks, mister."

Dexter frowned back, then turned to Jane. "You sure you don't have any coffee, not even instant?"

"No, sorry. Now, where was I?" said Jane. "I know—Dominic!"

She was answered by a low growl, which made her nervous—if Dominic was going to start growling, she really did need more help. But then the screen door opened, and out slid Hound in his hunting stance, his I-remember-you-and-don't-like-you-at-all voice rumbling in his throat. Following him was Batty, who, though not quite growling, had the same scowl of dislike on her face.

"*This* is Batty," said Jane.

"Oh, yeah." Dexter edged his chair farther away from Hound. "Where are her wings?"

"She gave them to Jeffrey last summer," answered Jane.

"Terrific. Just what the kid needs—fairy wings."

"They were *butterfly* wings and he did so need them," said Batty. Startled by her own courage, especially with Dominic right there, too, she clutched at Jane's hand. "Hi, Mercedes."

"Hi, Batty. That man thought I was you."

"He doesn't know anything. He's Jeffrey's stepfather."

"Oh, no!" Mercedes was horrified, and Jane was certain she was about to blurt out the bad things she'd heard about Dexter, which would not have a soothing effect on him.

The situation was becoming desperate. Jane needed to keep Mercedes quiet, and she had to keep an increasingly annoyed Dexter from going after

Jeffrey on his own. Dominic was no help. Batty was no help. Should she sing, or try a tap dance? No, she'd go back to where she always felt most comfortable—with Sabrina Starr.

"So, the Sabrina Starr book that came after *Sisters and Sacrifice* had her rescuing—"

Dexter stood up, his face red, his frustration frighteningly apparent. In Jane's frenzied state, he looked much bigger than he was, and more than a match for a dog, a not-very-bright boy, and three girls, two of them quite small.

"I don't have all day," he boomed. "If you won't wake up Jeffrey for me, get your father. Or at least your older sister, Rosalind, isn't it?"

Still Jane managed to stand her ground. "Daddy's in England, and Rosalind's in New Jersey."

"Who *can* you get? Is anyone in charge here?"

At last, and just in time, the proper reinforcement arrived. The screen door opened, and out stepped Skye—still rumpled from bed, her hair going in all directions.

"She's in charge," said Jane, sagging with relief.

The balance of power shifted immediately. Skye was not at all pleased to see the interloper from Arundel, and a displeased Skye could be a mighty force, especially when she hadn't had any breakfast. Dexter sat back down in his chair, and for a moment Jane almost felt sorry for him. She wouldn't want to be the one to return to a weeping and hysterical Mrs. T-D without Jeffrey. And by heavens, he would be returning without Jeffrey. Jane was sure of it, now that Skye was here. Jane pulled her aside and quietly explained everything, or at least the parts she understood, which meant not much about Dominic. And Skye, as the true OAP, quickly grasped the essential points and set up defensive maneuvers. She sent Batty inside to wake up Aunt Claire. She sent Dominic and Mercedes back to their grandmother to get coffee for Dexter—since that seemed to be so important to him. Last, she told Jane to go next door and get Alec. And bring him back as fast as you can, she said.

Jane hadn't seen Alec since before the golf-ball sale, so not since he'd had his revelation about Jeffrey and his life had turned into a tornado. She'd thought about him a lot, and of the things she wanted to say to him, about hope, the twisted ravages of fate, and how he'd make almost as good a dad as her own. But when Jane reached his house and found Alec sitting on the piano bench, facing the wrong way and staring unhappily at nothing, she simply hugged him and said what was necessary.

"Dexter's come to take Jeffrey back to Arundel. Hurry."

Alec knew how to hurry—here was another thing in his favor—and without even bothering with shoes, he took Jane's hand, and together they tore back to Birches, arriving just as Aunt Claire came out of the house and onto the deck, looking as dignified as is possible when your bathrobe keeps getting caught on your crutches. Skye stood on her right and Batty on her left, and Alec and Jane took up their position across from them.

Dexter was in the middle. There was no longer any balance of power. It was just sulky him versus all of Jeffrey's most fervent friends, and he hadn't a prayer. But he wasn't giving up—not yet. Warily he said hello to Aunt Claire, then tried to give Alec an intimidating sneer but managed only to look like a scared bully. Alec smiled calmly back, and Jane kept hold of his hand—he was her choice for a port in this storm.

"Where were we?" asked Skye, maintaining a re-markable serenity. "Oh, I know. Mr. Dupree was demanding to see Jeffrey so that he could take him away."

"'Demanding' could be too strong a word," said Dexter, losing even more ground. "It's just that the boy's mother misses him so."

"She does? Is that why you're here, Dexter?" Now this was Jeffrey, stepping out of the house and onto the deck. Jane thought he had never looked so brave and noble and, at the same time, exactly like his father. She smiled up at Alec, who had eyes only for Jeffrey, though Jeffrey carefully kept himself from looking back.

"He wants to take you away," said Skye.

"That's right." Dexter nodded at Skye, as though she'd said something quite wonderful. "So go get your golf clubs, Jeffrey. We're going back to Arundel."

Jane held her breath and leaned against Alec, who was holding his breath, too.

"No," said Jeffrey. "I'm not leaving."

Everyone breathed again except for Dexter—gasping would be a better description of what he was doing.

"You have to." Gasping or foaming. Jane was almost certain that Dexter was close to foaming. "Your mother's worried about you."

"Tell her I'm fine."

"This isn't a choice. We've already told your driver not to come back for you on Saturday. It's go with me today, or—" Dexter stopped, not certain of the threat he'd gotten himself into.

"We'll drive Jeffrey to Arundel," said Skye.

"Of course we will," agreed Aunt Claire.

"Or Alec will," said Jane. "Right, Alec?"

"Yes," answered Alec, and gratefully squeezed her hand.

Jeffrey flushed, still ignoring Alec, but stood firm. "You see, Dexter? I'm not your responsibility. And, by the way, I don't have the golf clubs anymore. I gave them to Batty."

This was the biggest blow so far. "You gave them to *Batty?*"

"And I sold them because I need a piano," said Batty. "Don't be mad at Jeffrey. He was being generous."

"Generous," choked out Dexter, his face as red as Alec's house.

"He's teaching me to play the piano," said Batty, growing ever bolder, "and also the harmonica."

Batty pulled out her harmonica and was playing "Taps" before Skye could dive over and take it from her.

"Sorry," said Skye, tossing the harmonica to Alec, who caught it and held it out of Batty's reach. "She's become a music lover."

But "Taps" had done Dexter in. Whatever fight he'd had was gone. Even the arrival of Mercedes with a half-spilled and lukewarm cup of coffee couldn't help.

"You refuse to come back with me today," he said to Jeffrey. It wasn't a question.

"Yes, sir, that's about it."

"It's on you, then, kid. Before I go, though, I have a message from your mother." Dexter looked around, as if he expected the others to go away. They didn't. "She apologizes and says that she did the best she could."

"Thank you. And you can tell her—" Jeffrey stopped, not knowing how to finish the sentence.

To Jane's delight, it was Alec who came to his rescue. "Tell Brenda that Jeffrey's doing the best he can, too."

With that, the battle was won. There was field cleanup to do—washing away of the gore and working out the details—but that was for the grown-ups to handle. Jeffrey melted back into the house and the four girls followed him, and when he sat on the couch, they sat there with him, two on each side, squashing him in so tightly no one could have pulled him out, if indeed they'd dare approach his ferocious Amazonian bodyguard to try it.

"Dexter was a little upset about the golf clubs," Jane said after a while.

"He was apoplectic," said Skye. "I loved it."

This got a ghost of a smile from Jeffrey, but it didn't last. "I'm wrecking this vacation for everyone. Maybe I should go with him."

"No!" cried Batty and Mercedes, and Jane and Skye squashed him in even tighter just in case he was foolish enough to try to leave. They all sat quietly that way until Aunt Claire came back inside and sat in the chair across from them.

"Dexter is gone and he won't be back," she gently told Jeffrey. "I promised him that you'll be delivered back to Arundel on time, and he accepted that."

"I won't fit in your car," he said, "and I don't want to ride with Alec."

"Alec and I have already worked that out. He'll take some of our luggage in his car, and Hound, and maybe one of the girls. You'll ride with me. All right?"

Jeffrey nodded, miserable.

Aunt Claire went on. "And Alec has decided to move out of his house until we need him for transportation. He thinks you'll be more comfortable here for your last few days without bumping into him, and this way you can use the piano whenever you want. He said you're probably missing the piano."

"I don't want to be any trouble."

Aunt Claire stood up from her chair and shoved her way onto the couch, then put her arm around him and held him close. "You're not any trouble, Jeffrey. Not to Alec, not to me, not to any of us. You must believe me."

"I'm trouble for Dexter."

Skye snorted. "It's a badge of honor to be trouble for Dexter."

"Alec won't be far away," said Aunt Claire, "just up the coast with his friend, the one who owns that boat, the *Bernadette*. If you decide you'd like to see Alec or just talk to him, or if we need anything at all, we can call him and he'll be here in a half hour. But, Jeffrey, he told me specifically to tell you this—you have all the time in the world. He will never give up on you or stop loving you, no matter how long you take to figure out what you want. Do you understand?"

Jeffrey stared straight ahead, not answering, looking so sad, so frightened and lonely, that Jane started crying and Skye would have, too, if she hadn't pinched her arm so hard she left behind a black-and-blue mark.

"No, I don't understand," he said at last.

"Well, then, it's our job to show you how worthy you are of being waited for," said Aunt Claire. "Someday you'll understand. I promise."

An hour later, Alec was gone, too. Jeffrey had silently watched from the window as the car pulled away, then just as silently gathered up Batty and Hound and headed next door for the solace of music. Others scattered, worn out by the drama. Jane went back to the deck and Sabrina Starr. Mercedes wandered down to the beach to search for tiny snails. Aunt Claire, all out of jigsaw puzzles, started the Paris one all over again.

But Skye wasn't ready to calmly recuperate. Seeing Dexter, talking to him, being *polite* to him, had sullied her soul, and she had only one solution—she would clean Birches from top to bottom. Aunt Claire protested that Dexter hadn't even gone inside, but Skye didn't care. He'd been on the deck, he'd breathed the air—if she could have, she would have cleaned all of Point Mouette.

She began outside, scrubbing the chair he'd sat on, then ritually rinsing it with bucket after bucket of water. Next, naturally, she had to rinse the entire deck—Dexter had walked on it—which drove a protesting Jane inside. Where Skye soon followed, attacking the kitchen, surface by surface, just managing to keep herself from sweeping the ceiling. The living room came next, and after she'd asked Jane and Aunt Claire to lift their feet for the broom a half dozen times, Aunt Claire decided that it was an excellent time to practice driving the car with her sprained ankle. Glad for an excuse to escape Skye's cleaning frenzy, Jane offered to go along, then fetched Mercedes from the beach so that she could go, too. Just in case Skye finished with Birches and attempted to scrub the beach.

Being left alone in Birches was an invitation for Skye to go completely mad. With broom and bucket, sponge and scrub brush, she whirled around, straightening and scouring until the living room should have cried for mercy. Its windows hadn't been so clear in years, nor had the rugs been laid out on the seawall and beaten, or the couch turned upside down and its cushions aired on the deck. Skye even polished the baseboards and this time let herself have a go at the ceiling.

A lesser mortal, or a less tormented one, would have stopped there, but Skye was moving too quickly to stop. She wouldn't invade Aunt Claire's privacy, but she had no such compunction about small sisters. A Hannibal of housecleaning, she marched into Batty's room, which didn't look too awful on the surface. But underneath the bed was a revelation.

There, crumpled into a ball, was Batty's favorite

T-shirt with the horse on the front, the one that had been handed down through all four sisters. Batty had sworn she'd left it on the beach at low tide and hadn't remembered until it was swept away by high tide. And here was a stash of golf balls that Batty had kept out of the sale, a pile of beach rocks, and an even bigger pile of shells spilling their sand onto everything. Behind the shells were Hound's treasures: a hard-boiled egg from two days earlier and an empty box of Cheerios. Then way in the back behind a damp towel and yet another pile of beach rocks, Skye discovered a big inflatable plastic duck, forlorn and forgotten. She remembered that Rosalind had packed it into Batty's stuffed-animal box—but how it had ended up under the bed was a mystery, until Skye found some signs of chewing along the edge. Hound, of course. But because he'd managed to avoid actual puncture wounds, she decided to take a break from cleaning and inflate the duck. Because she was also remembering that Rosalind had specifically told her to blow it up when they reached Maine. Skye had even written it down on her list. *Blow up*—

And suddenly she was whooping and laughing and bonking herself on the head like the fool she was. She snatched up the duck and rushed out into the living room, dying to tell everyone that she'd been wrong and they'd been right. Not now, not ever, was Batty going to explode in any possible situation.

"It was just the duck," she cried, but since she'd driven them all away, there was no one to hear her. She ran outside, looking for anyone—anyone at all—and found Dominic Orne sitting on the edge of the deck.

"Look at this duck!" she yelped at him. "I have to blow it up!"

"All right," he answered.

"You don't understand how exciting—" But Skye stopped herself. Dominic didn't have the imagination to grasp the significance of this most glorious duck. "Why are you here again?"

"Jane said a lot of stuff earlier about empty shells and stealing."

"Did she call you an empty shell of a boy who cares only for his skateboard and stealing kisses?"

"That sounds right. I was hoping she could explain what she meant in, you know, normal language."

It wasn't an unreasonable request. Skye threw the duck at him. "Blow this up and I'll tell you. Here's why. Because you lured Jane into falling in love with you—"

"What?"

"You have to blow up the duck," she said, and waited until he'd started. "After you lured Jane into falling in love, you rejected her love and, even worse, you rejected her poetry when you sent back that ode she wrote for you."

He stopped blowing. "I don't even know what an ode is. Your sister is too smart for me. She writes books! I never knew what she was talking about."

This rang true. "Then why did you kiss her?"

He lowered his voice as if telling a great secret. "My brothers dared me to kiss as many girls as I could in French Park this summer."

"This was all about a *dare?*" Skye was appalled. "Jane was right—you are an empty shell of a boy. And so are your brothers. Empty shells and pathetic igno-ramuses."

Unfazed, Dominic went back to blowing and didn't stop until he'd brought to life a fully inflated and rather goofy-looking duck.

"All done," he said.

"Thank you." She grudgingly accepted it from him. "I will concede that you don't understand Jane. Almost no one does. Now please leave. I have impor-tant things to do."

Still, he lingered. "So Jane really liked me?"

"Liked, as in the past tense, as in now she thinks you're dirt."

"But if she liked me before—"

Skye leaned toward him, wishing she had some-thing more threatening to wield than the duck. "Do-minic Orne, if you ever mess with my sister again, I will tear you limb from limb. I have no intention of getting another haircut for months."

"You know I don't understand you either, right?"

"Leave!" And he finally did.

Now there were two things to celebrate—the duck and the fact that she'd managed not to murder Dominic on the spot—and Skye simply had to tell someone. She raced across the beach to Alec's house and found Jeffrey and Batty at the piano, working on adding harmony to a song.

"Batty, you're not going to blow up!" she crowed, waving the duck. "And Dominic is an idiot!"

"We know all that," said Batty.

Jeffrey looked up from the keyboard. "No one else has come for me, have they?"

"No one else has come," answered Skye. "And if someone does, we won't tell them where you are, I promise. We'll protect you."

"Good. Thanks." He went back to his music.

CHAPTER SIXTEEN
Batty's First Concert

A ND PROTECT HIM THEY DID. From discussing his past or answering questions about his future, from hearing the words *stepfather, abandonment, secrets,* or *Arundel.* They praised him and coddled him, and when he got tired of that, they teased him gently, and when he got tired of that, Skye punched him or Jane kicked soccer balls at him until everyone went back to praising and coddling.

Then there were all the phone calls from Mrs. T-D. Two of them, a third, and after the fourth, everyone lost count. Because Jeffrey refused to talk to his mother, Aunt Claire took over—woman to woman, she said—and stayed on as long as she could stand it. Although she never once complained, after each call she had to stump outside on her crutches and swing herself around Birches several times before she was calm again.

Because Jeffrey felt safest and most content when he was playing Alec's piano, they made sure he was next door as much as possible. Batty always went along, too. There was still her concert to practice for, scheduled for the very last night of their stay in Maine. This was now only a few days away, and all the recent chaos had put them behind with practicing. So they worked on that, and sometimes they just goofed around, playing nonsense songs, and sometimes they looked through the box of old photographs that Alec had left out on the piano, in plain sight, where they'd be sure to see it.

Since many of the photographs had names and dates penciled on the back, they were able to pick out Alec's parents, and Alec and his brothers at different ages. While Batty liked seeing the pictures of Alec— since he looked so much like Jeffrey—she still didn't quite understand how or why he and all the others suddenly belonged to Jeffrey, any more than she understood when Jeffrey explained pentatonic scales to her or, for that matter, why Skye was so thrilled about the plastic duck. Batty supposed it was nice that Jeffrey had found his father, since his father happened to be a person she liked very much, but the idea that parents could get lost in the first place bothered her. She discussed this with Hound when they were alone, and it bothered him, too. They kept their worries to themselves, but it made their longing for home grow and grow, until they even talked about walking back to Massachusetts, and might have tried to walk at least past the dock and a little way up the hill as an experiment, if it hadn't been for the concert and if it hadn't been for the moose. Jeffrey tried to find the moose for her—he took her into the pinewood a few times to look, but the golf course was always full of golfers, not moose, which each time was a sore disappointment.

Very early one morning, not their last morning in Maine but the one before that, Jeffrey crept into Batty's room and gently shook her shoulder.

"Are we going home?" she asked sleepily.

He found her little sweatshirt and pulled it on over her pajamas. "Not until tomorrow. We can't go home before your concert."

"My concert's tonight!" How could she have forgotten? And Jane had promised to help her dress up for it.

He put on her sneakers. "We're going moose hunting. Give those old moose a chance to show themselves."

"Just you and me?"

"Just you and me. We'll even leave Hound here, so he won't bark at the moose."

Jeffrey wrote a note with Batty's green marker—*We*

have gone moose hunting, Love, Jeffrey and Batty—and left it on the kitchen counter; then off they went to the pinewood. Batty thought they'd dash right through the trees and onto the golf course but found that you couldn't dash when the woods were so dark, and the pine needles were extra slithery because you couldn't see where your sneakers were going. She wasn't sure she liked it but soldiered on until she tripped over a rock hidden under the pine needles. The rock hurt her toe and Batty thought about crying, but Jeffrey stooped down and told her to climb on, and riding piggyback is too much fun to waste crying, especially when the sun came up and the woods weren't as dark.

Up and up they went, until they reached the big rock above the lake. Jeffrey let her slide off his back. Then they looked down, and the moose were there, all three of them, wading into the water.

"You see them?" Jeffrey asked.

"They don't have antlers." The big moose at Moose Market had antlers. Maybe Jeffrey was wrong and these weren't moose at all.

"Mothers and babies don't have antlers."

Batty stored that away as something Ben would like to know. "Can we go down to say hello?"

"No, they're too big. They don't look like it from up here, but the mother is bigger than a horse. Bigger than that bull you met last summer."

That bull had been terrifyingly big, which meant that moose had to be gigantic. Batty slipped her hand into Jeffrey's, just to be safe, but kept watching. The cow moose was calmly plodding through the shallows, while the calves nibbled the tall grasses at the edge of the lake. Batty loved them already. She decided that these weren't the moose that Skye had seen. These were different ones, special for Batty.

"I wish I had my harmonica," she said. "We could play them some music."

"We can sing songs to them instead."

"Like what?" She didn't know any songs written for moose.

Jeffrey wasn't so literal, and he led her in a rendition of a song Turron had said was one of his favorites, "You're the Top." For the words he didn't know, Jeffrey used anything that rhymed with *moose*, like *goose*, *loose*, *juice*, *caboose*, and *Dr. Seuss*. Batty enjoyed it so much that they sang it three times, each louder than the last, until it was a miracle the moose didn't look up to find out what all the racket was about. Too soon, however, a riding mower appeared, making neat swipes through the grass. Back and forth it went, each time getting a little closer to the lake, until the mother moose decided to gather up her children and make for the shelter of the woods. Batty waved good-bye.

"Will they be safe?" she asked Jeffrey.

"Very safe." He picked her up and set her on the rock, then sat beside her. "It's time to have a serious talk about music, Batty. You know you don't have enough money for a real piano yet from the golf sale. You might have to start with a little electric piano, and that's only if your dad and Iantha say it's okay."

"They will," said Batty.

"I hope so. But if they do, I won't be there to help you anymore. You can mess around on your own, but if you're going to keep going, you'll need lessons from a real teacher in the next year or so. I didn't start lessons until I was almost eight, and that was only because Churchie found a teacher and paid her. My mother refused to . . ." He shrugged off the memory. "Anyway, by then I'd picked up bad habits and had to break them and start all over, which made it harder. I'll explain all that to your dad. He's a good listener, your dad."

Batty picked at a tiny hole in her sweatshirt. "He promised me a stuffed animal from England. I hope it's a tiger."

"You know that music is a lot of work, right? You'll have to practice and practice and practice."

"Like Skye and soccer."

"Just like that. She doesn't mind because she loves soccer, just like I don't mind because I love music. But sometimes it gets hard and lonely, and I get scared that no matter how much I practice, I won't be good enough, and then I have to keep going anyway. Do you understand?"

"Yes," she said, and wished she did.

"No, you don't, goofball." Jeffrey got her down from the rock and brushed off the pine needles she'd managed to collect. "Let's talk about your concert tonight. Aunt Claire will come, and Skye and Jane."

"And Hound and Mercedes."

"Do you want to invite anybody else? Dominic?"

She looked up to see if he was teasing, and he was. But Batty did have somebody else she wanted at her concert. Two somebodies. She'd start with the easy one. "I want to invite Hoover."

"Hoover, huh." Jeffrey took her hand and they started off down the hill. "Anybody else?"

"You know who."

He crouched and looked her straight in the eye. "Did your sisters tell you to invite Alec? Tell me the truth, even if they made you promise to keep it a secret."

"They didn't tell me, I swear. Penderwick Family Honor."

Satisfied, Jeffrey stood and they set off again. It wasn't until they were nearly out of the woods that he spoke again. "I'll ask Aunt Claire to invite Hoover and Alec for tonight. Okay?"

"Okay!" Much pleased at this swelling of her audience, Batty skipped the rest of the way back to Birches.

• • •

After hours of packing, cleaning, and getting ready to leave Maine the next morning, Skye could feel OAP-dom slipping away from her. She tried to hold on to it, reminding herself that she had another whole day left of responsibility, but there it went, slipping further and further, because there wasn't really a whole day left anymore—Skye looked at the kitchen clock—no, in only twenty hours they would be home and reunited with Rosalind, and several hours after that, the rest of the family would arrive from England, and Skye not only would no longer be in charge, she would be fourth in line for being in charge. The idea was exhilarating enough to make her jump and shout, and she would have if she weren't so worried about the upcoming concert. Just two songs, Jeffrey had promised. Two Batty songs, from start to finish—to Skye it sounded like being locked in a closet with a screeching hyena.

But she could make it through the songs—she'd already hidden cotton balls in her pocket if listening became too painful. No, her real concern was Jeffrey's happiness and his future. He hadn't talked about Alec since that day on the rocks, and Skye had no idea whether he would speak to him tonight at the concert—or ever. She kept having a nightmare that once Jeffrey got back to Arundel, Mrs. T-D and Dexter would never let him leave again, and though she knew the nightmare came out of one of Jane's books, it scared her anyway, and Skye hated being scared.

than ever for the end to OAP-dom, Skye made it up to Mercedes by going through all the cards with their blotchily individual flowers. They'd reached the eleventh card and Skye was running out of nice things to say when Aunt Claire came in from the sleeping porch.

"Ta-da! Prepare to see the miracle I've wrought," she said jubilantly, then over her shoulder added, "Stop groaning, Jeffrey, and leave your hair alone."

He sidled through the doorway, wearing black jeans and a white shirt, with his hair slicked back—all the usual sticking-up parts were flat. "She's brutal with a hairbrush."

"And it was worth it," said Aunt Claire. "You look elegant. Doesn't he, Skye?"

Skye was too busy laughing at the expression on his face to answer, but Mercedes thought Jeffrey so glorious she would have thrown herself at his feet if Jane hadn't popped out of Batty's room just in time.

"Wait till you see Batty," she cried.

A shyly radiant Batty now appeared. Jane had put her into one of Skye's skinny black T-shirts, tied at the waist with a mysterious white braided band that on later inspection turned out to be shoelaces swiped from various sneakers. The result wasn't exactly a black concert gown, but Skye found that if she squinted, it wasn't far off, especially if she could ignore Batty's flip-flops.

"You look beautiful," said Mercedes. "Oh, Batty!"

"And elegant," said Jeffrey. "Doesn't she look elegant, Skye?"

Skye squinted again, this time at Batty's face, so earnest and happy, so certain of her own magnificence. "Yes, I think she actually looks elegant. I'm impressed."

"So, are we all ready to go?" asked Aunt Claire. "Jeffrey, you're sure about this?"

"No," he said.

"I can tell Alec you've changed your mind."

He shook his head, and Skye was greatly relieved.

"Everything's fine, and I'm ready to go." He bent his arm for Batty, who took it as gracefully as if she'd been trained from birth. And they led the way.

The procession was slow because of Aunt Claire's crutches, and they took the long route, by road, not beach. This got them to Alec's front door, which they so rarely used that there was a lot of being clumped up and confused, and trying to figure out whether they should knock, until Hoover heard them from the inside and made such a racket that knocking would have been ridiculous, and Alec opened the door to let them in. All this was strange and uncomfortable, and if it hadn't been for Hound and Hoover, who were thrilled to be together after several days apart and had so much to discuss, so many smells to share, and so much wrestling to do, more than one of the people might have fled altogether. But by the time the dogs had calmed down, everybody had managed to make their way into the house.

Jane whispered to Skye, "How did we ever miss it?"

Skye knew exactly what she meant. Tonight the resemblance between father and son was stronger than ever. They had the same dark circles of sleeplessness under their eyes, and their jaws were set into identical lines of stubborn loneliness and pride. Jeffrey pretended to ignore Alec, and Alec pretended not to notice he was being ignored.

Now Alec cleared his throat and made nervous host–like motions with his hands.

"I don't know if anyone would like dessert first," he said. "There's blueberry pie."

Jeffrey signaled no to Aunt Claire with a quick thumbs-down.

"No, thank you, Alec," she said, a diplomatic go-between. "I believe we'll begin with the music."

Alec had the room nicely prepared for the concert, with a vase of fresh flowers on the piano, lit candles here and there, and a group of chairs arranged in such a way as to keep a respectful distance between performers and audience. Aunt Claire was settled into the comfiest chair. Jane, Skye, and Mercedes sat in a row beside her, the dogs piled on top of each other under the piano, and Alec stood off by himself in a dark corner.

Now it was time for Batty's great moment. Jeffrey

helped her onto the piano bench, where she sat to one side, her legs dangling, too short to reach the floor. He murmured to her, she nodded, and then he faced the portion of the audience that didn't include Alec. His hair was already escaping the bonds of Aunt Claire's handiwork—and Skye noticed Alec unconsciously smoothing down his own unruly hair.

Jeffrey began. "Tonight's concert will open with Miss Batty Penderwick—"

"No, no," interrupted Batty.

"My apologies," he said. "The concert will open with Miss Elizabeth Penderwick on the piano, accompanied by yours truly. Ladies and gentlemen, 'Summertime,' by George Gershwin."

As he sat on the bench next to Batty, Skye stealthily pulled the cotton balls out of her pocket but delayed stuffing them into her ears. Since it was just possible that what she was about to hear wouldn't be horrible, she'd give Batty thirty seconds before blocking it out. Getting ready to count the seconds, Skye watched as Jeffrey softly beat out the time for Batty— and the music began.

And it was beautiful. Batty carried the melody up where a voice would sing—her small hands confident on the piano keys—with a natural sense of this poignant hymn to sweet drowsy summers, past and present. Jeffrey supported Batty without overwhelming her, adding Gershwin's rich harmony. He did it brilliantly, so that Batty owned the music—and it was clear that she knew it, despite her goofy outfit, despite her age, despite the fact that Penderwicks just don't make music.

Skye wasn't surprised to see that Aunt Claire was crying. She felt like it herself without knowing why and concentrated on getting the cotton balls back into her pocket. Jane wasn't bothered with staying cool—her whole self was quivering with the music—while Mercedes cried along with Aunt Claire and hugged herself with delight.

Then the spell was broken. Jeffrey had abruptly stopped playing, startling Batty, whose hands dropped off the keyboard. He put his arm around her to soothe her, whispering until she nodded.

"All right?" he asked.

"Yes." She swiveled toward the corner where Alec was hiding. "Please, would you like to join us on your saxophone?"

The audience all knew what this meant and watched like hawks as Alec silently came out of the shadows, took up his saxophone, and looked to the boy at the piano for direction. Once again Jeffrey beat out the time, the audience relaxed, and the music started again. What had been lovely before was now luscious and heartbreaking. To Skye, it seemed that Batty and Jeffrey played even better than before, while Alec's saxophone roamed, impassioned, between her melody and his harmony, breaking into wild runs that made everyone shiver.

And again Jeffrey stopped playing. His hands hung limp, and he tried to whisper to Batty, but instead he sank forward until his head fell onto the keys with a discordant crash. With that crash, and the horrible wrenching sobs that followed, Skye and Jane were on their feet, Jane to scoop up a bewildered Batty and Skye to catch the saxophone that Alec threw aside in his haste to get to his son. In two strides, he reached him, pulling Jeffrey up and hugging him, hugging him, hugging so fiercely that he would never let go. It took a long time, but at last Jeffrey's sobs slowed down, and the two started to talk.

"I haven't forgiven you. Don't you dare think it's suddenly all better." This was Jeffrey, showing no signs of wanting the hugging to stop.

"No, I won't, I promise," said Alec, hugging and hugging.

"And I might never forgive you. I don't know if I even *like* you."

"I don't like me much right now, either," said Alec. "See, we have something in common besides the music."

"And don't be funny and nice. It just makes everything harder." Jeffrey started crying again, just to prove his words.

Thus ended Batty's first-ever concert, in midsong, with tears, happiness, and laughter. It was made up to her later, but not until all the crying stopped, and then everyone had to eat the entire blueberry pie and drink lots of milk—because crying can make people so hungry—while Aunt Claire called Turron to give him the good news. After that, Batty, Jeffrey, and Alec played "Summertime" once more, all the way through and without interruption. But this time they left out the drowsiness, turning the song into a lilting celebration of all the good summers to come, all the fun that would be had, and all the music that would be made.

Batty still got to finish off with a solo on her harmonica. She dedicated it to Mercedes, for her loyal friendship, which made Mercedes blush and cry all over again, and then Batty played "Taps" with soul and feeling—one final good-bye to Maine—and she did it so well that even Skye couldn't complain.

Much later, after Aunt Claire and Jane had taken the little girls away, Skye lingered on the beach, waiting for Jeffrey. He was still inside with Alec—they'd been talking for almost an hour now, but Skye didn't mind. She had the stars to watch, and black holes to dream about, and freedom to revel in. Freedom! No more secrets. No more worries. She hadn't ruined Jeffrey's life after all, or let Jane ruin hers, and though it turned out Batty really did have musical talent, Skye figured she could live with that, as long as the piano was far enough from her bedroom that she wouldn't have to listen to the practicing.

She picked up a shell and danced with it under the stars but quickly came to her senses and threw the shell into the ocean. After that, she was careful just to walk, up and down, sedately even, until Jeffrey finally joined her. He was smiling like he'd never stop.

"Tell me," she said.

"Mostly we talked about music."

"Jeffrey!"

"And his family. My family." He shook his head with happy disbelief. "My cousins are musicians, too. There's one my age, a girl who plays the cello."

Skye's head snapped around. "She doesn't play soccer, does she?"

"I don't know. Why?"

"No reason." She kicked off her shoes and waded into the cold water. She hadn't gotten so far as wondering about cousins and how much Jeffrey might end up liking them.

Jeffrey was shedding his shoes and socks, too. "Alec says he doesn't know how he'll ever thank you and Jane enough for figuring it all out—that we look alike. We do look alike, don't we, Skye?"

"What?"

"Alec and I, don't we look alike?" He waded into the water after her.

"Yes, you do look alike. Where do your cousins live?"

"I forget. The Midwest, maybe?"

"That's pretty far away," she said, cheerful again.

"I guess so. And Alec said that he and I will come back here together next summer. And I said that I wasn't sure if my mother—you know. But he said he'd take care of all that." He stopped, and Skye heard him catch his breath. "Is this all real, Skye? And true?"

"True and real." She punched his arm for the last time that summer. "As real as that."

"Good." He grinned wickedly, the way Skye liked it the best, and punched her back. "Alec also said that you have to come back next summer, too, but with the whole family this time. Half of you can stay in Birches and the other half at his house—there's plenty of room there."

"Great. We can do it all over again."

"I know."

"But with Rosalind, thank heavens," said Skye.

"Of course, except, Skye, you know you were a great OAP."

"But with *Rosalind*!" she repeated forcefully.

Jeffrey laughed. "With Rosalind."

CHAPTER SEVENTEEN
And Back Again

THE FIRST TO RETURN HOME was Rosalind, who immediately ran across the street to see Tommy. Who in turn was so overwhelmed to see her that he managed only two sandwiches for his afternoon snack, causing his mother to ask if he wasn't feeling well. When Rosalind was satisfied that Tommy not only felt fine but was still her very own, she was ready to go back across the street, take her luggage inside, and reacquaint herself with home.

At first the house shunned her, pretending to be an unfamiliar place—either too small or too big, and with the colors not at all what she remembered—but once she reached the kitchen with its big family table and Ben's high chair in the corner, all was once again as if she'd never left. She'd hoped to find Asimov the cat there, on his favorite sunny windowsill, but not only wasn't he in the kitchen, he wasn't anywhere else Rosalind looked for the next fifteen minutes. Finally she discovered him hiding under the couch, full of indignation about being left behind while everyone else went on vacations. It took her another five minutes to partially coax and partially drag him out into the open, after which he crashed onto his side in a pretend heart attack brought on by neglect and starvation.

"You've gained at least two pounds, Asimov," she said, picking him up. "So you weren't starved. And Tommy told me he was over here every day watching baseball games with you, so you weren't neglected either."

Asimov's answer was to droop heavily in her arms looking, if no longer dead, at least pathetic, and he kept it up until Rosalind hauled him back into the kitchen and opened a new can of tuna. After two bites he forgave her, and after another three he forgot all about being left behind, though he did forever hold on to his newfound interest in the Red Sox.

Rosalind checked the time—three o'clock. While Daddy, Iantha, and Ben wouldn't be home until that evening, the Maine contingent should be arriving soon. She took her luggage up to her room and dug around in it for the stuffed animal she'd bought for Batty in Ocean City, a squishy red lobster with huge eyes. She had a squishy toy crab for Ben, too, a stingray-shaped chew toy for Hound, and a miniature toy octopus for Asimov. She carried the lobster, stingray, and octopus back downstairs and tried to present the octopus to Asimov, but he leaped instead at the lobster.

"Bad cat," she said, holding the lobster high and kicking the octopus around, hoping its movement would catch Asimov's interest. When at last he deigned to poke at it dispiritedly, Rosalind went outside to sit on the front steps and await the travelers from Maine.

She'd missed them very much. She'd expected to miss Batty and so had been ready for that emptiness, but she hadn't expected to miss Skye and Jane as much as she had. She also, however, hadn't thought she'd enjoy being without all of them, even Batty, despite the missing. She'd tried not to feel guilty about it—Anna had said that for once she was being normal—and by now had forgiven herself. Because what she felt right this minute, sitting on the front step and waiting, was what mattered. She let herself be swept up in it, a grand and uproarious happiness that they would all soon be together again.

And then there was the curiosity. It hadn't escaped Rosalind that she'd never once in the entire two weeks talked to Skye. She'd talked to everyone else, including Jeffrey, including even a man named Turron, though she never quite figured out who he was. But Skye, no. The lack of Skye had been so apparent that after a while Rosalind asked Aunt Claire if she was still with them in Maine, and Aunt Claire laughed and said yes. There were other mysteries, too—events hinted at, people mentioned, then dropped. Like Dominic. Who was Dominic?

Commotion was breaking out behind Rosalind. Bored with the octopus, Asimov was meowing at her from inside the door, and when she resolutely ignored him, he launched himself at the screen and hung there, stuck and yowling. Sighing, she went back inside and took him to the kitchen for another look at his octopus, which she prayed he would finally take to. This time she got down on the floor and wiggled the octopus enticingly and made what she hoped were octopus noises. It was in the middle of one of the squishiest of these noises that Rosalind heard a car pull into the driveway, its horn blaring—they were home!

She tossed aside the octopus, raced outside, and hurled herself at Aunt Claire's car, shouting "Hello" and being shouted back at by Skye, who sprang from the car almost before it stopped.

"Your hair!" Rosalind cried to Skye, and when Jane leaped out, too, she said it again. "Your hair! Why did you cut your hair?"

"It's a long story," said Skye.

But Rosalind was now diving into the backseat, ready to bestow her lobster and her love and longing, but found it frighteningly empty of children and dogs.

"Where's Batty? Where's Hound? What's happened to them?"

"They'll be along in a minute with Jeffrey," said Aunt Claire, smiling in the front seat.

"But who's driving them?"

"Alec," said Skye. "He's a long story, too. Hold on. We have to get Aunt Claire out of the car."

Rosalind was reeling. Both her sisters seemed taller and so independent with their cropped hair. Had time moved more slowly in New Jersey? Had she been asleep for a year under the boardwalk? And why did Aunt Claire need help getting out of the car?

Jane got a pair of crutches out of the backseat, and Skye pulled Aunt Claire out of the front seat, and now Aunt Claire was on her crutches and reaching for a hug from her oldest niece.

"How beautiful you look, Rosalind," she said. "We all certainly missed you."

"But you said on the phone that it was a minor strain!" Rosalind refused to be distracted by compliments. "Are you all right? Why didn't you tell me how bad it was?"

"Skye didn't want you to worry," answered Aunt Claire. "None of us did. We were fine."

"How did it happen?"

"A shorter story. Hoover the dog did it," said Jane.

"Hoover?" asked Rosalind, then clutched at her hair. "Oh, I remember now. Batty kept talking about Hoover and how bad he is. I thought she was exaggerating."

"He's bad, all right," laughed Skye, "as you're about to find out."

Another car was pulling into the driveway, with more honking. Rosalind got a confused impression of the occupants of the front seat—besides Jeffrey, a man she'd never seen before and a blur of black-and-white dog with a squashed-in face—before she plunged into the backseat and found it delightfully and comfortably occupied by her most beloved youngest sister—another haircut!—who was unhooking her seatbelt as fast as she could and crying, "Rosalind, Rosalind," until the two of them, plus the red lobster, plus the dogs, all tumbled out of the car, with hugs and dog kisses and much loud homecoming exuberance, the loudest of which was Batty's insistence on playing her harmonica.

"Alec taught me the blues on the way home." Wrapped tight in a Rosalind hug, she wailed through several bluesy lines. "I can explain the blues to you, Rosy, if you want."

Rosalind held her at arm's length and marveled. "You're *glowing*, honey."

"I'm a musician now." Batty went back to her harmonica.

"Oh, yeah, that's another thing, Rosalind," said Skye. "Batty needs a piano. Another long story."

"A piano!"

Before she could try to absorb that shock, Jeffrey was giving her a hug. When he stood back, she saw that he looked taller, too, and more grown-up somehow, and again Rosalind had that curious sense that she'd been apart from these people for much longer than two weeks. But the most noticeable thing about Jeffrey was his luminous joy. What had happened in Maine? Whatever had happened?

Standing next to Jeffrey was the man who'd been driving.

"Rosy, this is Alec McGrath," said Jeffrey. "Alec, this is Rosalind."

"Hello," he said. "I've heard so much about you."

There was nothing special about the words he'd used, but there was something special in his tone that made Rosalind look more closely at this Alec. He seemed familiar, but not in a way she could describe.

"Have we met before?" she asked. "Is that why Skye says you're a long story?"

"I told you she was smart, Alec," said Jeffrey gleefully.

"Jeffrey also told me that I wouldn't be absolutely accepted without your approval." Alec dipped his head in teasing supplication.

Several people giggled and Rosalind gazed wonderingly around at her family. They were all watching her, waiting for something from her, something important. All the watching and waiting seemed to do with this man, Alec, so she turned her attention back to him. She liked his face and she liked the way he was smiling at her—I'm already your friend, he seemed to be saying—with his hands in his pockets and his head tipped a bit to one side. Jeffrey was smiling the same way, she noticed, and had his hands in his pockets, and his head—why, his head was tipped just the same way. How strange. How very . . .

"Jeffrey, I'm having the most peculiar idea," she said.

"What is your idea?" he asked, smiling more than ever.

"I'm thinking that he—that Alec—oh, Jeffrey," she breathed. "Have you found your father?"

"Yes," he said. "Yes, Rosy, I most certainly have."

It was very unfair, and only a girl as strong as Rosalind could have waited as long as she did to have her curiosity satisfied. A father for Jeffrey! Let alone a mysterious piano, new haircuts, and Aunt Claire's sprained ankle. But before any stories could be told, Alec, Jeffrey, and Hoover had to be sent on their way to Arundel, with many hugs and promises to see each other as soon as possible, preferably for a weekend stay at Alec's apartment in Boston. Then Aunt Claire needed to be put on a couch to rest, because driving across New England with a sprained ankle is tiring, and then the car needed to be unpacked, and then

Hound had to be fed and Asimov had to be fed all over again.

But at last, Rosalind ordered her sisters upstairs to her room, because she couldn't stand the suspense anymore.

"I want to hear everything," she said, wrapping her arms around Batty and the new lobster—already named Lola—and how good it felt to have her littlest sister right back where she belonged.

"I need a piano," said Batty.

"All right. Start with the piano."

"It's hard to explain the piano without explaining Alec and Jeffrey," said Skye, "and Hoover."

"And we have to tell how Dominic made us get haircuts," said Batty.

"He didn't make us," put in Jane. "It was all my fault. Or the Firegod's."

"Oh, definitely, let's pin everything on the Firegod," said Skye.

Rosalind waved her arms at them. "You're getting nowhere. Firegods! Good grief."

"Maybe we should just start at the beginning," said Jane.

"Yes, please."

So Skye, Jane, and Batty started at the beginning and, with lots of interweaving, overlapping, and interrupting, told Rosalind the tale of Point Mouette. Rosalind, holding fast to Batty, listened, and exclaimed, and absorbed. The piano went down more easily than Skye had feared it would, maybe because Rosalind had more memories than the others did of their mother's love of music. Hoover she was rather glad to have avoided spending too much time with, and Dominic she was very glad to have missed altogether. But from what her sisters told her, she hoped to meet Turron in the future, and Mercedes, too. Naturally, though, Rosalind was most touched by how Jeffrey had finally found his long-lost father.

"And Mrs. T-D won't try to keep them apart?" she asked.

"She can't," answered Jane. "They're bonded now, father and son."

"Besides, she's got no legal grounds for doing it," added Skye. "Turron asked a lawyer."

Rosalind sighed happily. "This is a wonderful story. All the stories are wonderful, except maybe the ones about Dominic."

Jane nervously cleared her throat. "I haven't yet told you the last one of those."

"Oh, no," said Skye. "You didn't go to French Park and kiss him again, did you?"

"I did not go to French Park, and of course I didn't kiss him again. He has proved himself unworthy of me. It's just that he stopped by yesterday to give me this." Jane pulled a grubby and much-folded piece of paper out of her pocket and handed it to Rosalind.

"It looks like the beginning of a poem," Rosalind said after carefully unfolding it. "May I read it out loud, Jane?"

"I guess so."

"Here goes," said Rosalind.

> "I'm glad I met Jane.
> She isn't plain.
> She's a slick
> Penderwick."

Skye let out a groan that could have been heard all the way back to Maine, but Rosalind was laughing, so Skye couldn't help but laugh, too, and although Jane tried hard to be fair and kind about Dominic, she ended up feeding the poem to Hound, who appreciated it much more than she had.

"And now that we're through all that," said Skye, "I'm officially handing back the reins of OAP-dom to Rosalind. Long may she live. Amen."

"You were a good OAP, though, Skye," said Jane.

"Yes, you were," added Rosalind. "Thank you."

"I did okay," said Skye. "At least Batty didn't blow up."

"Why would—?"

Rosalind was interrupted by Hound suddenly charging the window, barking ecstatically and crashing his big nose against the screen. Everyone knew what that meant, and their hearts soared.

"They're home! They're home!" cried Batty.

She rushed from the room, and Hound followed, and charging after him went Jane and Skye. Rosalind held back for a moment, still puzzled about people blowing up. But then she heard car doors slamming, sisters shrieking, Iantha and Aunt Claire laughing, Ben shouting, and—above all that and better than anything in the world—her father's deep voice asking for Rosalind, where is Rosalind, and thoughts of blowing up were gone, never to return. She flew downstairs, and the Penderwick family was back together again.

The Penderwicks was Jeanne Birdsall's first novel, and it won the National Book Award for Young People's Literature. The sisters' story continues in *The Penderwicks on Gardam Street*, the second in the series. When it was time to write her third book about the Penderwick family—and decide where they'd go for summer vacation—Jeanne visited Maine for research and fell in love with the place, and she keeps going back, though the Penderwicks have headed home to Gardam Street.

All the Penderwicks books have been *New York Times* bestsellers, and the girls' adventures have been published in twenty-six languages.

Jeanne lives in Northampton, Massachusetts, with her husband, two cats, and an overeager Boston terrier named Cagney. You can find out more about Jeanne (and her animal friends) on her website at jeannebirdsall.com.